Gillian Appleb

Fear was a normal hu
was different. This feeling was slow and it
was hundreds of miles from anything familiar,
alone in the wilderness with a man who might
be a killer. A man who made her uneasy on a
deep, instinctive level.

A man who looked touched by some pagan god,
gilded as he was at this moment by the dying
sun's copper blaze. He was spectacular.

After a moment, he spoke. "I owe you,"
Rafe Stormwalker said. "You wouldn't be in this
fix if not for me. Your skill kept me alive when
you landed the plane. I'll keep you alive in the
wilderness."

Somehow Rafe's words persuaded her to move
forward, toward him and the shelter he'd found.

This was definitely not what she'd dreamed
it would be like, the first time she slept with
a man....

Dear Reader,

Have you noticed our special look this month? I hope so, because it's in honor of something pretty exciting: Intimate Moments' 15th Anniversary. I've been here from the beginning, and it's been a pretty exciting ride, so I hope you'll join us for three months' worth of celebratory reading. And any month that starts out with a new book by Marie Ferrarella has to be good. Pick up *Angus's Lost Lady;* you won't be disappointed. Take one beautiful amnesiac (the lost lady), introduce her to one hunky private detective who also happens to be a single dad (Angus), and you've got the recipe for one great romance. Don't miss it.

Maggie Shayne continues her superselling miniseries THE TEXAS BRAND with *The Husband She Couldn't Remember.* Ben Brand had just gotten over the loss of his wife and started to rebuild his life when…there she was! She wasn't dead at all. Unfortunately, their problems were just beginning. Pat Warren's *Stand-In Father* is a deeply emotional look at a man whose brush with death forces him to reconsider the way he approaches life— and deals with women. Carla Cassidy completes her SISTERS duet with *Reluctant Dad,* while Desire author Eileen Wilks makes the move into Intimate Moments this month with *The Virgin and the Outlaw.* Run, don't walk, to your bookstore in search of this terrific debut. Finally, Debra Cowan's back with *The Rescue of Jenna West,* her second book for the line.

Enjoy them all, and be sure to come back again next month for more of the best romantic reading around—right here in Silhouette Intimate Moments.

Yours,

Leslie J. Wainger
Senior Editor and Editorial Coordinator

Please address questions and book requests to:
Silhouette Reader Service
U.S.: 3010 Walden Ave., P.O. Box 1325, Buffalo, NY 14269
Canadian: P.O. Box 609, Fort Erie, Ont. L2A 5X3

THE VIRGIN AND THE OUTLAW

EILEEN WILKS

Silhouette®

INTIMATE™MOMENTS®

Published by Silhouette Books

America's Publisher of Contemporary Romance

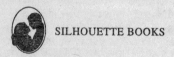

SILHOUETTE BOOKS

ISBN 0-373-07857-9

THE VIRGIN AND THE OUTLAW

Books by Eileen Wilks

Silhouette Intimate Moments

The Virgin and the Outlaw #857

Silhouette Desire

The Loner and the Lady #1008
The Wrong Wife #1065
Cowboys Do It Best #1109
Just a Little Bit Pregnant #1134

EILEEN WILKS

is a fifth-generation Texan. Her great-great-grandmother came to Texas in a covered wagon shortly after the end of the Civil War—excuse us, the War Between the States. But she's not a full-blooded Texan. Right after another war, her Texan father fell for a Yankee woman. This obviously mismatched pair proceeded to travel to nine cities in three countries in the first twenty years of their marriage, raising two kids and innumerable dogs and cats along the way. For the next twenty years they stayed put, back home in Texas again—and still together.

Eileen figures her professional career matches her nomadic upbringing, since she has tried everything from drafting to a brief stint as a ranch hand—raising two children and any number of cats and dogs along the way. Not until she started writing did she "stay put," because that's when she knew she'd come home. Readers can write to Eileen at P.O. Box 4612, Midland, TX 79704-4612.

My thanks to Tom Beasely for his expert advice about small planes and pilots; to Bonnie Pearson for setting me straight about guns; to Fernando de la Rosa of the Midland Hispanic Chamber of Commerce; and to Deputy U.S. Marshal Greg Dewey for "just the facts, ma'am." Any mistakes in the book have crept in despite the efforts of these people to keep me honest.

Prologue

The blood was still warm. So was the body.

One man knelt beside the cooling body of another. Boxes, crates and shadows crowded the two of them on one side. On the other side was a small office, separated from the rest of the warehouse by dirty glass.

The dead man lay in the middle of a puddle of blood and the square of light cast by the brightly lit office. Death hadn't mussed him much. His brown hair was as nicely styled as ever. Even the two small holes in the center of his Ralph Lauren shirt were deceptively tidy. Almost all the blood had come from the much bigger holes the bullets made when they tore out of his back.

A small scrap of purple cloth lay next to the dead man's hand, just outside the spreading puddle of blood.

The living man wore scuffed boots, old jeans, a plain T-shirt and a three-thousand-dollar watch. His hair was long, shiny and black. His features had the stony grace of an Aztec carving, immobile and bluntly masculine.

A portable heater in the office clicked on, the sound obscenely loud in the empty warehouse. Rafael Stormwalker jerked, a sign of nerves not mirrored on his face. The motion pulled his hand away from the dead man's throat.

Rafe looked at his fingers, red and slick from his foster brother's blood. He shuddered. He'd accidentally put his hand in the gory puddle when he'd knelt. His right boot nudged that puddle now, and crimson stained Steve's neck where Rafe had searched fruitlessly for a pulse.

Which meant his fingerprints were captured in garish color on the cooling flesh. Maybe elsewhere, too. Rafe didn't clearly remember those first few moments after seeing Steve's body sprawled on the cold cement floor.

But it didn't really matter, did it?

He looked at the dark metal of the gun that lay on the floor a couple yards away. It was a German make, a SIG-sauer P226, a semiautomatic with a rough grip and a smooth barrel.

He'd last seen the SIG two days ago in his desk drawer at home.

Rafe had seen death before—even violent death—but he hadn't expected to see it here, in his warehouse, in the sprawled body of his foster brother. In spite of the games Steve had been caught up in, both those he'd chosen and those Rafe had forced him to play, Rafe hadn't expected to walk in here tonight and find Steve lying in a pool of blood. Maybe he should have.

The bullets that killed Steve had been fired from Rafe's own gun. The scrap of cloth…

Rafe picked it up, needing to be sure. When he saw the crudely drawn device on one side of the cloth, a cold wind swept though him—the cold, cleansing wind of rage.

The last haziness of shock shredded in that wind. Steve had been *his*. Maybe Rafe's foster brother had been weak—more of a burden than a brother—but he'd been *Rafe's* burden. His to deal with. His—just like the company, the warehouse and the trucks that those bastards had used to smuggle their filth into the U.S.

They'd used Steve, his flaws and weaknesses, when Steve was alive. They were using him now, dead.

Someone was going to pay for that.

Rafe hesitated only briefly before wiping his hand on the soft cotton of Steve's designer shirt. He had no time to be squeamish.

He stood. They'd be here soon.

It was easy enough now to see how he'd been set up. He'd come to the warehouse in response to Steve's phone call, a call that had probably been forced at gunpoint. His enemy would have had someone nearby, watching, ready to tip off the police anonymously once their target walked into the trap. Any second now Rafe expected to hear the blare of a police siren. Or would they glide up, sirens and lights off, trying to catch him unaware?

Circumstantial evidence alone would get him locked up. If that happened, he was a dead man.

He moved quickly, bending to retrieve the Sig. He checked the clip—two shots fired, the two that killed Steve—and stuck it awkwardly in his jeans at the small of his back. The barrel was cool against his skin.

The distant wail of a siren floated into the shadowed warehouse. Rafe froze, listening intently. It sounded like they were heading up from the city, seven or eight minutes away.

He ran. It occurred to him as he threw open the front door that he was now exactly where a lot of people had always expected him to be—on the run from the law.

There was no moon yet, but Orion the Hunter was up, leading the pack of winter stars across the sky. Rafe slid behind the wheel of his Jeep and jammed the key into the ignition. An APB would be out on this vehicle in twenty minutes or less, he estimated—but in twenty minutes he wouldn't be in the Jeep anymore. He'd be on foot, crossing the last few miles of scrubby hills between here and the line drawn in the dirt by the muddy trickle of a river.

That line had divided the fates of millions of people over the years. Tonight it would divide Rafe's past from his future. If he had a future. People on both sides of the line would try to take it from him.

If he didn't get to them first.

An hour and forty minutes after finding his foster brother's cooling body on the floor of his warehouse, Rafael Storm-walker crossed the border into Mexico. The linked circles drawn on the scrap of purple cloth had made it clear the killer wasn't the only person responsible for Steve's death.

Rafe carried his own burden of guilt. So did the man he sought.

In the twenty-five years since his mother's death, he'd never been tempted to break the promise he'd given her. Now he waded across a muddy river in the dark of night determined to find a man he'd sworn never to contact, a man who might help him find evidence against Steve's killer—if he didn't decide it was simpler to kill Rafe instead.

His uncle.

Chapter 1

"See you later, José. Don't forget to check the pressure on that left engine."

The mechanic muttered something in Spanish about uppity women. Gillie laughed and waved at him as she hurried out of the hangar. José was no different from mechanics the world over. He hated to be told his business by a mere pilot.

Afternoon heat shimmered up from the dark tarmac she crossed. Gillie was a small woman, her arms and legs bared by her shorts and sleeveless shirt, her heart-shaped face browned by the sun. The brown hair that spilled out the back of her red baseball cap bounced with her quick steps. She had an assured way of moving that gave the impression of abundant confidence and energy. That impression was mostly right. Gillie had always had energy to spare, and she was always confident—about planes.

All Gillian Appleby really wanted from life was the sky. On that Thursday at the tail end of January she was closer to achieving her goal than she'd been since her father died.

She headed toward the little airport's terminal. Like many of the buildings in San Luis del Corba, Mexico, it was made of cement and painted a cheerfully bright color. The town spread out beyond the little airport, as colorful and random as a child's scattered building blocks.

Her stomach growled as she reached the terminal. It was after one o'clock. She'd flown a party of *turistas* in from Baja that morning, and breakfast was an endless five hours in the past. She pushed open the door on the west end. Cooler air blew out, courtesy of the building's antique air-conditioning.

Gillie stepped through the doorway and saw the man in chains.

He was as startling in the everyday setting as a puma would have been—as startling and just as magnificent. Both were sleek, muscular creatures made for strength and wild places; neither belonged in the waiting area outside the offices of Ventura Aviación. An army surplus shirt with several buttons missing did a poor job of covering the man's copper-colored chest. One chain circled his middle. It bound his handcuffed wrists close to his waist. A second chain ran from the first to the manacles at his ankles.

Gillie's breath caught in her chest, tangled up with a sense of wrongness. Surely something was horribly wrong for such a man to be in chains. Her gaze slid up to his face, and her thoughts stopped along with her breath.

A red bandanna held long, black hair out of eyes as dark as a shadow at midnight, eyes that met hers with the flat, dangerous patience of a caged predator.

A shiver slid up her spine and woke her from her brief trance. Only then did she notice the other man, a more ordinary man, who sat beside the one in chains. Despite his dress shirt and the suit jacket he carried over one arm, he was no businessman. Along with his neatly knotted tie he wore the subtle aura of a cop.

The handcuffs on his prisoner were a pretty good clue to his role, too.

One of the office doors opened. Timothy Lee came out. The Mexican sun had bleached his strawberry blond hair to a peculiar pinkish color that went well with the peeling sunburn on his nose. His white shirt matched Gillie's down to the pilot's wings embroidered on the breast pocket, except that his was larger and had been recently ironed.

"Gillie!" he cried. Timothy Lee had never had a lukewarm reaction to anything in his life. His wide mouth looked made for smiling, but was tight with worry now. "Thank goodness you're here. You can take a flight to El Paso, can't you?"

She frowned. "I just got back." And she was in a hurry. She'd been saving so long for her own plane. The Piper she'd heard about wouldn't be around long, not at that price.

"Yeah, but that was just a flight to Baja and back." He waved a pudgy hand dismissively. "Less than an hour each way. That's nothing for *you*. You'll take this one, won't you? Raul won't be back until tomorrow, and this flight's a rush and Mr. Montaldo wants me to go, and I *can't*. Not with Maria so close to her time."

Gillie loved kids of all ages, but she had a major soft spot for babies—those already born and those about to be. Timothy Lee knew it, darn him. "Maria's not going to go into labor the minute your wheels leave the ground."

"But I'd have to be gone *overnight*."

Gillie frowned hard and kept her mouth closed so she wouldn't say something stupid like "Sure, I'll go." She didn't want to go—and maybe not just because of the Piper, either. She had the oddest feeling, as if disaster were nibbling at the edges of her brain, just waiting for her to invite it in.

Ridiculous, she told herself firmly.

"Please, Gillie? You'd be back in time for the game Friday."

He was talking about the sandlot baseball team Gillie pitched on. The team's American component included Timothy Lee and a U.S. sales rep and a nanny. The rest were Mexican nationals, except for the Czech baker who played first base.

"Undue pressure, Timothy," another voice said in English with a whiff of a Mexican accent. The new owner of Ventura Aviación stood in the doorway of his office. Arthur Montaldo was a Mexican citizen, but his mother had been from Illinois. His thin face, thinning brown hair and first name reflected that half of his lineage. "Gillie has taken one of your flights already this week."

"I don't mind," Gillie said, then stopped, embarrassed by the way she'd automatically disagreed.

She didn't like her boss. She didn't like his neat little Zorro mustache or his neatly manicured hands. She had no better reason for her dislike—unless, like her neighbor Raquel claimed, she was determined not to like any man who made her feel like a woman.

Ridiculous. True, ever since Montaldo took over the little airline two months ago he'd acted *interested* in a way that flustered her, but Gillie was sure that wasn't the only reason she didn't like him.

Maybe she was just prejudiced against men who spent more on a single dress shirt than she did on a month's rent.

The cop spoke. "If there's a problem, Mr. Montaldo, let me know now."

"No problem, Marshal," Montaldo assured him. "I know Ms. Appleby looks young, but she's actually the most experienced of my pilots with this airline. Not that Mr. Lee isn't fully capable of flying you to Texas. And it is his turn to go up." He gave Timothy Lee a warning look.

"There are two other charter services here, I understand."

"They can't offer you pressurized cabins. True, you could fly over the Sierra Madres without a pressurized plane, but you'd be looking at more flight time. The pilot would have to take a longer route to limit the time at high altitudes, probably stopping to refuel along the coast. And using oxygen masks might be awkward with a prisoner. Particularly a dangerous prisoner."

Gillie's eyes darted to the one man who hadn't spoken—the man they were talking about. His face was expressionless.

"True," the marshal said, "and speed is important. But if this young woman isn't ready and your other pilot can't take the flight for personal reasons—"

"Mr. Lee will certainly fly if he's told to."

"But Mr. Montaldo—Maria could have that baby any minute!"

Gillie sighed. She'd already figured out that Montaldo wasn't a man who liked to be told no. It would be a shame if Timothy Lee had to go looking for another job when he had a new baby due to show up any day.

Not that it was any of her business. She was over her stupid compulsion to take care of everyone around her, wasn't she?

"I'll take the flight," she heard herself say.

Montaldo frowned. Whatever he'd been about to say, though, was interrupted when the door behind Gillie opened and a raspy male voice said in Spanish, "The Cessna is fueled."

Gillie jumped. She stepped aside, because she didn't like having her back to the man who'd just come in.

Jorge smiled at her. He was a round little man, bald on top, with incongruously bushy eyebrows that crawled along his forehead like a pair of woolly caterpillars. He had small, soft hands and the kind of half-dead eyes that set off alarms in Gillie's mind every time she saw him.

He was Montaldo's private chauffeur/pilot/flunky, and another reason to dislike the man.

"All right," Montaldo said, but he didn't look happy—displeased, no doubt, with having anyone interfere with his plans. Timothy Lee, however, was overjoyed. He bounded over, grabbed her hand and planted a big, smacking kiss on it. "Thanks, Gillie. I owe you, I really do. You just let me know what I can do to pay you back. You just name it."

"Lunch." It didn't look like she was going to get the shower and change of clothes—or the airplane—she'd planned on, but at least she could make sure she got fed.

"A couple burritos from Mamacita's stand out front, maybe?"

"I can get those for you, Gillie," Jorge said, smiling.

It was all she could do to repress a shudder. Fortunately, Timothy Lee insisted on buying her lunch, and Montaldo told his man to go do the preflight check on the Cessna. She watched with relief as the creepy little man left.

"You like the chorizo burritos with extra cheese, right?" Timothy Lee said.

"Right."

Timothy Lee hurried away eagerly. Gillie told herself that a free lunch was better than nothing. Maybe the Piper would still be there when she got back. She'd only be gone two days, after all.

She squared her shoulders against disappointment and turned to the cop. "I gather you're in a hurry, Marshal—ah, I didn't catch your name."

"Winston." He looked at her dubiously. "I am in something of a rush."

Gillie ran into this sort of attitude often enough. She put it down to her small stature and youthful appearance, rather than her gender. Gillie never expected others to really notice that she was a woman. "I'm familiar with the route," she told him reassuringly. "I'll have you Stateside in about four hours."

"Can we leave right away?"

"The plane will need to be—"

Her boss interrupted. "Didn't you hear Jorge? The tanks on the Cessna 414 have already been topped off, the flight plan is ready, and he's doing the preflight."

Montaldo was sure in a hurry. She nodded, though she would, of course, do her own visual inspection before she got in the plane. Pops would come back to haunt her if she ever got so sloppy she didn't do her own preflight check. "All right, then. We ought to be ready to go in about fifteen minutes, Marshal. I need to check out the weather and grab some things for an overnight in El Paso." She needed those burritos from Timothy Lee, too. She had no intention of flying on an empty stomach. "I'm Gillian Appleby, by the way."

"Glad to meet you, Ms. Appleby."

Some demon made her turn to the other man. The one in chains. Her heart gave a funny little hop as she met those waiting, watchful eyes. "And your name is—?"

"It's best," Winston said, "if you don't speak to the prisoner, ma'am."

"My father always said a good pilot knows what her cargo is. I want to know who this man is, and I'm not going to act like he isn't here." Though his name wasn't all she wondered about. She wanted to know why she was afraid.

Maybe this was what her earlier foreboding had been about—this man, with his watchful eyes and his chains. Because surely it was fear that made her feel so alive when she met the prisoner's eyes, fear that fizzed in her veins when she looked at his body, a body strong enough to break hers easily, even casually.

Though it was an odd sort of fear. It made her flesh feel tight and warm and strange.

Uh-oh. She *was* looking at his body, wasn't she? She jerked her gaze up.

His features were unmoved, but those dark eyes were lit faintly with knowledge and...humor? Was he laughing at her?

"Stormwalker," he said in American English, and his voice wasn't what she'd expected, not at all. It was smooth, not rough—as smooth and coolly provocative as silk rubbing along her exposed skin. He shifted his feet, and the links of the chain rattled. "My name is Rafael Stormwalker." His mouth turned up in the barest hint of a smile. "Call me Rafe."

Winston spoke sharply. "That's enough from you. Ma'am, I'd rather you don't have any dealings with the prisoner."

Irritation brought Gillie's chin up. "I just asked him his name, not whether he'd like me to bake him a file in a cake."

"That's our Gillie," Montaldo said patronizingly. "She's not always respectful, but she'll get you where you're going. Now, if you'd like to board your prisoner, I'll be glad to show you to the plane."

"Wait a minute," Gillie said. "I've got one more question."

Here it comes, Rafe thought as he waited for the question he knew was inevitable. The little brown wren would ask what he was wanted for, and Winston would tell her.

The marshal wouldn't have to ask her again not to talk to his prisoner.

"Get to your feet, Stormwalker," Winston said, standing.

It didn't matter, Rafe reminded himself as he stood—carefully, because the manacles around his ankles kept his feet just a little too close together for a man his height. True, the woman had treated him like a human being instead of an object, and her embarrassment when he caught her admiring his body had given him a moment of amusement. He could appreciate those gifts without letting her opinion of him matter.

No doubt her courtesy arose from sheer, youthful ignorance. Although she had to be older than she looked. With her ponytail and scrubbed-clean face, she didn't look old enough to drink legally in most places…or to participate in the other activities Rafe's body was reminding him of.

"Gillie, I'll fill you in on whatever you need to know after I get the marshal settled." Montaldo sounded irritated.

The ache in Rafe's groin didn't matter, either, but it irritated him. Damned poor timing. He'd gone without sex for longer than this. Why did his body decide to torment him now? And why her? She wasn't his type. Too skinny and too innocent.

Rafe had little patience with innocence.

Though she did have unusual eyes. He didn't think he'd ever seen eyes quite that shade of blue, a blue so vivid they didn't seem to be quite of this world.

"Just one question," the blue-eyed wren repeated stubbornly.

And her face was…surprising. At another time, in another place, he might have taken the time to find out what it was about her face that intrigued him.

"Why are you in such a hurry?" she asked.

He blinked in surprise. That was the wrong question. Or the right one—the one she ought to ask—but he hadn't expected her to realize that. Maybe there was a brain behind those unworldly eyes.

Winston and the other man exchanged glances. Rafe abruptly lost patience with them. "Aren't you going to tell her?"

"You don't get a vote, Stormwalker," the marshal said.

"She's got a right to know." Rafe wasn't sure why he was pressing the issue. He was every bit as interested as his keeper in getting airborne quickly. More so, probably. He knew who was after him, and he damn sure didn't want the wren to change her mind about getting them out of here.

Montaldo spoke impatiently. "Speed is important because the marshal has reason to believe his prisoner may have been targeted by a local drug gang."

Rafe shook his head. "You ever worked for the government, Montaldo? You've got a nice way with euphemisms." He looked at the woman who was splitting her frown between him and her boss. "The drug gang isn't just local, and the marshal 'has reason to believe' I've been targeted because his partner was shot this morning while they were bringing me in from Huajicoti. He's probably in surgery now."

"We'll be fine as long as we don't delay," Winston said. "Our rental car is being driven into Mazatlán by the federal police as a decoy. Our original flight was booked through the airport there, so if the gang's still after Stormwalker, that's where they'll look."

Maybe the wren didn't have much sense, after all. She didn't seem worried by the idea that someone was gunning for her "cargo." Just disgusted. Her upper lip curled. "Drugs." She looked at the marshal. "That's what he's wanted for?"

"No, ma'am," Winston said. "His only federal charge is fleeing the country to avoid arrest, but the original warrant is for murder."

Gillie was the only pilot in the airport's small locker room that afternoon. She whistled a snatch from Beethoven's Third as she sorted through the contents of her locker, looking for clean clothes. Her passport was already tucked into a pocket of the screaming-green nylon backpack she used as a suitcase. So were five hundred U.S. dollars and a thick wad of pesos.

Her father had always said, "Pack light and pay cash." His axiom had proved its worth more than once. Pop's wanderlust hadn't always led them along predictable paths.

A music lover could have been forgiven for not recognizing the theme Gillie whistled. Her ear for music was as bad as her ear for accents. Gillie had grown up in a fistful of countries scattered all over the world. She'd learned four languages before she was thirteen, but no one who heard her speak those languages ever mistook her for anything but an American.

She pulled out a shirt, looked it over, and saw a ketchup stain. *"Madre de un lechón,"* she muttered.

"You talking to yourself again, *chica?"* someone nearby said in Spanish. "Why don't you listen to me speak of your beautiful eyes instead?"

"Hey, Enriqué," Gillie said companionably in the same language to the short, heavy man with a shiny-bald head and a bandito's mustache who entered. Enriqué was ticket agent, baggage handler and general oddsbody for one of the two regional airlines with regular flights in and out of San Luis.

He was also the most happily married man she knew, and the worst flirt. "How are the kids?" she asked.

"Berto," he said proudly of his nine-year-old, "says he is saving himself for you. Maybe because of your eyes—like two jewels fallen from heaven." He winked. "Or maybe because he likes your motorcycle."

Gillie laughed. Her ancient Honda wasn't the most reliable transportation, but it was good on gas and cheap to fix. Gillian had better things to do with her money than pour it into a vehicle that never left the ground. "I think he just likes my fastball." Gillie's second passion, after flying, was baseball.

"Tell Berto I'll wait for him." She found an old, yellow sweatshirt and folded it more or less neatly before stuffing it in the backpack. El Paso was apt to be chilly at night. They'd even had snow there a couple years ago.

Gillie had seen snow. She hadn't approved. She did not like to be cold. Frowning, she packed a second shirt as well.

"Here," Enriqué said. "Timothy Lee, he said to give you this." He held out a white paper bag. Wonderful smells of peppers, onions and meat made Gillie's stomach growl.

"I'm starved." She grabbed the bag. Mamacita's burritos were fantastic. She unwrapped one and bit into it, chewed quickly and swallowed. The peppers burned all the way down. "Did Timothy Lee send me anything to drink?"

Enriqué held out a six-pack of Coca-Cola. "Slow down,

slow down," he said as she bit off another big bite. "All these years you've lived in my country, and you haven't learned to stop rushing."

Slow was not Gillie's best speed. "Didn't Timothy Lee tell you? I've got a flight."

"But you just landed. You're not—no, no. Tell me you are not taking Timothy Lee's flight."

She shrugged uncomfortably and took another bite. Her inability to put her own needs first embarrassed her.

He frowned at her fiercely. "I will speak to Señor Montaldo. He should not have allowed you to take that flight. It is a man's job, with that outlaw on board."

She would have laughed if her mouth hadn't been full. She chewed and swallowed again. "Enriqué, I don't know when I've heard you say anything half so silly. What's the harm? I'm flying the plane, nothing more."

"I know how trouble looks. That one is a bad man. Trouble."

Gillie thought of her unsettling reaction to the prisoner. She remembered that even Montaldo hadn't looked happy about her taking the flight—but then, her boss didn't care for opposition. No doubt he'd just been put out that things hadn't gone as he'd planned. "I've already taken the flight, so it doesn't matter."

He muttered something she didn't catch. "And I know why you take this flight. You want the money for your plane, yes? Why do you not listen to me? Better to save for your dowry instead of for buying a pile of cold metal. Metal won't keep a woman warm at night, *chica*. You are a pretty woman. With the encouragement of a nice dowry, you'll have no trouble finding a good man."

She rolled her eyes. Enriqué had played this tune before, and she was getting tired of the refrain. "I don't want a man."

"You are still young. Whatever man was foolish enough to break your heart, you will forget him soon."

Temper sparked. "No one broke my heart. Men just take up too much of a woman's time." And some women simply weren't meant to have a man, not in a permanent, personal way. Gillie had accepted that about herself years ago.

"Your papa should never have let you grow so old unwed. You are too stubborn."

"Haven't I mentioned that this is none of your business?"

"What about babies?" he demanded. "You will choose a plane over babies?"

In spite of herself, Gillie smiled. "But my friends who are parents delight in letting me borrow their babies—don't you, *amigo?*" She grinned and patted his arm, her anger evaporating as quickly as a puddle in the hot Mexican sun. "Why do I need to have my own? I can play with yours, then, after a few hours, I give the little one back and go flying."

She turned to her locker and grabbed a pair of jeans. Enriqué muttered something about foolish women and selfish men. "Your papa was a fine pilot, but he was selfish, too caught up in his own—"

"Enriqué," she said sharply. "That's enough." Her fingers lingered on the last item to be packed—an intricately carved wooden box from Indonesia about the size of a shoe box. The feel of the deeply incised petals of a flower were dearly familiar. This box went on every overnight trip with her, like the extra cash. Just in case. "Pops was a great father. He may not have been exactly conventional, but he was a great father."

There was a moment of silence. "Of course he was, *chica.* Of course he was."

Gillie tucked the box in her backpack carefully, making sure it was protected. Then she zipped the backpack and slung it on her shoulder, smiling brightly at her friend. "Don't worry about me, Enriqué," she said. "I know what I'm doing."

It was hot in the oversize metal cigar that was supposed to carry Rafe back to the States and a cell. Hot and cramped and airless. Rafe had been in smaller planes, but not often. Three seats lined either side of the plane's narrow aisle, two facing front and one facing the rear.

Handcuffs and chains were a damn sight more confining

than the little prop plane. Rafe's jaw clenched. He hadn't known that he'd be taken back in chains, when he'd contacted the embassy two days ago.

Never let the bastards know they're getting to you. He'd learned that before he was nine. "You said I'd get a hand free during the flight," he reminded Winston.

"That was before my partner got hit. We'll see." The marshal faced the front of the plane on one side of the aisle. Rafe sat on the other side of the aisle, facing rear. It gave them both some legroom, while letting the cop keep an eye on his prisoner. Winston glanced outside and frowned. "What's she doing now?"

Rafe looked out the window. The wren was making a slow circuit of her plane. "Looks like a preflight check."

"Dammit, her boss already did that. He told her he would."

Winston's vehemence made Rafe look at him closely. Winston's face was flushed from the heat trapped in the plane's metal body. Sweat beaded on his upper lip, and his eyes were restless. Too restless.

The marshal hadn't been this shook up when a sedan pulled alongside them this morning on the highway and the passenger opened up with a semiautomatic. "You getting jumpy about being a target, Winston? Beginning to think maybe I wasn't lying, after all?"

"Getting shot at proves someone doesn't like you. It doesn't prove anything else."

"It ought to suggest that someone is pretty damned interested in keeping me from getting to the States."

"Maybe. That still doesn't make you one of the good guys."

Rafe didn't bother to respond. Nothing would ever make him "one of the good guys." Not as far as most of the law-abiding citizens of Dolores, New Mexico, were concerned, anyway. But their opinions didn't matter. Not now that he'd sent the list of bank accounts and dummy corporations to his DEA contact. Relying on someone else to do what had to be done made Rafe nervous, but it couldn't be helped. With luck, he wouldn't spend more than a night or two behind bars.

With luck, that wouldn't be long enough to get him killed.

"Damn, how much longer is she going to take?" Winston exclaimed.

Their pilot chose that moment to climb the two steps into the plane. She wore black wraparound sunglasses and carried a neon green backpack. Her brown hair swung in a shiny ponytail from the back of her red cap.

Rafe expected her to blow a big, pink bubblegum bubble any minute.

"We've got good weather for the takeoff," she said cheerfully. "No wind to speak of." Two steps took her to the rear of the little plane. She opened a locker and stowed the garish backpack inside.

"No wind? No air, you mean," Winston muttered. "It's about time you showed up. It's damned hot in here."

"Sorry about that." She moved back to the open door, bent and pulled up the stairs, which became the bottom half of the cabin door. "Can't get the air-conditioning going until I start the engines. It'll take a while to cool off in here, I'm afraid." With a few practiced motions she had the top half of the door down and locked in place.

"I saw you outside. Your boss said he did the preflight already. I don't appreciate unnecessary delay."

She straightened. Her eyebrows went up. "Who takes care of your gun?" She held a notebook, a map and a six-pack of Cokes as she started up the aisle. Her eyes stayed carefully away from Rafe.

He almost smiled. She was not at all happy about the way she felt around him, was she? Poor little wren, attracted to a bad man.

"I don't see what that has to do with anything," Winston said.

"When I'm going to trust my life to a piece of equipment," she said, "I like to be the one to check it out."

Winston gripped the armrest on either side of him tightly, as if someone might try to wrestle his seat away from him. "I guess I should apologize."

She paused next to him. "Are you not a comfortable flyer,

Marshal? Is it the size of the plane that's bothering you—or the pilot?''

He hesitated. "I don't much care for small planes."

She nodded sympathetically. "A lot of people feel that way. You do bounce around more in a plane this size than in a 747, but I promise you I know what I'm doing. I've been a licensed pilot for eleven years, and—''

Rafe's chuckle surprised him as much as it did the others. "You started flying when you were four? Or five?"

Those black sunglasses swung around to face him. Her pointed chin went up haughtily. "I was sixteen when I got my first U.S. license, but I'd already been flying for years. I'm currently licensed to fly in four countries."

Maybe it was something about the way the glasses hid her eyes, focusing his attention elsewhere. Maybe it was only his body's currently deprived state. But her lips looked suddenly, intensely appealing. Soft, naked lips. Tender. Almost virginal.

He stared at those pretty lips. He knew exactly what he'd like to do to them. He could think of things he'd like them to do to him, too—although, in spite of her laying claim to twenty-seven years, he doubted she knew how.

Suddenly the idea of teaching an innocent didn't seem boring. Not boring at all.

"Can we get this thing in the air?" the marshal said testily.

She blinked startled eyes. "Sure," she said, and hurried the last few steps to the cockpit. Rafe watched her go, his face unsmiling and blank, his body fiercely, futilely aroused.

Gillie scowled as she tossed her map, flight log and sack of canned Cokes in the empty copilot's seat and slid into her own.

It was perverted, that's what it was. Staring like that at a man who was probably a murderer, and getting so flustered she forgot the marshal was even there.

Flustered? Try *hot,* she amended mentally as she flicked the mags on. She was embarrassed for herself.

She punched the first Start button and flipped the primer switch—left engine, toggle left. The engine started with a throaty growl.

Just because he stared at my mouth like he wanted to kiss it or something. Good grief, what would happen if he—

No, she was not going to think about that. Or him.

The oil pressure looked good, so she repeated the procedure for the right engine, paused to listen and to check her gauges, then continued the start-up procedure. Alternators—check. Wing flaps up, locator beacon armed, bus switch on, radio set. She slipped on the headphones and talked to the tower.

Of course she didn't know for certain he was a murderer, she thought as she listened to the tower's instructions. Just that he'd been accused.

"Fasten your seat belts," she called out to her passengers, and briefed them on the flight as she taxied to the end of the runway, speaking loudly to be heard over the engines. "We're going to be flying high, about twenty thousand feet, to get above the turbulence along the mountain range. We should arrive in El Paso around six forty-five local time, since we jump over a time zone on the way."

She wondered if Rafael Stormwalker dreaded reaching El Paso, if he wished the flight could take twice as long. She wondered if he really was a murderer. He looked, she thought, like a man capable of killing.

Gillie shivered and set all thoughts of the man called Stormwalker firmly aside. She set the plane's brakes, throttled up the engines and ran her final checks. Excitement sang in her blood as she prepared to take to the sky, a feeling as stirringly familiar to her as a lover's touch might have been to another woman.

The buried hum of apprehension was foreign. She ignored it.

Ten minutes later the little Cessna leaped into the air.

Takeoff didn't agree with Winston. He looked green and said little as the small plane's nose pointed at the sky and they climbed, hard and fast, toward the mountains, bumping along from one air pocket to another like a speedboat smacking against choppy waves.

Once they leveled off, though, the marshal's nerves seemed

to ease along with the turbulence. Thirty minutes into the flight, Gillie was able to pass him the news relayed to her from the ground: his partner was out of surgery and in good condition.

Two hours and five minutes later, Gillie shook her head at those unsettling twinges of foreboding she'd felt earlier. Pure silliness. She sipped at her warm, flat Coke and hummed an aria from *Carmen*. Between the engine noise and the headphones she wore she couldn't hear herself at all, but that didn't matter. Humming or whistling helped her hear the music inside her head.

This was turning out to be an ideal flight, long enough to satisfy her craving for the sky, challenging enough to keep her alert. Her passengers had been so quiet she could almost forget they were there.

Almost. Gillie suspected Winston had a touch of claustrophobia. Every so often he'd get up and move restlessly the few paces that took him up and down the aisle. Sometimes he spoke to her, sometimes he didn't.

The other man hadn't spoken since they took off. So why was his invisible, unheard presence so much more distracting than the marshal's pacing?

It was almost time to switch to the auxiliary fuel tanks, leaving just enough fuel in the main tanks for their landing in El Paso. Gillie set down her half-full Coke and smoothed out the map that lay spread out on the copilot's seat, ready to check her position.

She liked to see how stingy she could be with her fuel, balancing airspeed, elevation and distance against other variables like cargo and the presence of headwinds or tailwinds. Pops had started her playing the game as soon as she could do the math and read the charts. Such a game had a serious meaning to any pilot, but especially for one like Ned Appleby, who'd flown his plane on a shoestring budget most of the time.

She thought of the Piper her father had flown for the last several years of his life. She'd had to sell it to cover his medical expenses.

Gillie frowned, impatient with herself. There was a time for grief, but that time was past. She had no interest in examining the muddier emotions that tagged along with some memories. No, she wasn't about to spoil this moment, while she flew above some of the most ruggedly beautiful country on God's earth, with those unwanted feelings.

She looked at the rolls and ridges of earth far below, teasingly revealed by the scattered cloud cover. It looked like some impossibly huge cat had clawed the mountains, gouging long, deep strips from the earth, which had bled a misty cover of clouds to cover its wounds. She checked her map and her fuel gauges, and smiled. Aside from the time she'd gotten a push from a hurricane, this was the best mileage she'd made on this route.

Hitting every other note as she hummed a passage from Beethoven's Fifth, she reached down and hit the switch to change the right engine to the auxiliary fuel tank, then the left.

She didn't see the marshal get up and start pacing. She felt it, though, in the slight quiver of the plane. When he spoke from behind her she slipped her headphones off. "What did you say?"

"Looks like rough country down there," he said.

"We're over the last of the Barrancas del Cobre," she said, "the Copper Canyon area. It's rough, all right, and about as remote as any spot on this continent. Pretty, isn't it?"

His grunt might have meant agreement.

"The Indians have a lot of legends about this area. They say—" she broke off, listening.

"What?"

Her right engine coughed again, then cut out for a couple seconds. "Go sit down."

"Ms. Appleby—"

"Sit down! Now!" Her gaze flew over her instrument panel.

The plane yawed sharply in the same second the right engine belched black smoke. The marshal left, stumbling as the plane tilted. She heard him, but paid no attention. She had none to spare.

Fly the plane. The words came to her in her father's voice.

Ned Appleby had drummed the rule into her over and over: in an emergency, don't think about cargo, crew, passengers or the possibility of crashing. Just fly the plane.

The engine was clattering and pinging now, but her gauges said everything was normal—no, wait. The cylinder temp was high.

She pulled the throttle back to idle. The engine still shook, and the plane shuddered with it. Black smoke streamed from the engine casing. With her left hand on the yoke, Gillie fought the violent pitch and yaw of the small craft. Her heart pounded as hard as the damaged engine.

Something had to give.

Winston yelled a question. She ignored him, grabbed the prop control and feathered her right propeller, turning it sideways to cut the drag. Then she shut off the engine.

In the suddenly quieter cabin she heard the marshal clearly. "What the hell is going on?"

Gillie wished to heaven she knew. Swiftly she reset the wing flaps to compensate for single engine flight. "The right engine's shot," she called out. "I've had to shut it off, but we can fly on a single engine." Not easily or well—she'd lost eighty percent of her performance when she shut down one engine—but the Cessna would fly. "We won't make it to El Paso, though."

"Where, then? Someplace close? Dammit, I want you to get us down now!"

The hysterical edge to Winston's voice worried her, but she was too busy to deal with it. She sorted though her options, fighting to keep the plane's nose up while spreading the map out in the copilot's seat. Could she make it to Chihuahua?

Winston was ranting about her getting them down. A deeper voice broke in. "Shut up and let her concentrate. She can't put us down on top of a mountain."

A quick calculation told her Chihuahua was too far. Cuauhtémoc? She'd never landed there, but they had an airstrip. It should be about—

The left engine knocked. Sputtered.

"Well, hell," she said.

Gillie scanned her gauges. What was wrong? What would make both engines...*both* engines. Right after she switched to the auxiliary tanks.

Bad fuel.

Acting half on logic, half on desperation, she reached down and switched the left engine back to the main tank, and held her breath.

It continued to run rough but it was running. For now. She'd left half an hour's worth of fuel in the tanks for the landing, but that was half an hour with two engines running smooth. She had one engine ruined, one damaged, little fuel and less time.

The cold clutch of fear made her belly cramp, but her mind stayed clear. She had maybe fifteen minutes to descend between twelve and fifteen thousand feet and find something resembling clear, level ground to put this plane down on.

Fly the plane.

"Looks like you're getting your wish, Marshal," she called over the noisy left engine. "We're going to land now, one way or another. If you're a religious man you might start praying."

Clouds shredded around the plane as she took them down fast, fast enough to make her ears ache and her stomach jump. Faster than was safe, but she had little choice. She had to lose both altitude and airspeed quickly.

When the noise of some kind of commotion back in the cabin reached her dimly, she ignored it.

Fly the plane.

She did. With no one to admire her skill but God and whichever angels rode those wings with her, she put in the best thirteen minutes of flying of her life. But all she saw as she pulled out of her dive was mountains—wooded, rocky, steeply stumbling, up-and-down slopes with cliffs and gorges, boulders and trees. Nothing flat. Nothing clear.

When she spotted the ridge between two gorges she had—maybe—two minutes of powered flight left. The flattened mountaintop was partially wooded, but almost level. And it was long enough. Maybe. If the trees slowed them down without gutting the plane, tipping it, or sending it tumbling down the mountain....

She made her decision and banked.

As they dropped toward the ridge the engine hiccupped and died. With nothing to listen to but the screaming of the wind outside, Gillie fought to keep the plane steady while flicking off the mags, the engines, everything else that might start a fire.

This was going to be one hell of a messy landing.

Seconds to go. No clearing. She pointed the nose between two trees and hoped she'd sheer the wings off cleanly instead of flipping the plane and playing Jack and Jill all the way down the mountain. And she said her own hasty prayer.

She was too busy flying the plane to hear Winston screaming as they hit.

Chapter 2

Gillie hurt. She hurt everywhere. Somewhere on the other side of that pain was a voice urging her to wake up, but that didn't sound like a good idea. No, she'd just slip back into the hovering grayness...

"Wake up, dammit. Unless you want to play crispy critter when this thing catches fire."

Fire? Alarmed, she opened her eyes.

Bad idea. She closed them again, but carried the image of a man's face with her—a rough, dangerous man with a predator's eyes. "Is there a fire?" she whispered.

"Not yet," Rafael Stormwalker said grimly.

She'd just rest a minute, then. "My head hurts," she explained in another whisper.

"I don't think you're badly concussed. You weren't out more than ten minutes, and your pupils are the same size."

It occurred to Gillie that she was alive. She forced her eyes open again, and her mouth stretched up. "I did it. I did set us down on top of a mountain."

"So you did." Something flickered in those dark eyes.

Maybe it was a smile. "I still don't see how, but you did it. Are you injured anywhere other than that knot on your head?"

She shifted, and grimaced. Her left hip hurt. Her shoulder throbbed. Every bone in her body ached, and her head...she raised a shaky hand to the side of her head. The lump there felt huge.

Obviously she'd bounced off something harder than her skull.

Gillie had no memory of the impact, but she could guess what she'd hit. The windshield and instrument panel were a lot closer to her than they should be. The man who knelt beside her was wedged into an awkwardly small space because the copilot's seat was filled with crumpled metal.

"I'm okay. What about you?" Shakily she reached for her seat belt.

"Nothing major."

The buckle didn't want to cooperate, but she managed to fumble it open. "So where's the marshal?"

"He didn't make it."

Oh, damn, damn, damn—

"Not your fault," he said coolly. "He was hysterical at the end. Wouldn't stay in his seat. When we hit, he bounced off something and broke his neck."

Gillie swallowed. "He seemed like a good man. He didn't deserve—"

"Life has damned little to do with what we deserve. Can you move or not?"

"Sure." He was right. The chance that fire would break out lessened with every minute, but it didn't go away. She turned in her seat.

The world turned, too, but in the other direction, making everything spin in a slow circle.

"Damn you, don't you pass out on me again." Hard hands gripped her shoulders.

Her head throbbed the way her big toe did when she stubbed it. "I'm fine." She pushed at his hands. "Move back so I can get out."

He looked disgusted, but he did drop his hands. Slowly he

rose, though he was unable to straighten in the crumpled cockpit. He seemed to be favoring one leg. "If you can get up under your own power, do it."

"Right," she said, and took a steadying breath. Her eyes were almost level with his waist, and his shirt hung open.

He had a large gun tucked into the waist of his pants.

Surviving the landing hadn't exactly ended her troubles, had it? "My map," she said. "We'll need the map. It's on the seat behind you."

He grimaced. The map would be hard to locate in the cramped space. He had to twist around to do it. While he was looking the other way, Gillie tried hard to think past the pounding in her head.

She was stranded in some of the most isolated country on the continent, alone with a man who was probably a murderer. A man who had been in chains until now. But the chains were gone, weren't they? So were the handcuffs and the manacles on his legs. Which meant that he'd gotten the key for them off the marshal's body, along with the marshal's gun.

The marshal's *dead* body.

Just how had Winston died?

He turned toward her again, map in hand. "We have to get out of here."

"Okay." With one hand on the back of her seat for leverage, she leaned toward him as she started to rise—and as she stood, she pulled the gun out of his waistband.

Then her head fell off in a Technicolor explosion, and she passed out again.

Night falls fast and cold in the mountains in late January. Even in Mexico, a winter night at six thousand, five hundred feet can kill the ignorant, the unprepared or the injured. In terms of climate, vegetation and wildlife, the Sierra Madres had more in common with their northern cousins, the Rockies, than they did with the rest of Mexico.

Rafe wasn't ignorant, but he was unprepared and injured. He'd been slowed by the thin mountain air, by his knee, badly swollen now and nearly useless, and by the woman.

She was pretty much useless, too, at the moment. But he'd be dead, not just crippled and cursing, if not for her flying skill. Little in Rafe's life had surprised him as much as the moment when, after the plane finished bouncing off trees and boulders, he realized he was still alive.

The wren had turned out to be one hell of a pilot. Rafe figured that, of the three of them, she had most deserved for fate to perform a little sleight of hand in her favor. But he'd never seen life give the innocent any breaks before. Once he'd gotten over his shock at being alive, he'd expected the worst.

He'd called her name. Even before he got untangled from his seat belt and went after the keys in Winston's pocket, he'd called her. She hadn't answered, and he hadn't wanted to look in the cockpit.

But she'd made it, too—a second amazement in a day already ripped loose of all predictable moorings. She'd even woken up long enough to try and steal the .45 he'd taken from Winston's body.

Rafe leaned against the trunk of a pine tree, Gillie's limp body cradled against him for warmth, and let his mouth curl up in a smile. She was scrappy, all right. Stubborn. He respected those qualities.

Getting her out had been a royal pain. She didn't weigh much, but it was enough to finish wrecking his knee. He'd fallen once before making it to this straggly ponderosa pine fifty feet from the downed plane. Then he'd sunk to the ground, pulled his unconscious burden close for warmth and cursed his knee and the temperature. He guessed it was about forty-five degrees right now.

It was going to get a lot colder.

Rafe had a few other sore places, too, but the pain from his knee drowned out the other aches…except for one. Not that he should have been capable of that particular ache under the circumstances. But the woman he held was soft and warm. She'd lost the red cap she'd worn earlier. Her hair fell loose and silky over his supporting arm, and his body craved the life in hers.

She was also unconscious. The ground beneath him was

cold, and the woman he held was small. Heat would drain
from her body a lot faster than his, just like the coming night
would leach any lingering warmth from the thin mountain air.
He couldn't rest his knee for long. That peak to the west would
cut off the last couple of hours of sunshine.

The plane wasn't likely to explode into flames now. The
fuel tanks were in the wings, and the wings were gone. Reluctantly he laid the woman down, pushed to his feet and
hobbled back to the little Cessna.

Inside the plane's canted body he turned to the rear. Winston's body lay across the aisle between the door and the
locker that was Rafe's goal.

Rafe looked down at the ungraceful sprawl of the corpse.
Death didn't leave a man much dignity. He knelt and said a
few words in a tongue neither English nor Spanish—the barely
remembered scrap of a prayer his mother had spoken over him
when he was small and afraid of the dark.

Then he began stripping the corpse. The living had more
need of warmth than the dead.

Rafe had seen death when he was in the army, but he'd
never dealt intimately with a body. Undressing one turned out
to be as frustrating as it was unpleasant. He turned up a real
prize, though: a pocketknife. He did smile when he found that.
A knife raised their chances considerably.

The rear locker held another prize, a first aid kit, as well as
the woman's neon green backpack. He stuck one inside the
other, then used his knife to slit three of the seats open. He
needed the padding.

Then he paused.

Winston's glasses were under the seat. They'd survived the
crash in better shape than the man. Rafe put them back on the
dead face, tucking the earpieces behind the ears. It was a foolish act, as pointless as most sentimental gestures were, and he
was irritated with himself for wasting time.

He climbed out of the plane carrying the backpack, Winston's suit jacket, shoulder holster, socks and tie, and an arm-
ful of stuffing from the plane's seats. He was wearing the dead
man's shirt.

While he was in the plane the sun had begun to set. Lucid orange light flooded the ridge, light so pure he could almost drink the color out of the air. Across the clearing, the woman was awake. She was sitting up, hugging her bare arms around herself and looking at him. Some trick of the slanting light turned those blue eyes of hers into a color he had no name for.

Those unlikely eyes met his from twenty feet away.

A peculiar sensation stopped him in his tracks, a jolt like when a sleeper dreams of falling and the waiting body wakes with a startled jerk. He shook his head. After a moment he got himself moving again, trying to keep his weight off his injured knee.

Her face was pale. She shivered and looked away when he reached her. He dropped his load next to her, bent, and took her face firmly in one hand. Her skin was soft and warm. He wanted to pet it the way he'd pet a cat.

"Hey!" She tried to pull away. "What do you think you're doing?"

"Checking your pupils." He kept her face turned to him in spite of her squirming. Her pupils were still the same size. Good. He ran the fingers of his other hand lightly over the side of her head. She winced.

He nodded, satisfied. "That's a nice, big lump you have."

"You sound awfully happy about it."

"A knot on your skull is better than a dent. That would mean a depressed skull fracture."

She shivered again.

Rafe was deeply relieved that she'd woken again and didn't seem to be suffering anything worse than a headache. When she'd passed out the second time, he'd worried. It could have meant she was bleeding inside her skull—bad news, very bad. Even if the hemorrhage didn't kill her right away, she wouldn't have been able to travel. And she had to be able to travel. He couldn't leave her behind. He owed her.

Rafe lived by two laws: he did what was necessary to survive, and he paid his debts.

She stared up at him. "You're wearing the marshal's shirt."

"Yes." He lowered himself to the ground a few feet away. "You can have his jacket." He tossed it to her.

She flinched.

"Being squeamish can kill you in a survival situation," he told her and reached for the backpack, taking out the first aid kit. Carefully he emptied it on the ground. Bandages, peroxide, adhesive tape, aspirin, medicines for motion sickness and nausea, gauze…and, yes, thank God, iodine. If—when—they found water they'd have to purify it. Iodine tasted nasty, but it worked as well as boiling did.

So far he hadn't found any matches. You couldn't boil water without a fire, and he wasn't sure he could start a fire without matches.

The box itself was metal and would make a decent digging tool. "The temperature is going to drop to freezing or below tonight. Put the jacket on, and everything else you've got in that bag of yours."

She grimaced, but reached for the backpack.

He moved a few feet away to a hollow next to a ragged granite outcropping. With grim haste he began scooping away the sandy soil, first with his hands, then with the metal box, heaping it alongside the hollow.

"Oh," she said. "Oh, thank goodness."

He glanced over his shoulder.

She was holding a carved wooden box. Her face glowed with relief. After looking inside, she set it aside carefully, as if the contents were valuable.

He looked back at his task.

"So what are you doing?" she asked. He heard her dressing behind him—a rustle of cloth, the soft crunch of pine needles as she moved. The sounds were almost as erotic as if she'd been removing clothing instead of adding more.

Rafe grimaced at the dirt in front of him. "Digging."

"I can see that." More cloth-rustling sounds, followed by sharply drawn breath. "Damn head," she muttered. For a moment there were no sounds, either of pain or movement. Then she asked in a careful voice, "How did you say Winston died?"

He stopped digging and looked at her. A little rush of heat zipped through his system, as if she'd run her fingers along his zipper.

His reaction was ridiculous. She looked like a ragamuffin. He couldn't even see those pretty legs of hers anymore. She wore Winston's suit jacket over a yellow sweatshirt, which in turn covered a plain white shirt. It looked like she'd sensibly pulled her jeans on over her baggy shorts. Her hair trailed halfway down her back without a hint of curl—an ash brown waterfall, soft and inviting.

Irritated, he snapped, "What happened to your hat?"

"I guess it's still in the plane. How did Winston die?"

He realized, suddenly, why she was asking. Funny. It hadn't occurred to him she might think he'd killed the marshal. Under the circumstances, though, it was only smart of her to wonder.

Even odder that it would bother him. "I told you. He broke his neck."

"Just before we landed there was some kind of ruckus between you, wasn't there?"

He shook his head. Just when he was ready to give her credit for good sense, she went and got stupid on him. "You should be trying to persuade me you're not suspicious of me, not asking me whether I killed the marshal or not."

"Did you?" she persisted. "Did you kill him?"

Rafe scowled. "Yes." He turned back to his digging.

For several minutes there was complete silence except for the sighing of the wind through the pines, a wind chilly enough to make Rafe glad of his borrowed shirt and the exertion that kept him warm. He didn't look at the woman. Survival was what mattered, not the opinion of one foolish wren.

His improvised digging tool scraped rock. This was as deep as he could go, then. Not deep enough. He'd have to try building a wall of rock and dirt opposite the natural wall of granite.

When she finally spoke again, the sound of her voice startled him—but not as much as her words did. "I don't believe you."

"All right, don't." The stupid woman would believe whatever she wanted, not from logic or a sense of fair play, but because it suited her. That's how people were. Apparently she wanted to believe she was safe with him. "Have it your way. I didn't kill him, but I was responsible for his death."

"How did he die, then?"

Rafe owed her his life, but he didn't owe her any explanations. He set aside the box and reached for a rock half the size of his head, grunting as he shifted it into place in the mounded earth next to the trench he'd dug. Then he reached for another one.

"Winston wasn't exactly a happy flier," she said.

"No kidding."

"I think he was claustrophobic. He didn't sound completely rational toward the end."

"Rational? He went nuts." Rafe dragged another rock into place. "When you said to start praying, he came unglued. He jumped out of his seat, yelling that he had to stop you from getting us killed. I stopped him instead."

"How?"

Rafe stood. Why was he talking to her? Because she made him hard? Surely not. He hadn't been that brainless since he first discovered hormones.

There weren't any more rocks the right size within grabbing distance. He limped a few feet away.

She scrambled to her feet. "How did you stop him?"

"How's your head?" He bent and picked up two decent-size rocks. "Any dizziness?"

"It hurts, but I'm not dizzy."

She was pale, though. "Get another rock about this size," he told her, hefting a stone he knew it would take her two hands to lift. Maybe if he kept her busy she'd shut up.

He barely had his two rocks in place when she brought him another one—bigger than either of his. She held it in both hands, all right, and her face looked pasty. He shook his head. Idiot woman. "Give it here."

She did. "Why are we moving rocks around? Why did you dig a hole in the ground?"

"I'm trying to keep the two of us alive tonight."

Her nose wrinkled skeptically. "With a hole in the ground?"

"This is where we'll sleep."

The expression on her face was hilarious—almost enough to make him forget the ache in his knee…and elsewhere.

"There?" she squeaked. "In the ground? Together? No." She shook her head, which must have made her head hurt. She reached up to cradle her head in one hand, her eyes tight with pain. "No, I don't think so. You can sleep there if you want, but not me. I'll be in the plane."

"The plane looks safer because it's a piece of civilization," he said, mounding dirt around the rocks he'd placed, "but we're not in a civilized situation now. Thinking in those terms is dangerous."

She frowned at him. "So how do you know so much about this, anyway?"

"Two hitches in the Army Special Forces a few years back. Primitive camping since."

She looked around, as if further study of the area might turn up some other option. No Motel 6 popped up out of the rocks. She looked at him again. "So why is a hole in the ground better than a slightly crumpled airplane?"

"Our bodies can heat a small, insulated space. They can't heat the interior of the plane. Dirt is a good insulator." He wished he'd been able to dig deeper, but the low wall he was building opposite the natural one would help.

She watched him. "How did you stop Winston?"

God, did she never let up? "Go get me some more rocks."

"Tell me how you stopped Winston."

"I tripped him. Is that what you wanted to know? I stuck my legs out into the aisle. He tripped and he hit his head. He didn't pass out, but he was disoriented, too groggy to get back in his seat before we crashed. That's why he broke his neck."

She was silent for as long as it took him to finish heaping dirt around the rocks already in place. Then she said, "We didn't crash. It was a forced landing, not a crash."

Rafe almost smiled. It scraped her pride to call their landing a crash, did it? He understood about pride. Because he considered it almost as important to survival as water and warmth, he didn't argue with her. He just kept digging.

Gillie watched the man digging in the dirt in front of her. She was afraid.

Fear was a normal, human emotion. It came in lots of different colors, including the grinding gray she'd lived with as her father slowly coughed his life out in a Venezuelan hospital bed. But this fear was different. This feeling was slow and icy. She was hundreds of miles from anything familiar, alone in the wilderness with a man who might be a killer. A man who made her uneasy on a deep, instinctive level.

A man who looked touched by some pagan god, gilded as he was at this moment by the dying sun's copper blaze. He was spectacular.

She didn't know what to do.

"If your head's better," he said, standing and looking around—for more of his rocks, no doubt, "try doing something more useful than staring at me. If your head isn't better, sit down. Can you take a couple of aspirin dry?"

"No," she said, and shuddered at the idea. *Think,* she told herself. But her brain wasn't working right. The dizziness was gone, but her head still throbbed like the inside of a kettle-drum.

If she couldn't think, she'd act. "I'm hungry. I'm going to see what I can find."

He shot her a withering look and limped over to another small pile of rocks. "Run on down to the market and bring me back something, too, why don't you?"

She grimaced. "I *meant* that there should be something in the plane. Crackers, at least. We stock those for people who get queasy." And there were her Cokes. She could take the aspirin with one of those.

"It's too far to walk with a concussion. You won't be any use to me if you keel over again."

"It's too far to walk with a bum knee, too, but you did it. Look," she said. "I can function. You're stronger than me, so you stay here and play with your rocks while I see what's in the plane."

After a moment he nodded. "All right. But if you feel dizzy, sit down until it passes. I might not bother to haul you out here again."

She started to take off the jacket.

"What in the hell are you doing now?"

"You should have this. I've got two shirts and a sweatshirt on."

"It doesn't fit." He picked up another two rocks.

She eyed him skeptically. "The shirt does." Sort of. It only buttoned part of the way up his chest.

"The jacket doesn't," he said curtly.

She gave up and turned away.

The ridge she'd landed on was fairly narrow, and roughly the length of two football fields. The ground fell away sharply on the north and west, less steeply to the south and east. The altitude and the rough, rocky ground had discouraged all but the hardiest conifers.

What remained of the Cessna lay about fifty feet away, crunched up against a granite outcropping.

Gillie had loved that little plane. Looking at what was left of it hurt. Both wings were gone. They'd snapped off cleanly, just as she'd planned. One of them lay near the edge of the ridge. The plane had sheared a short, violent path from there to its final resting spot.

She walked slowly. It was getting colder, so movement felt good, even though it made her head pound. *One thing at a time,* she told herself. Food and shelter came first. She had to see what she could find aboard the crumpled Cessna.

And then? Was she really going to curl up with Rafael Stormwalker in his hole in the ground? Did she believe him when he said he knew what he was doing, that he'd had Special Forces training?

Did she believe him when he said he hadn't killed the marshal?

Of course, he hadn't said that. First he'd claimed he killed the marshal, then that he was responsible for the man's death. But if Rafe was telling the truth, Winston had brought about his own death. They would all have died if Rafe hadn't stopped him. Any distraction during those last, impossibly tense moments of landing would have resulted in a real crash, the kind no one walked away from.

That claim of responsibility wasn't what she expected from a murderer. It implied that he was troubled by his part in Winston's death.

Did killers have consciences?

Gillie reached the little plane's tilted body. After a pause to gather her courage, she pulled herself through the doorway.

Rafe's head came up when Gillie reached the Cessna. He watched her hesitate as the last of the orange sunset faded into the soft gray of twilight, watched as intently as a cat at a mouse hole when she swung inside.

The temperature was dropping rapidly.

He stood and limped toward the wrecked plane.

Gillie's arms were full when she headed to the exit. It made her progress across the plane's tilted floor awkward. She decided to set the sack down next to the doorway so she could toss out the—

"Give me some of that stuff you're carrying."

His voice made her jump. She started to slide backward.

He reached up, grabbed her around the waist and lifted her down. His big hands felt as inflexible as the manacles he'd worn earlier in the day.

She landed on her feet in front of him and realized all over again how large he was. Not handsome. No, not even good-looking. Both words were ordinary, and he was extraordinary. She didn't like noticing that, but she did. In the gathering gray of twilight he wasn't as spectacular as he'd been earlier, but he was still an incredible male specimen.

And large. Definitely large. She shivered.

He let her go.

"Thanks," she said warily, and took a step back.

"The blankets will help."

"They're small, I'm afraid."

"And the pillows?" One of his dark eyebrows twitched up. He held out a hand imperatively. "All the comforts of home."

"I don't see anything wrong with comfort. And pillows are insulation, too." She hesitated. He *couldn't* know what she'd planned to do. It was only her guilty conscience that made her think he looked so...knowing. And what did she have to be guilty about, anyway? She'd intended to share the food and blankets before closing herself up in the plane, leaving him sole ownership of his hole in the ground.

She could still do it. "There's a couple more things I need to get from the plane," she said craftily.

"Forget it. I'm not about to let you hole up in there and freeze to death. I'm going to need your body warmth tonight almost as much as you'll need mine."

Her mouth dropped open.

He shook his head. "You have an incredibly transparent face, you know. Give me the blankets and pillows."

Reluctantly she handed them over.

"What else did you find?"

"Food," she said fervently. "Raul—he's one of the other pilots—he snacks a lot. I found four packages of instant soup, half a jar of peanut butter, some crackers, three candy bars and a big bag of M&M's. And I had some cola in the cockpit." Gillie fell silent, wondering if—no, when—she'd see Raul again. And Enriqué. And Timothy Lee, Berto, Maria, Raquel—heavens, she'd even settle for seeing Montaldo's oily face.

Speaking of faces... "You put his glasses back on," she said.

He scowled. "What?"

"Winston's glasses. They must have fallen off when we landed. You put them back on him."

"So?"

"You took his shirt and jacket, his socks and shoes and tie—and put his glasses back on."

"I didn't need the damned glasses." He moved away, toward the back of the plane. "Didn't your boss load Winston's suitcase somewhere in the tail?"

"Probably." Rafael Stormwalker was not an easy man to figure out. She frowned and followed him. "I don't know if we'll be able to get to it, though. Everything is pretty messed up back here.'' She ran her hands over the dented section that was supposed to open to reveal a small storage area. ''Are you afraid it makes you too human?''

''What?''

''Putting the marshal's glasses back on him. Do you think that caring about the dignity of a dead man makes you too human?''

He stared at her in disbelief. ''You have to be the nosiest female I've ever met.''

Gillie didn't think she was nosy, exactly, but she was a bit more direct than most people. She shrugged and tried the release. Jammed, just like she'd thought. ''If I don't ask, people won't tell me what I want to know. Look, this panel isn't going to open without a pry bar.''

''I doubt that will stop you,'' he muttered. ''Just keep asking it why it won't open.''

But they couldn't get the luggage compartment open, not in the short time they had left before night fell. Rafe went into the plane to get the last of the stuffing from the seats, and they started back toward his hole in the ground with their arms full. The world was awash in deepening shades of black and gray. It was cold, and getting colder.

Gillie's head was hurting pretty badly by the time they reached their ''camp.'' She dropped the blankets and pillows she'd carried and stood, swaying slightly.

He put an arm around her. ''Dammit.''

He was hard and warm along her side. So why did she shiver? ''I'm fine. It's probably my blood sugar. I told you I was hungry.''

''You have hypoglycemia? Low blood sugar?''

''No, I just get hungry a lot.'' She admitted, ''My head does hurt a bit.''

''Sit. No, here.'' He moved her where he wanted her, a couple of feet away. ''On the log. It'll keep you off the ground.''

Gillie hated to admit it, but sitting did seem like a good idea.

He moved away, dug through her backpack and came back. "Here." He held something in the palm of one hand. His other hand held out a Coke.

She couldn't see the aspirins, but she felt them when she brushed her fingers across his palm. His hands were warm. Hers weren't. She took the aspirins and then drank gratefully, trying not to be greedy, while he got something out of the food sack.

He handed her crackers and peanut butter. "Make us some supper."

"Give me the knife, then."

"No." He turned and walked away.

She glared at his back as he retreated into the dimness. "Where are you going?"

"To put the rest of the food in a tree and take a leak."

She blushed, opened the peanut butter, and used her finger to start spreading it on crackers.

It sure was dark now, as well as cold. "Did your army training include how to rub a couple of sticks together to make fire?" she called out. A campfire sounded like a great idea. The light would be as welcome as the warmth. It would keep animals away. "Oh, no."

"Now what is it?" His voice told her he was coming back.

"I've heard there are cougars in these mountains. And bears. And what about snakes?" she demanded.

"No snakes," he said. "Not this high and not in winter. Even the rattlers will have moved lower. As for the rest— that's why I put the food in a tree. Animals generally avoid man, though. And," he added, "I have the gun."

Oh, yeah. The gun. "I suppose you learned about guns in the army, too."

"They encourage that sort of thing."

She peered at him through the darkness. Could the granite man have a sense of humor? No, she decided, handing him several of the crackers she'd fixed. Humor and sarcasm weren't the same thing. "So, do your survival skills extend to building a fire?"

"Not unless you found some matches."

Great.

By the time they finished eating and had shared the rest of the Coke she'd opened it was completely dark. The moon wasn't yet up, but the stars—oh, the stars were incredible, so bright and clear Gillie felt she could almost touch them. They gave her dark-adjusted eyes enough light, barely, to make her way apart for a moment to empty her bladder.

"It's almost as good as flying at night," she said when she returned. "Being this high and this far from any city, I mean. The sky looks so…" She ran out of words. She'd never had words for what the sky meant to her.

He stood. "We need to get covered up," he said, "while we've still got some body heat left to conserve." Two steps took him to his hole in the ground. The blankets and the rest of the stuffing were piled next to the hole, ready to be pulled over the two of them.

He knelt.

She didn't move.

His face was a paler blur in the darkness when he looked over his shoulder at her. "What is it now?"

Gillie didn't really think Rafe was going to attack her. He wouldn't have to wait for her to climb in their strange "bed" to do that. But she knew, too, that a woman's looks—or lack of them—didn't always have anything to do with sexual assault. And they would be nestled together very cozily in his hole in the ground, cozy enough to give him ideas he maybe hadn't had yet.

She couldn't make herself move.

After a moment he spoke. "I owe you," he said. "You wouldn't be in this fix if not for me. Your skill kept me alive when you landed the plane. I'll keep you alive here in the wilderness."

It wasn't a promise. He sounded more irritated than reassuring, but that very irritation somehow persuaded her to move forward, toward Rafe and his hole for two.

This was definitely not what she'd dreamed it would be like, the first time she slept with a man. Not what she'd dreamed of at all.

Chapter 3

Morning comes early in the mountains. Gillian woke to the smudgy light of predawn and a chorus of birds trying to chirp the sun up over the horizon. That part was okay. She was used to waking up early, though normally she woke to the smell of coffee, not dirt.

She wasn't used to waking up with a man's hand on her breast.

Even through three layers of material, his hand felt warm. Just like the rest of him, snuggled close along her back. Really warm. The heat from the large, efficient furnace of Rafe's body, trapped by the walls of their sunken bed, had kept them cozy all night, just like he'd claimed. Not comfortable, exactly—not when they lay on rocky ground covered with lumpy padding. But the only cold places on her body were above the neck.

Her nose, for example, was cold. Not her breast. No, that part of her was definitely not cold.

Maybe she could move his hand before he woke up and noticed where it was. That would be almost the same as if he'd never held her breast. If he didn't know where his hand had been, she wouldn't be so embarrassed.

His fingers squeezed.

She scrambled out of their sunken bed as if she'd been shot.

Moving quickly didn't seem like such a good idea once she was shivering in the early-morning air. Every sore spot on her body had stiffened up overnight. She rubbed her aching hip and glared at him, trying to ignore the tingles still racing through her from his caress. "I thought you were asleep."

He lay in the middle of the shredded stuffing, smiling up at her in great good humor. "I woke up."

His smile changed him—changed his eyes, his mouth—seemed, even, to change his body, though he didn't move a muscle. For that one moment he looked like another man. One who had never been chained.

"Yeah, well, keep your hands to yourself," she muttered, her cheeks hot, and turned away. Her body felt odd. She hugged her arms, wondering if he could *see* tingles, if they showed the way her goose bumps did.

"I wonder how long it will take them to find us," she said, hobbling over to her backpack. She unzipped it and took out her hairbrush and got started. *Ouch.* She learned not to brush anywhere near the knot on her head.

"I was hoping you could give me some idea of that." He levered himself up and out, moving even more stiffly than she had.

"Your knee's worse, isn't it?"

"I need to bind it. How's your head?"

"Better." Compared to yesterday it was great, in fact. At least one thing had improved overnight.

Gillie didn't figure any woman would actually choose to have stick-straight hair like hers or small breasts, but there were advantages. She could go braless without anyone knowing like she had for this trip, and her hair never tangled badly. She finished brushing it and put it into a quick braid, fastening the end with a covered rubber band, then dug around in the backpack for her toothpaste and toothbrush.

She glanced at her first-ever bed partner uncertainly. It seemed rude not to share.

"Go ahead," he said. "I'll wait and see if we can get Winston's suitcase out. May I use your hairbrush?"

The civilized request in such uncivilized circumstances made her grin. While she brushed her teeth he brushed his hair, pulling it back in a ponytail he fastened with his red bandanna. Their grooming session reminded her of sleepovers when she was a girl...except, of course, they were on a remote mountain, not in a snug bedroom.

And Rafe was definitely not a teenage girl.

She put her things up and glanced longingly at the three remaining Cokes. "I could sure use some caffeine. Do you think I could open one of the Cokes, or had we better save them and try to find water?"

"There's no water on this ridge. We can split one of them now and another at lunch." He limped toward her. "Do you have any idea how long it might take searchers to find the plane?"

"I'll check the locator beacon today to see if it's working. I should have done that last night, but..." She shrugged. "I couldn't check it out in the dark. Even if it is working, though, the mountains will block the signal unless a search plane flies directly overhead."

"What about your flight plan? Won't they follow that?"

"It's too general for anyone to track us to this specific ridge, though it should give the searchers a rough idea of what area to cover. Truthfully, I think we're going to be here awhile. Several days, at the best." She smiled so she wouldn't panic. "You sure you don't know how to make a fire?"

"We won't starve," he said, "and we won't freeze."

She grimaced and rubbed her arms. "I hate to be cold." Cold, to Gillie, meant a big brick house with white trim and white columns in front. Cold was being twelve years old and spending the winter in that red brick house with people who didn't like the way she dressed or talked or ate. People who wanted her to be someone else.

Gillie had tried. That winter she'd really tried to please her mother, but she'd failed. She hadn't tried again.

Suppressing the twinge of memory, she popped open the Coke.

Rafe watched the woman whose survival had become his obligation. The part in her hair was crooked. Her cheek was smudged with dirt, and her clothes were dusted with it. And he wanted her. His palm still tingled with the memory of the shape and feel of her breast. He watched her swallow and wanted to nibble on her exposed throat.

He turned away, heading for the fir tree where he'd stashed their food. He thought about how pretty she'd looked, standing there all flushed with embarrassment as she glared down at him. He shouldn't have teased her, though, not unless he was ready to go ahead and seduce her, and there was no time for that. Not now.

The paper sack looked undisturbed. He chinned himself on a branch, then pulled himself high enough to reach the sack.

Last night had been bad enough, lying next to her, sharing warmth and covers and a hard, crowded bed. He'd be a fool to encourage his body's unruly urges. He had to focus on surviving.

Rafe dropped back to the ground. He heard her approach and turned.

"I'm starved." She held out the Coke. "Thirsty?"

From what he could tell, she was always starved. "Here," he said, exchanging drink for food. "We'll split one of the candy bars for breakfast."

They ate right there, standing up. It didn't take long.

"I'm going to take another stab at getting the luggage compartment open," he told her. They were going to need everything they could find for their trek down the mountains. He wondered how much trouble she was going to make about leaving the plane.

Gillie licked a last smear of chocolate from her thumb. "There might be some tools in the wing storage. Nothing as useful as a crowbar, probably, but I might find a wrench or something else you could use."

He nodded. "I'll come with you."

That wasn't exactly what Gillie had in mind. She wanted to get away from him for a while, away from those dark, watchful eyes. He unnerved her. She turned abruptly and started across the ridge. Movement felt good.

He kept pace easily in spite of his injury. And he was still watching her. She frowned. "Didn't your mama ever tell you that it's rude to stare?"

"Was I staring?"

"It's rude to answer one question with another one, too."

"I guess you'd know about that."

She glanced at him suspiciously. His expression was as unrevealing as ever. "Is that supposed to be funny?"

"Do I look like I'm joking?"

Her mouth twitched. "About as much as that rock does. Did you hear the one about the cop, the nun and the copy machine?"

He lifted one eyebrow ever so slightly. "No."

"Darn. I keep hoping to find someone who has."

He chuckled.

The unexpected sound charmed her. She felt as if she'd been looking for spilled pennies and found diamonds instead. She wanted him to do it again.

She was an idiot.

As they neared the broken-off wing, he veered to the right, heading toward the nearby cliff. Gillie looked away. She was glad she wouldn't have to go too near that vertical drop-off. A stiff, constant updraft blew along the cliff face. That wind chilled her even this far back.

She stopped about six feet away from her target, her nose wrinkling.

Rafe went right to the edge. "The other wing is on a ledge about thirty feet down," he said, looking down. "It might be possible to get there, but I'd rather not try it without gear."

Gillie frowned at him. He looked perfectly capable of bouncing over the edge of a mountain with a rope in his hands and no more expression on his face than showed right now.

"I suppose, for a fun weekend, you climb rocks when you're not living off the land, eating lizards and grasshoppers."

"Lizards aren't a good source of protein. What's wrong?" He started for her.

"I smell fuel. One of the tanks must have ruptured."

"It's not likely to catch fire just sitting here, is it?"

"No." No, that wasn't what was bothering her. She walked forward slowly. "Did I tell you what went wrong with the plane?"

"I assumed it had something to do with the engines."

"Bad fuel." She explained briefly how she'd reached that conclusion as she knelt beside the wing. She bent over to look at the auxiliary fuel tank. The rupture in the metal was easy to spot.

When she ran her fingertips over the wet surface, they came away slick. Oily. The feel of the liquid confirmed what she'd smelled. "Jet fuel," she whispered.

"Is that bad?"

"Bad?" She laughed—but it wasn't a happy sound. "Jet fuel in a prop plane is sure disaster. It's a wonder we made it down at all. If this had been in the main tanks as well as the auxiliaries, we'd be a smear on the ground a few miles outside of San Luis."

He was silent a moment. "How do you think the mix-up happened?"

"I can't imagine. Most of the planes that operate out of the San Luis airport are props. Only one of the regional airlines flies a jet in regularly, so there's just the one tank for jet fuel, clear on the other side of the field from where Ventura's planes are fueled and serviced."

"I see." He nodded. "Yes, that explains a lot."

She looked skeptical. "It does?"

"It explains why the jet fuel is only in the auxiliary tanks. Whoever did this didn't want us to crash where we'd be easily found and the substitution discovered."

She frowned. "What do you mean, 'whoever did this'?"

"The person who sabotaged the plane."

She stood quickly. "Don't talk nonsense." True, she didn't

see how jet fuel could have been used accidentally—but it couldn't have been deliberate. That would mean someone had tried to kill her. "Good grief," she said, "that's crazy. I know those people."

"When there's enough money involved, we can learn things about people we'd rather not know."

"But I've worked with everyone there for over a year. Well, everyone except Montaldo, but—"

"Your boss was in a hurry to get us off the ground, as I recall."

She stared at him. "If you're implying that my boss was the one who did this—good grief, it's his plane sitting in pieces here. Have you got any idea of what a Cessna like this costs?"

"I'm sure it was insured. But what's important right now isn't who sabotaged the plane. It's the fact that the plane was sabotaged." He moved closer. "You're in trouble because of me, and I'm sorry as hell about it. The only way I can pay you back is to take you with me."

"Contaminated fuel I could understand," she muttered. "It happens. Not often, but it does happen. But jet fuel..." Yet the greasy feel of the spilled fuel was unmistakable.

Belatedly, what he'd said caught up with her. "What do you mean, take me with you?"

"We can't stay here. The people who did this will be coming to check on their handiwork."

"We can't do anything else! Listen, leaving the plane is the worst thing we could do. We're in the middle of a mountain range that covers some of the roughest, least populated country on this continent! There aren't any phones or roads or—"

"That's in our favor, actually. They won't be able to get to us quickly. Which is fortunate, because we won't be able to move fast."

She stared at him a moment longer, then shook her head. "Even if you were right about the plane being sabotaged— I'm not agreeing, mind you, but let's say you're right—no one is going to come after us except the search and rescue people. We're too damned hard to find." She knew what he was really worried about, of course. He didn't want to be recaptured and taken back in chains. She didn't really blame him.

"They'll come," he said grimly.

She stood, grimacing at the oily feel of her fingers. "You think you're that important, do you?"

"What I know is important. A matter of life and death for some people. A matter of money—large amounts of money—for others."

"Oh, right. Next I suppose you'll tell me you didn't really kill anyone, and you had nothing to do with this drug gang that's gunning for you. You're just an innocent bystander, right?"

His face had as much expression as the stones around them. "You've made your mind up already. There's no point in me telling you anything, except that we do have to get out of here. Today."

"Forget it. I'm not going anywhere."

He didn't answer. But the way he looked at her chilled her more than the steady breeze from the cliff.

Gillie found a small toolbox in the wing storage. Rafe used the claw hammer to pry open the luggage compartment. But once he had Winston's suitcase, he set it down without opening it and went back inside the plane. He didn't say why. She didn't ask.

Her head hurt. Her stomach wasn't entirely happy with her, either. Normally she didn't have a problem with altitude sickness, but normally she wasn't concussed. She sat down to look through the contents of Winston's inexpensive canvas bag.

A dress shirt. A pair of slacks. Two pairs of thin dress socks. Briefs. A shaving kit. A wooden box that reminded her of her own treasure box, though this one was plain and smaller.

She opened the box, and found a pipe and a lighter inside.

It was the pipe, not the lighter, that drew Gillie's attention. Her fingers slid over wood smoothed from years of handling, and she thought about the man who would never enjoy this pipe after a meal again. Was there a woman somewhere who'd nagged Winston about smoking the way Gillie used to nag her father? Was that woman waiting now, desperate for word, for hope?

Tears stung her eyes. She blinked fiercely and set the pipe back in its place. "I hope someone finds us soon, so she doesn't have to wait too long."

"What did you say?"

She jumped.

Rafe swung down from the plane's open door.

"I wish you'd quit doing that."

"What?"

"Quit sneaking up on me." Her voice sounded husky. She cleared her throat and blinked a few times before she stood. Years of living in Third-World countries had made Gillie practical about some aspects of living and dying. "We need to bury Winston today. Even in this chilly weather, it won't be pleasant to wait any longer."

"No." He turned around to get something from the plane. "We don't have time, and besides, someone would only have to dig him up later to take him home. We'll make sure the door is securely closed before we leave so that animals can't get in."

Animals. She swallowed. He didn't sugarcoat his meaning, did he? "I'm not leaving the plane."

He limped over to her, carrying several lengths of webbing from the plane's seat belts.

"What are those for?"

"I'm not sure yet. What have you found?"

"Clothes," she said. "A lighter. A shaving kit."

He looked the contents over briefly, nodded and reached for the snap on his jeans. When her eyes rounded he said dryly, "I have to take my pants off to bind my knee. I thought I'd use strips from the shirt you found."

"Oh." Gillie watched him tug his zipper down. She turned around quickly.

He chuckled.

This time the sound didn't charm her at all. "Will you at least leave the lighter with me when you go?"

He didn't answer right away. She could hear him stripping.

Finally he spoke. "How do you think the jet fuel got in the tanks?"

"I—" Somehow that hadn't been what she'd expected him to say—maybe because her mind was occupied with listening to him take his pants off. "I don't know."

"What was the name of the man who came to say that the plane had been fueled?"

"Jorge." She shivered. Now that she thought about it, she could easily imagine that creepy little man sabotaging her plane...only not without reason. Not without orders from his boss.

Cloth tore. He was making the strips to bind his knee. Should she offer to help? She'd have to turn around. See him. Touch him. *A man in his underwear isn't any more naked than one in swim trunks,* she told herself.

She didn't move. "I don't much like Montaldo," she admitted, "but good grief! He's not a killer." It occurred to her that was probably not a tactful thing to say to a man accused of murder.

"As I recall, Montaldo didn't look happy when you agreed to take the flight," he said. "Maybe he was worried that you might do exactly what you did, and pull off a minor miracle. What kind of pilot is Timothy Lee?"

"He's okay." Reluctantly she added, "I'm better." She chewed on her lip, unhappy. She could hear him moving around behind her and wondered if he was putting his pants back on. "Ventura isn't into smuggling. I'd have seen something, heard something, if that was going on."

"You said you hadn't worked for Montaldo long. Maybe he plans to change things."

"Well, yeah, he just took over Ventura recently, but he's a reputable businessman. I mean, he owns three other little airlines..." Two of which, she recalled, were up near the border, in excellent position for quick overnight trips that didn't get listed in the company books.

Then she remembered something. "Wait a minute. No one knew you were going to be on that plane, Rafe. All the plans got changed after you were ambushed on the way to Mazatlán.

It's just too much of a coincidence to think you accidentally wound up at the one airport where there was someone who worked for this drug gang that's after you. No," she said, smiling with relief, "I don't know what went wrong, but the plane wasn't sabotaged."

"According to Montaldo, his airline was the only one in San Luis with a pressurized plane—the only logical choice."

"So? You were supposed to be flying out of Mazatlán, not San Luis."

"I think they herded us right where they wanted us. Look, Winston assumed the shooting happened where it did because that's when they caught up with us. Maybe not. Maybe they planned the attack so that, if they failed to take me out with it, they'd spook Winston into doing exactly what he did."

"If he'd gone ahead and taken you to Mazatlán anyway—"

"I doubt we would have made it there, but if we had, they would have had another plan."

"But why would they do all that?" she burst out. "My God, according to you, people all over the country are out to get you! Don't you realize—" She stopped. Accusing him of paranoia would probably not be a good idea. Especially if he really was paranoid.

"Have you ever read about the gang warfare in Chicago during Prohibition? This situation isn't much different. There are two gangs that make a great deal of money off illegal substances involved. One wants me dead. The other—" He stopped.

She spun around. "You're part of it. Part of the gang." Nausea rose, thick and rancid. She rubbed her throat, distraught and not knowing why. She'd reminded herself often enough that he was a prisoner, an accused killer. Why would it make her sick to think of him being part of a drug gang?

His eyes were hooded. "I've said too much already."

He had, she realized belatedly, finished dressing. Almost. He reached down as she watched and snapped and zipped his jeans.

She swallowed a rising panic. It *had* to be panic that fluttered around so wildly inside her. "Look, even if everything

you say is true, this gang of yours isn't after me. If you think
you have to go, then go. But I'm not leaving the plane.''

He sighed. ''And if it was your boss who sabotaged the
plane? You think he'll be happy you survived, knowing you
might implicate him?'' He came forward, not stopping until
he stood close to her—close enough that she had to tilt her
head back to meet his dark eyes. ''Even if there weren't some
very bad men apt to turn up here, we couldn't stay on this
ridge. There's no water.''

''We've got the Cokes.''

''The average person uses a gallon of water a day. We're
already slightly dehydrated.''

''I'm not going.'' *Stay with the plane.* That's what all the
experts advised if you had to make a forced landing away from
civilization. Gillie's instincts shouted agreement. She wasn't
about to go off into the wilderness with this man. ''Are you
going to leave me any of the Cokes? There's a wooden box
in my backpack, too. It isn't anything you'd need, so if you
would leave me that I'd appreciate—''

He moved fast. She reacted the blink of an eye too late, not
realizing what he was doing until he had a hold of her wrist.
He reached back and pulled something from a back pocket.
Something that glinted silver shiny.

The handcuffs.

Gillie threw herself backward. It wasn't the best tactic. He
didn't let go, so her weight toppled them both over. She landed
hard on her bottom, and he landed on top of her, sending her
sprawling.

She threw dirt in his eyes. He jerked his head back, but this
time *he* was too late. She'd blinded him temporarily, thrown
him off balance. She shoved hard against his chest and scrambled.

She almost made it. She got out from under him and got
her legs under her and was about to shove to her feet when
he tackled her.

His big body landed fully on top of her. She went flat. She
couldn't get a good breath. He grabbed her hands in one of
his and jerked them over her head. Then he shifted his

weight—not much, but enough. She dragged in air. Her hair had come loose in their brief scuffle, and one strand had gotten in her mouth. She spat it out and glared at him.

He didn't have a mark on him, dammit. Nor had his expression changed. Except for his eyes.

His eyes. Not expressionless now, they glowed as dark and hot and dangerous as the inside of a volcano. Gillie stared up into those eyes, swallowed, and realized something else.

The hardness she felt along an intimate part of her was *not* from something in his pocket. He wanted her. And she…she was throbbing, pulsing with the compulsive beat of jungle drums.

Slowly he reached up with his other hand, his eyes on hers. She felt caught, trapped, pinned in some essential way more threatening than the physical. Yet she was incredibly aware of him, physically. When he moved his arm she felt the movement all along her own body in the subtle shift of hard, male muscle pressed against her.

She was still breathing fast, but no longer for the same reason.

Cold metal slid around her wrist and snapped into place.

Rafe managed to tune out the woman's complaints and curses while he finished getting their gear packed. For some reason, though, he couldn't tune out her silence.

Silence shouldn't have a presence, a weight. Hers did. She'd yelled and tried to hit him when, after cuffing her, he'd dragged her to her feet and forced her over to a tree. She'd insulted his ancestors when he fastened the other cuff to a branch. He didn't blame her. She was angry and frightened.

Then she'd fallen silent.

Rafe strapped on Winston's shoulder holster and slid the .45 into place. He would rather have had his own gun, but he and the wren hadn't found his things in the wreckage. Either they were thirty-five feet down a cliff in the other wing's storage compartment, or they were still in San Luis with the injured marshal.

He picked up the makeshift pack he'd put together out of

Winston's canvas tote bag and the seat belt webbing, grabbed her backpack and the sturdy limb he intended to use as a walking stick. He turned around, facing the tree where he'd left her.

She stared at him. Her eyes accused him of violation.

Rafe seldom bothered to regret necessity, but the need for those blasted handcuffs oppressed him. He'd hoped, when he went back in the plane after the cuffs, that he wouldn't have to use them. But their conversation had made it obvious she wasn't going to leave the plane unless he forced her to.

She didn't trust him. He could think of no reason why she should, or why her distrust should rankle. She had to come with him, that was all. If she stayed here, she'd either be killed by the people who were looking for him, or she would die slowly, of exposure. He couldn't allow that. He owed her.

Binding his knee and using a walking stick helped even more than he'd hoped. He barely limped when he approached her. She glared at him, but beneath the defiance he saw something else—a trapped look in her sky-colored eyes.

The wren was made for flying free. Not for chains. He knew only too well how the chains felt. "I don't want to do it this way," he said. "Be reasonable. I'm bigger than you and stronger. I can and will make you do things my way. If you'll give me your word to cooperate, I'll take the cuffs off."

He watched a crafty expression slide over her face. She looked like a cat just before it steals a piece of chicken off the table—just like she'd looked when she tried to trick him into letting her go back into the airplane so she could lock herself up inside.

"All right," she said, and heaved a sigh. "I guess I don't have much choice. I'll cooperate."

She was lying. She did it very badly, too. Rafe knew she planned to escape as soon as she could, so it made no sense, no sense at all when he reached out and, with one quick twist of the key, set her free.

Chapter 4

Gillie slipped her hand out of the horrid silver bracelet. Rafe was staring at the key in his hand with the oddest expression on his face, as if he'd never seen it before. "I suppose you want me to take my backpack," she said brightly. "Is that box in it? The one I mentioned?"

The dazed look faded, replaced by that spark of amusement she'd seen before in his dark eyes. "Yes," he said. "It's there."

Thank goodness. Gillie knew it would be foolish beyond belief to delay her escape because of a few trinkets, but she just couldn't bear to leave her treasure box behind.

Rafe stepped forward. Automatically, she stepped back.

He reached for his shirt pocket and pulled out her map, neatly folded. "Show me where you think we are."

Reluctantly she moved close enough to take the map from him. It was a standard aviation map, with rivers, highways and towns marked, and a few elevations. It also had some pencilled notations Gillie had made about landmarks she'd found useful or interesting on other flights.

"We're somewhere around here," she said, making a small

circle with her fingertip that covered a couple hundred square kilometers. "I wasn't keeping track of our location toward the end, so I can't be more specific."

"You've flown over this region before. Which direction do you recommend we go?"

"I recommend we stay put," she said. "But if you refuse to listen to sense, then head east-northeast. See, these mountains are kind of like a giant step that lifts the land up into the central Mexican Plateau. You don't want to go west. The land between here and the sea is all chopped up by cliffs and canyons. What you want to do is to get over the hump to the eastern side of the range."

She pointed at a penciled line on the map. "I've sketched in the way the divide runs. We should be pretty close. We'd nearly made it over before the engines went out."

"This side of the mountains catches more of the rain, though. How much drier is the eastern side?"

She hadn't thought of that. "I don't know. The higher parts look pretty green from above, but the plateau itself is desert." She shook her head, wishing she could tell him more. What he planned was risky, very risky, but he must know that. He wasn't a stupid man.

Which meant he truly believed it was more dangerous to remain close to the plane.

More dangerous for him, she amended mentally. No doubt he considered being recaptured worse than any hazards the wilderness offered. She could understand that. She just didn't intend to let him drag her along on his escape.

Or not very far along, at least. She'd have to start out with him, but once he believed she wasn't going to make trouble he'd relax his vigilance and she could get away.

"I'm used to the desert," he said, refolding the map before sliding it back in his pocket. "I can keep us alive until we run into a village or a road."

"Up here there aren't really any roads to run into. Most ground travel across the western Sierra Madres is still by railroad."

He nodded. "But we might make use of some of those train

tracks, if we come across them. And there are paths used by…the natives."

She frowned. "How do you know all that?"

"I'm a businessman," he told her, bending to pick up his pack. "I have to know how the goods I buy are shipped."

He stood there watching her with those patient eyes of his, a big, bronzed man with black-as-sin hair pulled back in a ponytail, his torn camouflage shirt partly covered by a dead man's dress shirt. He looked more like a cross between a biker and a warlord than a businessman. In fact, Gillie had never seen anyone who looked less like a businessman.

Unless, of course, that business was smuggling drugs.

"Let's go," he said. "I want to find water before dark."

Reluctantly, Gillie bent and picked up her own backpack. It was heavier than it should have been. She frowned. Had he put anything in it that he'd need in order to survive after she escaped? "What's in here?"

"I can't carry everything in my pack." He turned and started for the eastern edge of the ridge. "I have to keep as much weight as possible off my knee."

She opened her mouth to protest that she hadn't been complaining about the weight, then closed it again. She couldn't very well explain, could she?

Gillie started off behind Rafe, humming her favorite aria from *Carmen* to keep her spirits up.

An hour later she wasn't humming anymore.

The route Rafe chose was steep, but not impossible. Gillie had to watch her footing carefully, though, and the exertion brought back yesterday's headache. After an hour of slipping, sliding and scrambling around she decided she'd never in her life paid this much attention to the ground beneath her feet.

She didn't like it.

Dirt crunched beneath her tennis shoes—crisp, crumbly, really *dry* dirt. "Wouldn't you know it," she muttered. She hit a patch of scree. Her feet tried to skid out from under her, so she grabbed at the branch of a scraggly juniper. The jerky motion increased the pounding in her head.

"What's that?" he asked without looking back.

So far, he hadn't looked back once to check on her, though he paused sometimes to let her catch up. Gillie wanted to be pleased by this. His disinterest should help her get away when they reached a more heavily forested area and she faded back out of sight.

That was her plan—to fade out of sight. She'd wait until they got far enough from the plane that he wouldn't bother to come after her, then she'd just sort of disappear into the woods...once they reached some woods.

For some reason, though, Gillie wasn't pleased to know that Rafe didn't care whether she went down the mountain on two feet or rolled down it like a bony barrel. She made a face at his retreating back. He was a vastly irritating man. In spite of his injured knee, he handled the rugged ground much better than she did. "Wouldn't you just know that the one and only time in my life I have to make a forced landing away from civilization, it would be the dry season?"

"The rainy season has its own hazards." He stepped from one crooked bit of rock to another with the assurance of a big cat, using his walking stick to brace himself. "The loose dirt and gravel you're sliding around on now would be even more difficult if rain had turned it to mud."

"Yeah, but where do you think you'll find water in the dry season?"

"If we're lucky, at the bottom of this ravine. But it's more likely that we'll have to follow the ravine to see what it drains into. We may have to follow more than one dry watercourse before we find one that still holds water."

In other words, he didn't expect to find water anywhere near the plane. Gillie frowned unhappily. She was going to need water. Maybe she should go with him all the way to whatever water he found. Only she didn't want to wait too long to make her break. She might get lost on the way back.

If she didn't just pass out. "My head hurts," she told Rafe's back. "I need to rest. I think I have a touch of altitude sickness."

He didn't turn around. "I think you have a touch of concussion and are slightly dehydrated. Unfortunately, we can't stop yet.''

''Well, when can we stop?'' She was all too aware that going back up the slope would take even more energy than scrambling down it had. She really needed to rest before she did that. Once they were sitting down she could come up with some excuse to see what was in her pack, too, so she could be sure to leave him anything he was obviously going to need.

''When we find water.''

Gillie didn't like his broad back or his attitude or the way he didn't get tired like any normal human being. Most of all, she hated the niggling thought that she might be better off staying with Rafe, that it really didn't make much sense to stay by the plane when she had no water, and it might be several days or several weeks before rescue came.

Panic welled up, a sick and shapeless mass, at the thought of leaving the plane completely behind. She bit her lip and forced herself to pay close attention to the ground.

That's how she noticed the smudged imprints crossing her path. They were shaped like kitty-cat paws, except they were big. Really big. Her breath caught and her feet stopped. ''These tracks—did you see them?''

''I've seen a lot of tracks.'' He kept heading downhill.

''These are awfully big.''

He stopped and turned around at last. ''I saw them,'' he said. ''They look like puma tracks.''

She stared at the dirt and swallowed. ''I guess it could be worse. They could be grizzly tracks or something.''

''You needn't worry about grizzlies. The black bear population is pretty healthy, but grizzlies haven't been seen in these mountains for thirty years.''

Her head came up. Her eyes narrowed. ''So how do you know these things, anyway? About the dry season and bears and the lack of roads in these mountains? How come you know so much about this part of Mexico?''

The blasted man turned around and started walking again without answering. She had little choice but to follow, stepping over the puma's tracks rather than on them. It seemed more respectful.

Once they found water, she promised herself, she'd escape. He'd go his way, and she'd go hers. She'd come back to the water hole every day or two, and surely it wouldn't be too terribly long before she was rescued.

Within ten minutes he was quite a bit ahead of her, which was just the way she wanted it…later, when she was ready to fade back into the woods. Not now, when she'd just crossed a puma's path. So she hurried to catch up, hit a patch of loose topsoil, landed on her bottom and slid a few feet.

It hurt. Her hip was still sore from the landing yesterday, her head throbbed miserably and she didn't want to be there, sitting in the dirt at seven thousand feet with an aching head, a sore bottom, no water and a murderous drug dealer for her guide…a murderous drug dealer who was apparently going to walk off and leave her sitting on her backside.

She wasn't going to cry, though. She was definitely, absolutely *not* going to cry.

Several feet down the slope, Rafe finally did stop and turn. "You're going to have to be more careful. I can't carry you if you twist an ankle, and there's no point in sniveling about it."

Sniveling? *Sniveling?* Anger did a good job of blotting up the tears she had not been crying. It got her to her feet, too. And then—quite without her conscious decision—it sent her running.

Uphill. Away from him, far away—she'd run or scramble or slither all the way back to the plane. He couldn't run uphill, not on that knee of his. She was going to do it, going to get away. She was—

Flat on her stomach with the wind knocked out of her. Pure panic skittered in as she tried to draw a breath and couldn't.

He turned her over and slid his arm behind her, supporting her so she wasn't sprawled on top of her backpack. Her face was scraped and cold from the ground. She stared up at him, terrified. Then her lungs started working again. She gulped in air, bemused by adrenaline, oxygen and flight.

His eyes, those dark, knowing eyes, shifted. He was looking at her mouth. Something inside her shifted along with his gaze, something tiny and vital and mysterious.

Gillie drew in another breath and realized she could smell him—a scent somewhere between spice and musk, a scent that made her think of dirt and the subtle green smell of growing things, of sun-warmed flesh and the hot blue of a tropical sky. She lay there staring up at him as she got her breath back, and with every breath she took his scent inside her.

"I'm sorry," he told her.

He didn't look it. He looked hard and angry as he dug the handcuffs out of his back pocket. It took him only seconds to trap her right hand despite her sudden, frantic effort to stop him.

She heard the click as the metal locked in place around her wrist, followed by a second click as he snapped the other cuff on his own wrist. He said it again, quietly this time. Almost softly. "I'm sorry."

But there was nothing soft or apologetic about the hand that cupped her face then, trapping it between those spread fingers and the arm that still supported her. His face came down.

Gillie stiffened, expecting an assault. That, she could have fought. But he fooled her. His mouth was hard but careful, as careful as it was determined. His hand moved, stroking down her cheek to her throat, the fingers calloused and warm and stirring.

The smell and taste of him raced through her like fate, bringing a hunger she didn't understand. She wanted to inhale him, to press her face into his neck and breathe in nothing but him. She wanted to push him and this moment away, far, far away.

She couldn't move.

His tongue invaded her mouth. She jolted. She felt as if she'd been lifted and snapped in the air like a sheet—one quick, hard billow erasing all her wrinkled thoughts. This new movement seemed to happen not just inside her, but everywhere, as if the whole world were being kissed along with her, being shaken and sent snapping in the air.

At last, fear flowed in. At last, too late, she turned her head away and pushed against his chest.

He pulled back immediately. In some dim corner of her mind where thoughts still formed, Gillie was surprised at how quickly he let her go, so quickly she had to put a hand out or tumble back onto her pack.

Rafe's head swam. He hardly knew what he did when he let Gillie go and sat back on his heels. Her hand followed his when he drew back. It followed because it had to, because he'd cuffed them together. He looked down at her face and saw the arousal, the confusion and the fear.

He wondered if she was more afraid of him because of what she thought he was, or because of what he'd made her feel. If he'd had any doubts about her innocence, that kiss had settled them. She knew nothing, nothing at all, that would protect her from a man like him.

Right now, right this minute, it scarcely mattered that she could give him, at most, a stunned sort of submission, not as long as her submission let him enjoy the secrets of her body.

Rafe drew back a few more inches. Her trapped hand followed.

His knee throbbed. Racing after her hadn't been good for it. He straightened that leg slightly, easing the ache, and took a slow, deep breath. He wanted to sound calm so he wouldn't frighten her further. "I shouldn't have done that."

She pushed herself into a sitting position slowly, watching him as if she expected him to jump her again. "So why did you?"

Good question. But then, the wren was full of questions, wasn't she? He shrugged. "An impulse." All he knew was that he'd looked into her impossibly blue eyes, at the fright and relief and awareness there, and he'd wanted her. It was that simple, and that hard.

She grimaced. "That's not much of an answer."

"Why did you run? Wasn't that an impulse, too?"

She looked away.

Her braid was coming loose. One long strand of hair brushed her cheek—her dirty, scraped cheek. She'd been hurt when he tackled her, and he hated that. "Look," he said, "you don't need any more bumps and bruises, and I don't need to be chasing after you on this knee. Just accept that I'm not going to let you go back and die beside that damned plane."

She swallowed. "If you'll promise me you won't do *that* again, I'll promise not to try and escape."

A glimmer of humor surprised him. "Just what is it you don't want me to do?"

"You know." Her hand made a vague arc in the air. "Grab me and—and all *that.*"

"Oh. *That.*" He considered lying. He was much better at it than she was. And yet... "Sorry," he said, choosing to speak the truth he'd been forced to recognize, "but I can't promise not to kiss you again."

She scowled.

"I won't force you, but I'm not going to pretend I don't want you. I'll take exactly as much as you'll let me have."

Alarm jumped in her eyes, giving him a certain grim satisfaction. About this, at least, she believed him. And she didn't fully trust herself.

Good. He'd warned her. It was up to her now to find a way to protect herself. He stood and held out his hand—the one that was chained to her. "Come on," he said. "We've got a lot of ground to cover."

It didn't surprise him when she rejected his help and stood on her own, though the handcuffs made that awkward. "So tell me," she said, brushing ineffectually at the dirt on the front of her jeans, "how did you wind up being accused of murder, anyway?"

He shook his head. "You really don't have much of an instinct for self-preservation, do you?" He started down the slope again, taking it easy both for her sake and his own. His knee throbbed.

The chain between them went taut before she stumbled into place beside him. When he reached out to steady her, the chain rattled.

"Well?" she demanded, pulling away from his grasp. "Are you going to answer my question?"

"I was in the wrong place at the wrong time." He wished she would let him keep holding her arm. He liked touching her, and she could use the help.

"Ah," she said, nodding. "Another of your detailed answers. Who is it you're supposed to have killed?"

"An irritating female who asked too many questions." Rafe watched Gillie's jaw set in a stubborn line. Her strength showed in that determined jaw, but he saw her vulnerability just as clearly in the tender spot beneath it.

He wanted to lick her there.

He sighed.

"I'm just making conversation," she said haughtily, stumbling over a rock. She jerked her arm away when he tried, again, to help her. "We may as well talk since we're chained together. You have heard of conversation, I suppose? It's a give-and-take kind of thing where I say something, then you do, then I do."

"There's a difference between conversation and nosiness."

"Questions keep a conversation flowing, especially when one of the conversers acts like he's going to run out of words if he uses more than three at a time. Let's try it. I'll start." She smiled brightly. "I've never killed anyone. How about you?"

He sighed again. It was going to be a long day.

It had been a very long day. Gillie stood at the bottom of a shallow-sided gully beside the man who'd handcuffed her, kissed her and ignored her. It was late afternoon, maybe five o'clock. Her calves ached from hours of unaccustomed up-and-down hiking. Her head ached worse, though maybe the ache arose as much from the thinking she'd done in the past few hours as from her physical efforts.

"This will be good enough," Rafe said. "We have a lot to do before dark."

Rafe had done everything he'd said he would. He'd kept them alive, kept her from going back to the plane and he'd found water...and he'd ignored or turned aside all her questions.

She thought she'd managed to answer a few of those questions for herself, though. "This isn't much more than a big mud puddle," she said, eyeing the couple of inches of water at the deepest part of the gully. Bushes grew near, but not up to, the muddy edge of the water. "Really, the water hole we passed a few minutes ago looked better, even if there wasn't much water in it."

"It looked better to you because it was cleaner, and it was cleaner because the bottom was rock. But there wasn't enough water there, and I couldn't deepen that hole. Here the soil is sandy and damp. It should be easy to dig deeper so more water can seep in. The water will have to be filtered and purified before we can drink it, of course, but at least we'll have enough."

Gillie wanted to make a sarcastic comment about how many words he'd squandered on that explanation, but she was too tired. She wondered how long all his preparations would take. They'd each drunk a whole can of Coke at lunch instead of splitting one, but she was really thirsty now. And tired. Lord, she was tired.

She jiggled her wrist, making the chain between them dance. "Are you going to take this off now?"

"Are you going to try to run away again?"

"Where would I go?" she asked bitterly. "I'm no wilderness expert. I have no idea where the plane is anymore." While she knew their overall direction had been northeast, he'd dragged her up, down and around until she was thoroughly lost. Maybe he'd done it on purpose, either to confuse her or the pursuers he was so certain would be after him. Gillie didn't know, and at the moment she didn't much care.

She did know that if she went off on her own now, she'd die. If he went off and left her, she'd die. The knowledge of her dependency left her raw and jumpy.

He pulled the key out of his pocket. She held out her hand, too stiff with fatigue to rejoice as much as she wanted to when the horrid cuff fell away. She rubbed her wrist.

"Do you feel up to digging?" he asked. "I'd like to get a couple of snares set at the other water hole before dark."

"Snares?" The thought of food made her stomach growl. "Does that mean we get to eat supper?" He hadn't wanted them to eat anything for lunch, saying that digesting a meal would make their bodies use water they couldn't afford to lose until they located more.

"We'll eat something. Rabbit, if we're lucky. There's plenty of game around," he said, slipping out of his pack and setting it on the ground. "You have any problems with eating rabbit?"

"Of course not." She'd eaten too many odd things in different countries to have many food prejudices. "I'm hungry enough to eat just about anything."

He got that look on his face again, the one that was almost a smile, as if she'd said something amusing. Gillie ignored him in favor of more pressing matters. For the last couple of hours she'd worked to forget the pack on her back. But if he could take his off, she could, too.

When she eased her arms out of the straps, it brought a quick, fierce ache to her shoulders. She bit back a groan.

"What is it?"

"Nothing." She let the backpack slide to the ground, then stood still for a minute and ached. Her head, calves, hip, shoulders—there didn't seem to be a part of her that didn't hurt. "I'm just sore."

He studied her a moment, then shook his head. "Never mind. Sit down. I'll dig out the water hole after I set the snares."

"No." She shook her head and made herself focus. "No, there's too much to do before dark and I'm thirsty. I can do it."

"Don't be stupid. If you can't—"

"No!" She needed to do something to take care of herself in this alien place, needed to not depend on him for everything. "I said I'd do it. I *can* do it."

He studied her a moment longer. She tried to banish her fatigue from her face.

"All right, then," he said reluctantly, "if you're sure." He bent and dug through his pack until he came up with the metal box he'd used the night before to dig their "bed." "Here," he said. "Dig out about a cubic foot of dirt if you can. I'll rig a filtration system after I've set the snares."

She took the box from him and looked from it to the muddy puddle, suddenly uncertain. "Is there a right way to do this?"

"Sure. Dig where it's wettest."

Thirty minutes later Rafe lay on his belly at the other end of the gully, setting the last of three snares he'd rigged from branches and some of the seat belt webbing. The snares worked by dangling a specially designed noose along a small-game trail. A rabbit's head would fit through the noose, but not its body. When the animal felt the noose and tried to get away, it would pull down the branch the noose was fastened to, and trap itself.

He inched away from the brush where he'd set the snare, then stood, chilled from lying on the cold ground. Sundown was about an hour away, and it would be another cold night. Fortunately he'd seen a hollow on a ledge in the south side of the gully. They could sleep there with little preparation.

Rafe thought about lying with Gillie, and hardened.

Maybe the night wouldn't be cold after all.

Rafe had learned patience in a hard school. Most people, he'd discovered, never learned it at all, yet patience was a very effective weapon, as any cat waiting outside a mouse hole knows. Yet something about Gillie destroyed his patience along with his scruples.

He wanted her, and he didn't want to wait.

He didn't trust the strength of his craving, but he didn't intend to fight it, either. What could be more natural than for a man who had narrowly escaped death to want a woman?

True, he didn't want just any woman. He wanted one with a trim little body, a smart mouth and impossible blue eyes. He wanted to make the heat rise and burst in those eyes, to see what they looked like when climax took her. But that, too, was instinctive. Gillie was dependent on him for her survival. On a primitive level, that made her his.

Rafe respected instinct as much as he did civilization. Because he was a man, he would let Nature have her way with him, just as he intended to have his way with the wren. Because he wasn't really a primitive man, he wouldn't force her.

He wouldn't have to. She responded to his touch so beautifully.

Soon. If not tonight, he would have her soon.

Right now, though, he needed to get his noisy human self away from the water so the rabbits would come down to drink. Since he'd lacked the running water of a creek to wash away his scent, he'd rubbed the snares with mud. He hoped his "deodorizer" worked. He was hungry, and Gillie needed the protein. She had fewer physical reserves to draw on than he did.

Of course, the wren seemed to always be hungry, whether she'd gone without food for a day or an hour. Such a big appetite for such a small body. Odd how appealing that was, he thought as he started down the gully.

A few minutes later he stopped on the path along the side of the gully, looked down at her digging in the muddy water and forgot about being quiet. "Good God, woman, don't you have any sense?"

She knelt in the mud by the water hole. She wore only her T-shirt and khaki shorts, and her arms and legs were wet and muddy. Her lips looked blue from cold. Those blue-tinged lips scowled at him. "What's your problem now?"

"You're wet and you're freezing and you've taken most of your clothes off!"

"If you knew of a way to do this and stay dry, you should have told me." She straightened, winced and rubbed the small of her back. "Is it deep enough, do you think?"

Rafe realized, belatedly, that he was an idiot. Of course she'd get wet digging out the water hole, and of course she'd be cold once she was wet. She'd undoubtedly taken off the outer layers of clothing to keep them dry.

He shouldn't have let her do this, he thought as he scrambled down the side of the gully. He'd known it galled her to be less than self-sufficient, but he hadn't realized she'd actu-

ally risk herself in order to prove her usefulness. Why hadn't
he stopped to consider how cold she would get?

"Dammit," he said, stopping in front of her. "You never
complain, damn you."

She knelt in the mud and glared at him. "You'd rather I
whined?"

He looked at her face closely now and saw the pallor. Exhaustion lay just below the surface, covered with a thin coating
of pure stubbornness. He hadn't paid enough attention to realize what her limits were, because when he did...

"Did you get your snares set?" she asked. "Do you think
they'll work?"

"Yes," he said. When he did pay attention to her, he started
getting hard again. Like he was right now. "I'm all done, and
so are you." He held out his hand.

She tried to get up without taking it, but her legs didn't
cooperate. He grabbed her arms and drew her to her feet.

She, of course, tried to shake him off. "I don't need—"

"Shut up," he said. "You might hate it like hell, but I'm
bigger and stronger. I can do more, and I can make you do
what you ought to have the sense to do on your own, which
is to rest and get warm."

She shivered and eyed him sullenly. "You said to take out
a cubic foot of dirt, but the sides kept sliding in. It's more
than a foot deeper, though."

"Good." Reacting instinctively to the shiver and to the
chilled flesh beneath his hands, he pulled her close, offering
the heat of his own body. She was stiff and muddy and cold,
and she didn't resist as much as he expected her to. Which
probably meant she was even more miserable than she looked.

More softly he said, "You did a good job, Gillie. I'll rig
the filtration system while you get dry and warm."

"Can we have a fire tonight?" she asked. "I'd really like
a fire."

She didn't ask for much, did she? He felt a rusty sort of
pain, as though something long unused had stirred inside him.
"Yes. I'll make us a fire."

"I'll get some wood." The stiffness was easing out of her body as she leaned into him.

"That would be good," he agreed, and drew her with him to where her pack sat. "As soon as you've rested a bit."

"Well...I could sit down for a few minutes, maybe." She shivered again.

He gave her one of the pillows to sit on and both of the blankets to wrap up in, then went to his own pack. He knelt beside it and took out what he needed.

Rafe used Winston's knife to cut the legs off the man's spare pair of slacks. He trimmed each cloth tube to a length of about eighteen inches and fitted one inside the other, then bound one end tightly with a shoestring from Winston's shoes. As he finished, he wondered how you went about repaying a dead man.

Maybe the marshal had had a family. As soon as possible, Rafe promised himself, he would find out. He'd make sure they got what they needed.

The other ingredients for his filtration system would be simple to collect—sand and gravel to pack in layers inside the tube, which he'd hang from a low branch. He'd pour water into the tube, letting it filter through the sand and gravel to drip from the length of cloth that dangled below the shoelace into a container. Once enough water collected, he'd boil it.

Before he did anything else, though, he looked over at Gillie to make sure the fool woman hadn't decided to stagger around collecting wood.

She'd fallen asleep sitting up.

Chapter 5

They ate rabbit that night by the orange glow of a campfire. The meat was charred on the outside, dry and overdone inside. It was delicious. Gillie could have eaten twice as much, and she suspected Rafe could have, too. For dessert, they split one of the candy bars.

They were camped on a rocky ledge partway up the rugged south side of the gully. As Rafe pointed out when he woke Gillie at sunset, he didn't want to be near the water hole when the nocturnal predators dropped by for a drink. Gillie had been groggy and achy, still cold, although she'd quickly pulled on her jeans, long-sleeved shirt and sweatshirt.

When she'd reached the camp a fire was burning, with water boiling cheerily in the bottom half of the metal toolbox from the plane. The top half of the toolbox had held more water, cooling. Rafe had given her a cup of instant soup made with the hot water, saying she needed it for warmth, and a couple of aspirins. With rest, food and drink, her headache had faded away.

Now a three-quarter moon rode low in the eastern sky, turning the night silver and the shadows a liquid black outside the orange glow of the fire. She and Rafe sat against the rocky face of a small cliff. It reflected some of the heat from the fire on their backs.

Gillie hugged one of the blankets around her shoulders and thought wistfully of a bath. "If we only had plumbing," she said, licking the last bit of chocolate from her fingers, "life would be nearly perfect."

Rafe didn't look up. Earlier, he'd skinned the rabbit they'd just finished eating—an activity Gillie had chosen not to watch—and he was now scraping at the hide with a rock. He had the other blanket draped around his shoulders, which pleased Gillie. It proved he did feel the cold.

"Have some more water," he said.

She glanced at him suspiciously. Filtering and boiling the water hadn't made it *taste* clean, but he'd nagged her into drinking lots of it, anyway, which had resulted in an awkward trip down the rocky slope and into the bushes. "That was a joke, wasn't it?"

He shrugged. "Not a very good one, apparently."

"That's all right," she said. "It's been a long day." A long day filled with a lot of climbing, scrambling, walking and thinking. Gillie considered some of the conclusions she'd reached, and some of the questions that still nagged at her.

Her feet were getting a little too toasty. She drew them back. "Why are you using a rock to do that instead of the knife?"

"I don't want to dull the knife."

She watched him work. His hands fascinated her. He had square palms, long, capable fingers and no rings. It occurred to her with a little jolt that he could be married. Sure, he'd kissed like he was unattached…but she wasn't going to think about his kiss, and how he'd made her feel. No, that was one of the things she'd already thought about too much.

Anyway, hadn't Pops always told her that for a lot of men, "If it itches, scratch it" were words to live by? One kiss proved nothing.

Firelight danced over Rafe's features, lending them the same sort of ruddy life it cast over the rocky cliff behind them. Gillie tried to imagine him married, and couldn't. She wanted badly to ask, but she knew he'd close up as solidly as that rock wall if she did.

There was so much about him she didn't know, so much she needed to know. For purely selfish reasons, of course. Her life depended on him. Naturally she wanted to know as much as possible about him.

She would, she decided, have to be sneaky. "What do you plan to use that rabbit skin for?"

"I don't know yet."

She scooted over slightly, trying to find a less rocky place for her bottom. "You know, you really have to learn to stop with these one and two-word answers. So, what would you wish for?"

"What are you talking about?"

"I wished for plumbing." she said. Now there was a pebble under her right hip. She reached beneath her and brushed the ground with her palm, rolling the pebble away. "What would you wish for?"

"Coffee."

"Coffee?" The quick, heartfelt reply delighted her. "You'd wish for coffee instead of something useful like, say, penicillin? Or mountain-climbing gear? If you had that, you could do the spider-crawl thing down some cliffs. I just know that would appeal to you."

He frowned and kept scraping. "What we really need is a canteen."

"But what you really *want* is coffee." She liked that answer better. It was more human.

"Wishing for what you can't have is a mistake. Out here it's a dangerous mistake. The most important tools in a survival situation are your mind and your attitude. The desire for comfort can keep you from doing what is necessary to survive."

"Oh, right. Like people can just stop wanting to be comfortable." She moved again. That blasted pebble seemed to follow her.

That almost-smile softened his eyes. "The Special Forces encourages us to think we can."

"That's where you learned all this survival stuff, you said. Were you in the army long? Did you get married then?"

He blinked. "What?"

"Oh, I just wondered—you know, the usual stuff." She gestured casually. "Like how long you were in the army, what you thought of it…whether you got married then or later."

"I'm not married, Gillie."

"Oh. I must have misunderstood something the marshal said." That sounded reasonable, she thought—except she wasn't sure, from the way he was looking at her, that he thought so. She pulled her knees up in front of her and wrapped her arms around them.

"I won't ever marry." He said it slowly, as if he were telling her something important, something that affected her personally. Which was ridiculous, of course. "I don't believe in tomorrows or in promises. All I can give a woman is money and pleasure. I've found that's usually enough."

"You give your women money?" she asked, shocked.

The sexual revolution had pretty much missed Gillie. She'd spent too much time in Third-World countries, where sex outside of marriage led to babies no one could feed, to take a casual view of intimacy. But in any country, no matter how traditional, the man watching her now wouldn't have to buy his women.

"I give them gifts," he said. "It's only natural to enjoy the things money can buy. And I give them pleasure, Gillie. Don't forget that. For many women, the pleasure is as important as the gifts."

His voice rasped across her nerve endings, rough and provocative as beard stubble. A restless feeling stirred low in her belly. It reminded her of the way her stomach flipped itself inside out when she pointed the nose of a plane at the ground and dived, fast and hard.

If she could just leave that feeling alone, surely it would go away. "Listen, I can understand you not wanting to be tied down. I feel kind of that way myself. There's always someplace new to see, isn't there? But how can you not believe in tomorrow? People have to have dreams." She thought about her Piper, the one she intended to buy. "If you don't dream, you don't go anywhere. You're just stuck, grounded."

"There's nothing wrong with having your feet firmly on the ground. And it's possible to have goals without inflating them into pie-in-the-sky dreaming."

She shook her head, unable to understand such an attitude. "As for promises—well, how much a promise is worth depends on who gave it, now, doesn't it?"

"Even good people break promises. They may not mean to, but life can make those promises impossible to keep."

She hugged her knees closer. "Who let you down, Rafe?"

He was silent a long time, so long she thought he wasn't going to answer. His hands stayed busy with his bit of hide, scraping and rubbing. Finally he spoke. "I tell you what. I'll answer one of your nosy questions—just one—if you promise not to ask any more tonight, and to answer a question of my choosing."

She thought that was an odd way to put it, but didn't hesitate. "Deal."

"Go ahead, then."

The question that crowded out wasn't the one she meant to ask, but maybe it had built up more pressure than the others. "How do you know so much about these mountains?"

He took his time answering. "My mother," he said at last.

That wasn't what she'd expected. "Your mother?"

"She was born in an *ejido* village about a hundred miles south of here." He watched his hands at their task. "The year her only sister died from an infection that a single shot of penicillin could have cured, her father lost his taste for what anthropologists call 'a traditional lifestyle.' Her parents moved to Juarez. But she remembered. She always remembered where she came from, and she told me stories about it."

Gillie had lived in Mexico enough to recognize the implications of his mother's being born in an *ejido,* which was land held in common by a native village. Over the years, greed, expediency and ill-conceived plans born of good intentions had whittled away at the *ejido* lands, until there were relatively few left.

She also knew how brutal life was in the cities for people wrenched from their roots. "What tribe is she from?"

He glanced up. His hands paused, then resumed their task. "Tarahumara."

"Oh." The Tarahumara were among the most stubbornly isolated of Mexico's tribal peoples. They had villages and farms scattered all over the Copper Canyon area. "We're on the north end of their territory right now, aren't we?"

"Yes." After a moment he added, "Many of them, perhaps most, will have moved to the canyon bottoms for the winter. We're unlikely to get any help from them."

Gillie bit her lip to keep the dozen questions tangled up on her tongue from all jumping out at once. Had he camped in these mountains before? What had happened to his mother? Was he raised in Mexico or in the U.S.? Why had he claimed that his knowledge of the mountains came from business?

But she was amazed that he'd told her this much. She didn't want to ask the wrong thing and watch him close up again. "What was your mother's name?"

"Tolopia. She went by Pia, mostly, after she came to the States." He gave her a quick, hard look. "She was an illegal alien."

Gillie thought about that. She knew that many women in border towns tried to have their babies in American hospitals because babies born on U.S. soil could claim citizenship. And who could blame those women? Not Gillie. Mothers were supposed to want the best for their children, after all. Many did, too. Gillie had seen that happen too many times to doubt it, just because her own mother hadn't been like that. "Did she cross the border to have you so you'd have citizenship?"

"No. By the time I was born she was a maid for a rich man who liked to hire illegal immigrants because they worked cheap and didn't dare complain. We lived in a little room behind the kitchen. But she started out as a migrant worker when she was fifteen."

"That's a hard life," Gillie said softly.

"Not as hard as turning tricks on the street. That was her only other option."

Gillie swallowed. Those kind of choices were part of life for many people in the world. She'd seen it. But she didn't want Rafe's mother to have lived with such desperation. She didn't want Rafe to have known it.

His hands stilled. His eyes caught hers, night-dark eyes with little orange flames dancing on their surface, twinned reflections of the fire. The air smelled of smoke and sweat, and his voice was low, the mocking tone of it shockingly civilized in their primitive setting. "Have you run out of questions at last? Don't you want to know if she managed to avoid whoring once she reached the States? Maybe you'd like to ask if I'm a citizen myself, or an illegal alien as well as a murderer."

She shook her head mutely.

"You asked more than one question, Gillie, but I thought you deserved a complete answer, because my question for you is personal."

"All right," she said, wondering what he would ask, what was important enough about her to have made him offer up so much of himself. "Go ahead."

He set down the hide and the stone he'd used to clean and soften it. "Are you a virgin?"

Her mouth dropped open.

Rafe enjoyed the shock on Gillie's face. He was glad he'd flustered her. He ached badly for her, and she seemed to forget, at times, that he was a man. "Well?" he said. "I answered your questions. You're honor-bound to answer mine."

"I can't believe you asked that." Shock faded into bewilderment on her face, then hurt. "Why would you ask something like that?"

He'd enjoyed shocking her, but he didn't like hurting her. Dammit, he shouldn't be able to hurt her. As far as she was concerned, he was the killer who'd kidnapped her, wasn't he? "Your questions were every bit as personal as mine."

"They certainly were not!"

"Oh? You don't consider it pretty intimate—not to mention stupid—to ask if I've ever killed anyone?"

"I was mad. You'd put those handcuffs on me and I wanted to get back at you. And I did, too, didn't I? But it wasn't kind of me, I'll admit that. Whatever dreadful secrets you're guarding—" she gave him a scornful look intended to let him know what she thought about him keeping secrets of any sort, dreadful or otherwise "—I had plenty of time today to think, and I did figure out that you aren't a murderer."

"You want to tell me just how you came up with that?" he demanded.

"You don't act like one."

He shook his head. "I can't believe you've survived as long as you have. There is no template for killers, little wren, no mold a man must fit in order to be capable of terrible things."

"I know that," she said impatiently. "Pops always said that the weak attack whoever is weaker, and I've seen decent people do things in the heat of the moment that they regretted later. But I didn't say you weren't capable of killing. Just that you aren't a murderer."

"The distinction makes some sense to you, I suppose."

"It's…" She gestured widely with one hand. "It's just not the same, that's all. I don't know how to say what I mean."

Rafe knew, though. Maybe he'd never put it in those terms, but what she said matched what he felt. Murder was an ultimately selfish act. A man might kill to defend his people, his family or those weaker than himself without being a murderer.

"You have your flaws," she pointed out. "You are bossy and arrogant and secretive, and not very friendly. But you're too controlled to kill in a fit of temper, and as for selfishness…well, you've gone to a ridiculous amount of trouble to drag me along with you. You've…taken care of me." She flushed, her gaze dropping, as if the idea of being taken care of embarrassed her. "Now, that just isn't the behavior of a man who would kill to make things easy on himself. I don't know why you're arguing about it. Did I mention that you're also perverse?"

He was perverse? "So you think you can trust me. Have you ever heard of the Stockholm Syndrome? Captives often decide their captors must be trustworthy because they can't deal with the alternative."

She sighed. "I wish you'd pay attention. I didn't say I trusted you. I said I don't think you're a murderer."

She looked cute, dammit. She looked dirty and stubborn and cute as hell sitting there arguing with him over whether he was a murderer or not. He wanted to smile, and he didn't like it, didn't like the blend of emotions she stirred, the amusement that somehow sharpened the arousal. "Maybe you think I dragged you along with me in order to serve my perverse desires."

She cocked her head on one side. "Is that another joke?"

"You aren't supposed to ask any more questions tonight, remember? You're supposed to answer mine."

She flushed. "It's a stupid question."

"I didn't pass judgment on your questions before I answered them."

"Well, I didn't ask about your—your sexual status!"

"I'm not a virgin." He felt a smile tug at the corners of his mouth, "I don't mind telling you that."

"Your sense of humor leaves a lot to be desired."

"So I've been told." It had bothered him at one time that other people thought him humorless. He was used to it now, though. "Are you going to renege on our deal?"

Her mouth opened, then closed. She looked away. "All right," she said, hugging her knees tightly. "All right, I am a virgin. There. Are you satisfied?"

"Damn." He'd hoped he was wrong, but he wasn't surprised.

She scowled. "I can't imagine what possible interest you can have in—"

"Come on, Gillie. You may be inexperienced, but you're not stupid. You know exactly why I wanted to know."

She looked away. "So, does this mean you'll keep your hands to yourself?"

"No." He shifted enough to pull the marshal's knife out of his pocket. "Here." He held it out.

The flames from the fire seemed to dance across her eyes as her head turned toward him. Her forehead wrinkled. "What? Why are you giving me that?"

"I won't force you. You have no reason to believe me, so you can keep the knife to reassure yourself."

"And if I stick that knife in you, who will keep me alive out here? You think I can start catching and skinning my own rabbits? A knife does not reassure me, Rafe."

"It's all I can offer."

She frowned at him. "What about a promise? You could promise not to force me. I think that would make me feel better than that stupid knife."

"I don't believe in promises, so I don't make them."

"You must. You're a businessman, you said. You make promises every time you sign a contract or make a deal."

"In a contract the penalties for default are established ahead of time. If circumstances beyond my control meant I couldn't fulfill a contract, I'd pay the agreed-on price for the failure." He shook his head. "The other kind of promises, the personal kind—a man can run up a terrible debt with them. And I'm already going to owe you."

"You don't owe me anything."

"I will," he said, "when I take your virginity."

The fire had burned down to mostly coals, but Gillie couldn't see it. All she could see was the faintest of glows in the darkness on the other side of the broad male back that penned her in.

They lay together in a hollow in the rocky cliff too tiny to be called a cave. There was rock above her, rock behind and beneath her, but it wasn't the hard surface that kept Gillie from sleep. It was the heat of the hard body beside her.

And, though she hated to admit it, the heat in her own body.

Oh, he was a terrible man. She didn't trust him. He scared her, but only some of the time, when she wasn't longing to punch him in the stomach so hard he wouldn't get his breath for a week. Or when she wasn't hurting because of his mother, or trying to figure out his peculiar sense of humor.

She hated what he'd said about the Stockholm Syndrome. Yes, she'd heard about it, and now she lay there and wondered how she could tell if her mind was acting funny on her. She thought she had a few things about him figured out, but what if she was just fooling herself?

He said he wouldn't force her. She believed him, too, even if he was too stupid to know that by giving her those words he'd already given her the promise he didn't believe in.

But he thought he was going to "take her virginity," anyway.

"You can't take it," she muttered.

"Go to sleep, Gillie."

"It isn't something you can take, because if you can't take something away with you, then you haven't taken it. That's only logical. And if you were to do what you want to do— which you aren't, but if you were—you wouldn't *have* my virginity, now, would you? So that means you can't take it."

Rafe lay with the reason for the relentless ache in his groin cuddled up against his back and wondered why in the hell he was smiling. "I guess not," he said.

"Not that I would let you, anyway."

But she would. He'd seen her response to him, the physical quickening that showed in her eyes, in her gestures, even in the pulse that beat at the base of her throat. Every time she'd shifted positions beside the campfire she'd ended up a little closer to him. Did she realize that? Did she have any idea of all the ways she gave herself away?

No, of course not. Her body wanted him, but her mind didn't, and she seemed to have no idea how powerful the body's cravings could be. It was hard to defend against the unknown, and in that respect her innocence would make it easier for him to get what he wanted.

Rafe knew that if he rolled over right now and kissed her, he could make her forget all the reasons she shouldn't let him touch her. He could have his tongue in her mouth and his hand under her shirt or between her legs in a few minutes.

It would be easy, oh so easy, to take her the rest of the way from there.

So why didn't he move?

"I was just thinking," she said. "Don't some Indian tribes

say some kind of prayer for the animals they hunt? Did you do that for our rabbit?''

"No, I didn't. Now go to sleep."

He wouldn't be betraying a trust if he touched her. Hadn't she told him she didn't trust him? And he had been honest with her, painfully honest, even telling her about his mother in order to keep the scales balanced.

He remembered the indignant way she'd denied trusting him with one breath, then with the next said she'd rather have his promise to protect her than his knife.

Stupid woman.

"I'll say one, then," she murmured sleepily. "But it would probably mean more if it came from you."

Tomorrow night, he told himself. He wouldn't wait any longer than that to seduce her. "Good night, Gillie."

Her voice was even softer now. "G'night, Rafe. How come you go by Rafe, anyway, instead of Rafael? Rafael's a nice name."

He found himself smiling into the darkness again, for no reason. "No more questions."

Off in the distance, a coyote howled. Another one answered from nearby. Gillie stiffened, then snuggled closer.

Rafe wanted to howl, too.

At noon the next day, the sun was a small, white ball overhead that did little to warm the thin mountain air. They'd followed a dry watercourse steadily upward for the last three hours, moving among ponderosa pine and Douglas fir. Frost clung to the ground in the pockets of shade they passed. They were higher than they'd been yesterday—too high, even, for cockroaches, but there were plenty of birds of different sizes and shapes to keep them company.

One of them was calling now. "Chewee, chewee, chewee."

"Oh, shut up," Gillie muttered.

Her head hurt. Her backpack was rubbing a blister on her left shoulder and her feet were sore. She felt like she couldn't get a decent breath of air no matter how hard she worked at it, and altogether, she'd had just about enough of this business of traveling on foot.

Not that she had any options. But she didn't like it, no, she didn't like it at all.

"Did you say something?" Rafe asked from a few feet ahead of her.

She glared at his back. She'd seen a lot of that back. Too much. She knew every stitch in the black tote he'd converted into a backpack. She'd memorized exactly where the strap from the shoulder holster crossed under his arm, and where the largest smudges of dirt were on the once-white shirt he'd taken from Winston's body.

She also knew how many colors hid in the shiny black of his hair, colors hinted at when the sun shone down hard on his head. Rafe might be every bit as dirty and scruffy as she was, but on him it looked good. On her… *It doesn't matter,* she reminded herself. It didn't matter at all that next to him she must have looked like something the cat had dragged in.

"What did you say?" he repeated, moving steadily uphill. He used his walking stick, but it seemed more a convenience than a necessity.

The man obviously wasn't bothered by anything as human as a lack of oxygen, sore feet or blisters. Maybe he didn't feel pain. "Nothing, oh, Man of Steel," she said. "Not a damned thing. Lead on."

Instantly he stopped and turned. "Is something wrong?"

She was cranky and embarrassed. "Did I ask you to stop?"

"No," he said, "but you'd be spread full-length in the dirt, dragging yourself along by your fingernails before you'd ask me to stop, so that doesn't mean much."

"I asked you to stop yesterday, and you wouldn't."

"Yesterday you were looking for a chance to run back to the plane. Once you couldn't do that, you quit asking."

"I'm fine."

"Yeah," he said. "I can see you are. We'll stop and have lunch."

"I'm not hungry."

He frowned. "Your head is hurting again, isn't it? Are you nauseous? Dizzy?"

"Yes, my head hurts. Yes, I've lost my appetite. No, I'm not nauseated or dizzy. And yes, I know what that means. I've got a touch of altitude sickness," she snapped. She'd never had it before, but because she'd flown plenty of unpressurized planes, she'd learned the symptoms.

His frown deepened. "You should have told me. Altitude sickness can be serious. In extreme cases it can even lead to pulmonary edema."

Oh, great, that was just what she needed to hear. Gillie wasn't sure what "pulmonary edema" was, but for once she had no urge to ask. "Whether the air up here agrees with me or not doesn't matter a dirty darn, does it? All I can do is keep going up until we get to where the land goes down again."

"You're angry. Weakness of any kind makes you angry."

"I'm not weak. I don't need to be pampered." She'd proved that long ago, proved it well enough to stay with Pops when her mother couldn't—or wouldn't. He'd never had to leave her behind. "I've been taking care of myself for a long time now. Don't slow down on my account."

His eyebrows lifted oh so slightly to express his opinion of that statement. "Right. We may as well keep going, then, since you're so full of enthusiasm. I wouldn't want to hold you back. Do you think we should readjust the loads in our packs? Maybe you could carry a little more."

She snarled at him.

He turned around, but not before she saw the corner of his mouth curl up.

If he'd been a couple of steps closer, she would have hit him. "Just what do you think is funny now?" she demanded, automatically falling into step behind him.

"I have an odd sense of humor, remember?" The ground grew rougher as they climbed higher, the sides of the little gully closing in on them. Rafe crossed a patch of scree by stretching out one long leg to step from one wide, flat rock to another.

"You sure do." The rocks he'd used so easily were too far apart for her. She had to jump, but she made it. The landing made her head pound miserably. "But that's partly because you want to keep it a secret when you think something's funny."

"Save your air for climbing," he said. "The going gets worse up ahead."

More good news. "You talk, then."

She waited, but he was, of course, silent. Gillie couldn't handle the quiet right now. She needed conversation, contact. Trying to keep her increasing breathlessness from showing, she asked, "So why do you go by Rafe, anyway? You never did tell me."

"You're not going to stop talking, are you?"

"Not unless you start. It keeps me from noticing…things." Like her headache, or the fact that she was getting a bit sick to her stomach. "Did they call you Rafe in the service?"

"Among other things. My nickname in boot camp was Snake."

She laughed. "You're kidding."

"No. It's not that I reminded anyone of a snake—at least, I don't think so. But one day we were standing in ranks outside, waiting to be inspected. It was Louisiana, it was summer, and it was nearly one hundred degrees. Someone had found a snake near the barracks the night before and saved it. He thought it would be funny to let the snake loose and see if anyone fainted or panicked."

"So what happened?"

"As usual, I didn't get the joke, so I picked up the snake." He stopped.

It looked like they'd reached the end of the gully they'd been following. The sides funneled to a point where the ground bent upward at an awkward angle, then tangled itself up in a jumble of rocks and boulders that blocked the pass.

"You did, huh? Then what?" She stopped next to him, chewing on her lip as she eyed the dead end.

"The drill sergeant didn't get the joke, either, but he thought I was the one playing it. Wait here while I go ahead a bit," he said, starting up the slope. The soil was loose, gravel and sand mixed. "This part looks tricky. I want to make sure this is the best way to go."

"Did you get in trouble for the snake?" she asked, tilting her head back to watch. Every step up he took sent dirt and pebbles sliding down, but he was making progress.

"I suppose it was funny," he said, stretching to reach one of the boulders. "The others thought so. I got the snake to strike at my cap so I could pick it up, then stood there holding it behind its head. The tail was lashing around like crazy, and the sergeant's face was a couple inches from mine while he yelled at me. I had a hard time getting his attention. He didn't want to listen until he'd finished yelling."

"So what did you tell him?"

He made it to the rocks. "That it wasn't my joke because I could tell the difference between a milk snake and a coral snake. And a coral snake just wasn't funny at all." He turned around. "I'm going to go a little farther ahead to see what kind of path we'll have."

"A coral snake?" she repeated, appalled. "You picked up a coral snake?"

"I knew what to do. The others didn't." He smiled, and for a moment, just a moment, he must have forgotten to keep himself secret, because it was a *real* smile, full and complete...and blindingly beautiful. "Besides, I was eighteen. It's not a very intelligent age."

Without another word he turned, and within seconds he'd vanished into the tumble of boulders. Gillie was left with the memory of that smile burned into her mind like an afterimage left from staring directly at the sun.

He was gone a long time. Too long. Gillie had too much time to picture all the calamities that might have befallen him. She restrained herself as long as she could, but finally she had to go after him.

The climb up the loose dirt of the slope that he'd called "tricky" turned out to be nearly impossible. She kept sliding down. Finally she backed off a bit, took a running leap and scrambled up far enough, fast enough to grab the rock he'd grabbed, and pull herself up the rest of the way.

Once she was among the boulders piled at the apex of the gully she paused, panting. It wasn't hard to see which way he'd gone. There was only one way to go. It involved a good deal of up-and-down scrambling, which she was heartily sick of, and a bit of sliding and grabbing, which she disliked even more.

Then, just beyond a big, rocky outcropping she saw the flash of a white sleeve, the flutter of long black hair in the wind. She felt that wind in her face, cold and harsh, and gulped at it as if she could get enough air that way. "Rafe," she said as she started moving again, "why are you just standing there?" She rounded the last of the rocks. "Why didn't you—*omigod*."

A scant foot past her toes the ground dropped away like God had taken a hatchet to it. Sky was everywhere. To her right. To her left, just beyond Rafe. In front of her, and way, way down. She was surrounded by blue, a blue purer than anyone but angels, birds and pilots normally saw.

Panic plucked at her with quick, hot fingers.

Other fingers—blunt, masculine fingers—wrapped around her arm. "Hey," Rafe said. "Your face is white as a sheet."

She stared straight ahead so she wouldn't be looking down at all that sky below her. "It's—I—you didn't come back. I thought—I thought something happened to you."

"I'm fine. I should have known—" He shook his head. "Never mind. I checked out the trail like I said I would. It took a while. The ledge is stable enough, but a bit narrow in places."

Ledge?

"But once we descend the first couple hundred feet it widens out, and not far beyond that is a little meadow. There's a freshwater spring, so we'll camp there," he went on. "The last part of the ledge is a bit steep, but—did you say something?"

She shook her head. "No. No, we have to find another way. I don't do ledges."

"You don't...Gillie?" He sounded incredulous. "Are you scared of heights?"

"Of course not," she said, clenching her jaw so her teeth wouldn't chatter. "I'm just shaking like this for the fun of it."

"But you're a pilot. How can a pilot be afraid of heights?"

"That's different." She gave up and closed her eyes. "Planes can fly. I can't. Anyway, it isn't heights that scare me. It's places with edges."

"Places with edges," he repeated, amusement threading his voice. "There is a bit of an edge here."

She wanted to kill him, only she wasn't willing to open her eyes. "I'd tell you to go jump off a cliff, but you'd probably enjoy it."

"Gillie," he said, "I've found water and a protected campsite. What I haven't found is another way down. We're on the divide. There are bound to be other passes, but we don't know where they are. We don't even know where *we* are. It might take days to find a route that didn't scare you—if we could find one at all."

It was too much. Just too damned much, what with plane crashes and dead marshals and handcuffs and digging for water and kisses that blew the top of her head off. No woman should have to cope with all that and a damned ledge, too.

Her lip quivered. Her eyes stayed closed tight. "I don't know if I can," she whispered.

Arms closed around her. Rafe drew her up against him, and he felt wonderful—so big and warm and solid. Maybe it was because she'd slept with this man for two nights now. Maybe it was because she seemed to have come to the end of her own strength as abruptly as she'd come to the place where the ground fell away. Whatever the reason, it felt natural to nestle into him and hide for a moment from the cold wind.

"Sure you can," Rafe said. "You're just tired."

"I'm all right."

"I know you are." One of those big hands moved, stroking her hair.

She almost wept, it felt so good. "I don't like this wilderness stuff. I really don't like it."

"I know," he said, his hand continuing to stroke her head gently, "I know. I think you should just keep your eyes closed. I'll hold on to you. I won't let you fall."

"I've never been able to handle *edges*," she explained to his chest.

"You can handle whatever you have to, Gillie. I've seen you doing just that for a couple days now. But you won't have to look at the edge. Just trust me."

Trust him?

Slowly some of the tension drained out of her body.

Chapter 6

The ledge varied between a foot and eighteen inches wide for most of the way. Easy. Rafe had already walked down it once without any problems other than the stress the slope put on his knee. The wind was a bit stiff, but not enough to cause a problem. He could have been sitting beside the spring right now, resting that aching knee, if Gillie hadn't turned irrational on him.

Instead, he inched along sideways, facing the cliff, with one arm around the stubborn woman inching along beside him. Her eyes were closed, her body stiff with fear. He carried her backpack slung over his other shoulder so she wouldn't have that weight upsetting her balance. It was awkward and tiring.

He didn't mind. He was probably crazy, but he didn't mind their slow progress. The nerves-of-steel pilot who'd landed their plane without power, without a landing strip, without even a clear patch of level land, was terrified of…edges.

Yet she'd stopped shaking when he told her to trust him.

Stupid woman.

His body had gone crazy when she relaxed against him, as if her trust signaled some sort of sexual surrender. Couldn't she tell he burned to violate that trust as soon and as thoroughly as possible?

She brushed against him now as they crept along. It was just as well her eyes were closed. One glance in the right spot would have told her more about his condition than she wanted to know.

"So how did your father get out of that one?" he prompted when she paused in the middle of one of her tales about her father. He'd turned the tables on his wren. This time he was the one asking the questions. If he kept her talking, she couldn't dwell on her fears. Oddly, he had no trouble coming up with questions. Maybe her nosiness was catching.

"The same way he got into it—he talked his way out."

"Talking a lot runs in the family, I guess."

She chuckled, then gasped as one foot skidded on a pebble.

"Easy," he said, drawing her more firmly against his side. "You're not going anywhere."

"Not very fast, anyway," she said wryly.

Holding her this close, he could feel the frightened thud of her heart belying her casual words. "Slow is okay. Especially for falling off cliffs. It gives you time to change your mind."

"Have I mentioned what an odd sense of humor you have?"

"Yes." Reluctantly he eased away a couple inches so they could resume their gradual progress. He had to look ahead, not back at her. They were coming up on a difficult stretch. "Most people don't think I have any sense of humor at all."

"Well, you are stingy with smiles. If you would let loose with a smile a bit more often, it would help. People might guess that you were amused then."

"Your father laughed a lot, didn't he?"

"Oh, yeah. Pops loved to laugh." The memory gave her pleasure. He could hear it in her voice. "'As long as you can laugh,' he used to tell me, 'you know you're alive.' Of course, he said the same thing about flying and enjoying a good cigar or a glass of bourbon."

She'd loved the man. Rafe didn't understand it. Ned Appleby had dragged his daughter to hole-in-the-wall bars and barely-there airstrips all over the world. He'd subjected her to primitive living conditions and, at times, even to danger. He'd died leaving her nothing but debts and the memory of his laughter.

Maybe, for a woman like Gillie, the laughter outweighed all the rest. The idea was hard to grasp for a man who couldn't remember the last time he'd laughed out loud. "I do smile," he said suddenly.

"In a chintzy sort of way, yes. Like you hope no one catches you at it."

He felt a rush of impatience, with her, with himself. He couldn't be other than what he was. "So life was just one adventure after another for you when you were a kid. What about school? Did your father make sure you went to school?"

As soon as Rafe asked the question, a sliver of memory worked its way out, sharp and clear as a shard of glass: the kitchen of the big house where his mother had worked.

The rest of the house had been off-limits, everything except the little room near the kitchen where he'd lived until his seventh year, but he'd been allowed in the kitchen. He remembered miles of spotless white countertops, a creaky wooden floor and the smell of onions and hamburger cooking on the stove. He remembered seeing his mother standing at one of those counters, cleaning something. She'd always been cleaning something.

In the particular memory sliver that had worked its way out, he was arguing with her about school. At six years old, with three whole days of the first grade under his belt, he hadn't seen much point to it.

"I took high school courses by correspondence," Gillie said. "Maybe I didn't get to do the cap-and-gown thing, but I did graduate. We were in Indonesia when my diploma caught up with me."

Rafe would have liked to push the sharp-edged splinter of the past back down, but it refused to go. "My mother valued education," he said. "I stayed in school for her sake at first."

Or for the sake of her memory, at least. He could see her clearly in his mind's eye. She'd been a young woman still, young and pretty, with her black hair coiled on top of her head. On that day when he'd argued with her about school, she'd been wearing her maid's uniform and a worried expression. Rafe had been wearing jeans from the second-hand store and one of the three new shirts she'd bought for him to start school in. The green one.

The bloodstains from his first fistfight on school grounds never did come out of that shirt.

He gritted his teeth and forced the past away. "Lean back just a little here," he warned Gillie. "There's a rock sticking out that will scrape your middle otherwise. Yes, like that. Good. So, what did you do before high school? Did your father tutor you?"

"On some stuff, like the math. He was great at math."

"Didn't you ever go to a regular school in the U.S.?" he asked. She seemed very western, very American, for a woman who'd never spent any time there.

"The States aren't the only place to get an education, you know."

"That doesn't answer my question."

"What does it matter where I went to school?" she asked irritably. "I went to lots of different schools."

Now, that sounded like she was evading his question. Interesting. The wren had secrets, too, it seemed, tender places she didn't want others touching. Her schooling was one, apparently.

Another one, he suspected, was her mother. He'd noticed that she never mentioned the woman, and wondered why. How long ago had she died? Gillie didn't have any trouble talking about her father two years after his death. "I guess it doesn't matter," he said. "Listen, I don't want to worry you, but we're coming up on a tricky stretch here."

She stopped dead. He had to stop, too, or drag her along with him. He turned his head to look at her.

"Define *tricky*," she said.

"The ledge narrows, then disappears—"

She gasped and clutched at his shirt with one hand, at the rock with the other. Her eyes popped open.

"Easy there. The gap isn't very wide, just a few inches, then the ledge comes back, nice and solid, but it stays narrow for a few feet. It gets wider after that." And extremely steep, but he thought he wouldn't mention that just now.

She leaned her forehead against the rock and closed her eyes again. "I'll be fine," she assured him.

He slid his arm up and down her back, trying to soothe muscles tensed as hard as the rock she clung to. "Sure you will. You may have to keep your eyes open for just a little bit, though."

"No problem." Her eyes stayed closed.

"Okay. I'm going to take a baby step toward that gap— c'mon with me, Gillie, it's just a baby step—good, that's good. Now open your eyes and watch how easy—yes, like that— you can do this."

"It's getting pretty narrow," she said nervously. Her eyes were open, but she wasn't looking down.

"You're fine." He squeezed her waist. "I'll help. We've got a few more baby steps to go on the narrow part." About six feet of baby steps, in fact.

By the time they crossed the foot-wide gap in the ledge, Rafe was sweating in spite of the chill wind. Not that the ledge had been difficult for him. In spite of the uneven load her backpack made, he hadn't had any trouble himself.

No, he was sweating with *her* fear. What had been easy for him was a nightmare for Gillie. Oh, she did everything he asked of her. She fought her fear valiantly, but the battle was taking too much out of her.

They paused on the other side of that gap. She swayed slightly. He knew she'd been worn-out before they set foot on the ledge, maybe light-headed from altitude sickness. Now she was exhausted. But they couldn't rest here. She wasn't going to regain her strength, not on eight inches of ledge.

"Come on, sweetie," he said. The endearment slipped out without his noticing. "Come on. That's it, you're doing great. Just a little farther." They had another hundred feet to go to reach the narrow meadow where he'd found the spring.

"Rafe, I'm afraid—"

"I know, sweetie, but you're doing fine."

"No," she said, "that's not it. I'm afraid that if I fall, I won't be able to let go of you. I'll take you over with me. I don't want to do that."

"I won't let you," he assured her. "I'm not going to let you fall."

"But if I do—"

"You won't."

"You don't know that," she said, her voice as thin and sharp as the wind that tugged at his hair, her hair, their clothes. "I might."

"All right, all right. If you do somehow manage to throw yourself backward hard enough to unbalance all 180 pounds of me, I'll pry your fingers off and let you go, okay?"

"Okay." She gave three quick, short nods, like punctuation. "Yes, you do that."

Rafe clenched his jaw against the need to yell at her.

His assurance that he'd let her fall relaxed her enough for them to finish their halting descent. She closed her eyes again for the last part of the way, even when they were able to walk abreast.

He stopped several feet into the meadow. "Hey," he said, turning her to face him. "Look around. We made it. No more baby steps. You did it."

Slowly her eyes opened. "Oh," she said. Her fingers flexed on his arm once, twice. "Oh, I did. *We* did." She gazed around the meadow with all the delight of a sinner readmitted to paradise.

Their haven was small and scrubby as meadows go, more like a wide place in a trail that ran between the rocky sides of two peaks. There were no wildflowers, and the grass grew in brownish tufts rather than a green carpet. Rocks, taller grasses and a few scruffy shrubs screened the grotto where he'd found the freshwater spring. A scattering of pines and a few stunted oaks dotted the sides of the field.

She looked down at the soft dirt, then up at him. A smile started. "This is better. Much better. No edges."

Rafe looked down into eyes as blue as the sky that would

have swallowed them both had they fallen from the ledge. Gillie's face was pale with exhaustion. Even her pretty lips were pale. He knew she was desperately vulnerable right now.

I'll wait, he told himself, dropping her backpack in the dirt, *until tonight.*

She was smiling at him. Trust and relief shone in those unworldly eyes. He looked at her mouth. Her tongue sneaked out, dampened her lips, then hid from him again.

Yes, I can surely wait, he thought as he bent slowly. He didn't have to have her right now, not right this very minute. He was a man accustomed to control. It would be unfair to seduce her now, and he liked Gillie. He wanted to be fair to her.

I'll wait, he thought as his lips brushed hers. Then he stopped thinking.

There was no control. Only need. Her lips were still damp from her tongue, so he licked them. She gasped and he came inside, tasting her deeply as his hands drew her tight against him. He wanted to touch her everywhere, to fill himself up with her.

''Gillie,'' he said, and that was all he could say, just that, just her name. He said it again, whispered it in her ear while his hands raced over her. There were so many places to touch, to taste, to feel. He bit lightly on her earlobe and she shuddered in his arms. He wanted to push inside her that very instant, but settled for sliding his hand up underneath the layers she wore.

The sound she made could have meant anything—protest, surprise, delight. She started to pull back.

''Shh,'' he said, pressing kisses along the line of her jaw. ''Shh, it's okay,'' he told her. ''Let me touch you. Please, Gillie.'' And he cupped her breast. Her nipple was hard, and he murmured his approval as he bent to suck lightly on her neck. He rubbed her hard nipple with his thumb, and she jerked—then arced in obvious, instinctive invitation.

He moaned.

The fire took Gillie without warning. Not the kiss, no— she'd had warning of that. She'd seen this kiss trapped in the darkness of his eyes when he bent over her, a kiss tangled up with the promise of storm, and she'd done nothing. She'd let him kiss her. She'd let him, because she wanted a taste of the storm.

She'd been a fool.

Heat flowed from him to her, liquid lightning that sang crazy songs in her blood. His hand kneaded her breast, and she moaned and pressed herself against it, wanting more. Needing more.

When he pulled her down with him, she went.

Here at the edge of the meadow there was little grass to cushion them. Yet after their stony bed last night, after the rocky ledge they'd just been on, the loose soil felt soft and welcoming to Gillie. She lay on her back in the dirt with Rafe on top of her, with his mouth eating at hers and his thigh heavy between her legs. His makeshift pack lay in the dirt a few feet away, next to hers.

Rafe pushed up her sweatshirt and the shirt beneath it, and she lifted herself up so he could do that. Then her breasts were bare, exposed to the chilly air and to his eyes. She shivered, and reason almost woke.

He bent and took her nipple in his mouth, and she came apart.

He sucked, gently at first, then hard. Harder. Her breath came in quick pants. Her hands fluttered at his shoulders, unable to rest, unable to hold on to anything in this new world of sensation. Hunger crawled through her, a terrible beast with wicked teeth and claws that raked her and made her shudder.

Then it was Rafe's teeth scraping lightly across her nipple. When he did, the hunger beast bit down and burst something open inside her, something that had always been hidden and *hers,* only hers, until now. It burst and flowed through her like syrup, flowed right up to her surface, up where Rafe could taste it and take it from her as he suckled and sucked.

She cried out. Above the drumming bass of passion, fear sang a clear, high note. "No," she said, and closed her hands on his shoulders at last. She pushed at him weakly—or maybe she pulled him closer.

"It's all right, Gillie," he told her, and his mouth nuzzled a path from one breast to the other. The nipple he left was wet and cold, so cold in the thin mountain air. "I'll take care of you," he said.

"Rafe?" She trembled.

"I know," he said, "I know." And his hand cupped her between her legs just as his mouth fastened on her other nipple.

She spun out of control. He licked and he rubbed, and she wanted him to keep doing those things more than she wanted to draw her next breath. And yet—and yet— "Rafe," she gasped. "You're going to hurt me."

"I'll be careful." He blew on her wet nipple. "I can't promise it won't hurt at all. I've never had a virgin, Gillie, so I don't know exactly what to expect, either. But I'll be very, very careful."

She gasped and she shivered and she sank her hands into his hair—and yanked his head back. He stared down at her. His lips were parted and damp. His eyes were dark as sin and twice as hungry.

"Y-you," she stuttered, her hands fisted in his hair, tears starting in her eyes. "You damned, stupid, arrogant *man*—do you really think I'm worried about *that* hurt?"

For a moment longer he stared down at her. His hand still cupped her intimately. A tear leaked out of the corner of her left eye and trailed down her temple.

She wanted his hand there. She did, and he knew it.

In one convulsive movement he threw himself off her. He lay on his back and cursed in two languages while she lay motionless beside him, her chest heaving as she fought for air and composure, fought to keep from crying out at the sudden loss.

She was cold without him. Her breasts were bare and damp from his mouth. Gillie managed to sit up and tug her clothing back in place. She took one deep, shaky breath before leaning her head on her knees, her face turned so she didn't have to look at him.

She didn't think about what had just happened. She couldn't, not yet.

Rafe stopped cursing. After a moment she heard him sit up, then stand. He didn't speak. She desperately wanted him to say something, anything—no, not just anything. She wanted tenderness. Oh, she was a fool, wasn't she?

Yet he'd been so patient earlier. She hadn't expected kindness from this man, yet that's what he'd given her as he led her along the ledge. He hadn't mocked her fear. Instead he'd soothed her, encouraged her, distracting and rescuing her one painful step at a time.

And as soon as he'd saved her from one edge, he'd shoved her off another one. She felt like she was still falling.

Her backpack landed in the dirt next to her. Slowly she turned her head.

As soon as he'd dropped her pack beside her, he'd backed off. He stood three paces away now. She looked closely, but couldn't see any trace of the man who'd begged her to let him touch her.

But Rafe *had* wanted her. She was sure of that. She could almost believe he'd needed her.

He stood watching her now with all the stony, remote beauty of the mountains he was forcing her to cross. "Sit on your pack," he said, "not on the bare ground. It will drain too much heat from your body." He turned and walked away.

It had been two hours or so after noon when they'd arrived at their mountain meadow. Gillie was amazed by this when she shrugged into her pack once more and glanced at the sky. The sun's position insisted they had hours to go before dark. How could so much have happened in little more than a single morning?

Because she had no choice she followed Rafe.

He waited for her fifty yards away, near one of the stony sides of the little valley. Her eyes widened as she approached. He was standing in front of a wall of dried mud bricks that looked like it closed off the mouth to a cave. "Rafe! Do you suppose someone's living here?"

"Not anymore. Not for several years, judging by the shape the adobe is in. It's still sound enough for us to sleep inside tonight, though."

Gillie peered in the open doorway. The interior was too dark to make out much detail, but the room shaped by one man-made wall and three natural ones was small.

Who had built it? she wondered. How long ago had they left, and why? She wanted to ask Rafe, but she couldn't. She couldn't bring herself to speak to him. Not yet.

This room was where they would sleep that night. Together.

He showed her where the spring lay hidden in a rocky grotto nearby, and they both carried water back to the campsite. He laid their campfire outside the little cave room. "We'll move our fire inside tonight," he said, "but the room will have to be cleaned out thoroughly first. Not just for sanitary reasons. I don't want a stray bit of straw catching the place on fire."

"All right," she said. He wasn't looking at her. Gillie was grateful for that. "I'll clean it." She needed to keep moving. There would be no keeping the thoughts out once she stopped.

"You need to rest."

"I'm fine."

He gave her a long, steady look. "As you please," he said. "But we'll eat first. We may as well finish up the peanut butter."

She turned away. "I'm going to go wash up."

"Feeling dirty, are you?"

She paused and glanced over her shoulder. "You know, you don't have to work quite so hard at being a jerk. I think you've got that role down pat." She turned and walked away.

Rafe watched Gillie escape.

He'd been aware of the way she tracked his every move with wary little glances while he built the fire. She'd watched him with the same careful attention any small creature gave to a predator.

She couldn't know he was more shaken by his loss of control than she was.

He knew why she needed to get away from him now. She couldn't get much distance, of course, but he'd let her have what he could. He had always understood the need for distance.

How odd to find that he didn't want to allow her any.

Gillie followed the trail through the bushes that led to a stone doorway formed by two leaning boulders. When she passed beneath the lintel into the grotto, awe widened her eyes and quieted her mind.

She'd felt like this before. Once, in a Gothic cathedral at Chartres. Another time, when she and Pops came across a tiny shrine hidden in the jungle in Indonesia. The spring itself was narrow and deep, walled in striated slabs of rock that glittered where streaks of white and rose quartz caught the sun.

The water itself looked and smelled pure, though they would still boil it for drinking. It was also as cold as justice untempered by mercy.

Avoiding her own thoughts was tricky, Gillie discovered, about as tricky as walking a ledge with her eyes closed. But there was no one to lead her along this path, a path that led in only one direction. To one person.

She washed her hands and face and wondered if Rafe had even seen the beauty of the little grotto. Maybe his eyes only marked the presence of water and the existence of game trails. Maybe he didn't notice the glittery streaks in the rock, or see how the thrusting, tumbled shapes formed a natural sculpture more spectacular than any merely human artist could create.

Could he be so dead to all but the essentials of survival that he didn't see anything else? She shivered.

Gillie used one of the empty Coke cans to bring Rafe water to wash with. They ate standing up while they waited for their drinking water to cool, taking turns scooping peanut butter out of the jar with the last of the crackers.

"I'm going to set some snares and scout around," he told her then. "I may be gone awhile."

She didn't look at him. "All right."

He hesitated as if he had something more to say, but left without saying it.

While Rafe was gone, Gillie gathered more branches for the

fire and thought about the coming night. Would he insist that they still had to sleep together for warmth? It seemed much warmer to her here, though they'd only descended a few hundred feet. Maybe the rock walls of the little valley trapped some of the day's heat. And they would be inside, after all, with a fire to warm them.

No one had collected the deadfalls for a long time, so she had no trouble finding firewood. It might have been better if she'd had to work a little harder. She might have been forced to keep her mind focused then. As it was, her mind wouldn't cooperate. It only dwelled on the subjects she wanted to avoid.

Like how it would feel to lie next to Rafe that night. How it would feel if their bodies touched. What if he touched her with his hands as well? What if he kissed her hard and deep again?

She shivered. Fear and desire fought and fused, making her stomach dizzy.

A fire and walls, she decided, would surely make it warm enough for them to sleep separately that night.

Gillie kept going as long as she could. She did her best to clean their sleeping quarters, but it was too dark inside for her to do a good job. While she pushed twigs and tiny bones and less identifiable debris outside with a branch, she wondered if this abandoned dwelling meant there were other people nearby.

Mostly, though, she wondered about Rafe. And about herself. She couldn't shut those thoughts out anymore.

She found two useful things in her cleaning—a pottery pot that was intact except for a broken place on the rim, and a shallow bowl. She set those things outside by the fire.

By then she was so exhausted she had to sit down. She was hungry, too. Feeling a mixture of defiance and guilt, she got a small handful of M&M's from the stash in Rafe's pack. She pulled one of the blankets around her, leaned against the crumbling, sun-warmed adobe and ate the little candies one by one.

Exhaustion sent the boundaries she'd built in her mind slipping. She could no longer deny what she felt. And what she felt was fear—a huge, unreasonable mass of fear, resting right below her breastbone.

She wasn't afraid Rafe would force her. He wouldn't. Why was she so sure of that? Just as she was sure he wasn't a murderer. Yet she didn't really know him. When she met him two days ago—only two days—he'd been in chains. She didn't know him at all, yet she'd let him touch her in ways no one ever had.

Logic, she thought fuzzily as her eyes closed, seemed to have little connection to what was happening to her. Her last thought as sleep dragged her down was a question. What was it, exactly, that she feared?

They cooked and ate outside. Rafe had snared two rabbits this time. Strips of meat from one of them hung above the fire to smoke. Gillie had used the pot she'd found to stew the other rabbit with some onions and small tubers Rafe had dug out of the remnants of a garden someone had once tended here.

It was very dark that night. Clouds had rolled in just before sunset, and the sky overhead looked like a dusty black blanket. The only light came from the orange dance of the campfire.

The man sitting Indian-style across the fire from Gillie looked utterly pagan and comfortable in the primitive setting. Gillie, on the other hand, felt ready to jump out of her skin. She finished the last of the bland tubers and set her bowl aside.

"Would you like more?" Rafe asked politely. Since they had only one bowl, he was eating directly from the pot.

"No, thank you." Gillie's hands felt itchy and empty. Her eyes had nowhere safe to light. She picked up a stick and began drawing idle patterns in the dirt.

"We could have a few of the M&M's for dessert."

She glanced at him. "I, uh, had some already. This afternoon. While you were gone." Her cheeks felt hot. "I'm sorry. I shouldn't have eaten anything when you weren't here to have your share."

Rafe made a disgusted noise. "Do you think you could quit acting like I'm about to beat you? Or rape you. Maybe you think I'm going to—"

"No," she said quickly. "No, I don't think that. I just don't know how to act. I don't know...much of anything." Not about him, and not about herself, either. She drew a big question mark in the sand.

"What," he mocked, "no questions?" He leaned sideways to set the pot aside, straightened and met her eyes. "I have a question, Gillie."

She held herself stiff, her eyes averted, and waited.

"Why are you a virgin?"

She blinked. "I—why—good grief, Rafe!"

He leaned forward, resting his hands on his thighs. Light and shadows played along his skin, throwing his cheekbones into relief. His hair, drawn back into a ponytail again, was as impenetrably black as the sky overhead. "Is it love you've waited for, or marriage?"

She squirmed, uncomfortable. "Why does it have to be either one? I mean—" she waved vaguely with the stick "—look at me. I've never had to beat men off."

"That's because you've found other ways of keeping them at arm's length. Do you know how appealing—no," he said, shaking his head. "Of course you don't, and you won't believe me. But the fact is you're waiting for something, either the safety of marriage or the illusion of love."

Stung, she tossed the stick aside. "What does it matter to you? I don't imagine you're going to offer me either one."

"That's right," he said quietly. "But you said I was going to hurt you. I don't want to do that, but I do want you, Gillie. Maybe if I know what matters to you, I can avoid hurting you."

Her heart beat faster. She licked her lips nervously and saw that his eyes followed the movement.

Rafe did want her. She didn't think it was just lust—at least, not the indifferent sort of appetite that sent men into bars or bordellos. He wanted *her*. Gillie felt as if she'd caught a glimpse of something shiny and glorious that waited for her just the other side of the fear.

She swallowed. "You know what? I guess I do have a couple of questions."

His slight smile was reflected, like the glow of the campfire, in the darkness of his eyes. "Do you, now?"

She nodded. It would be safer, far safer, to go on knowing as little as possible about this man. Yet she couldn't do it, not when looking at that faint smile in his eyes made something inside her start to soar. "We could trade answers again."

"Do you always bargain this way?"

No, not this way. This way was new to her. She shrugged. "I guess I'm used to bargaining. People do that, you know, all over the world, though they give you funny looks if you try it in the States."

"Did people give you funny looks, Gillie?"

"Definitely." She chuckled. "I mean—picture it. I was twelve, and my mother had given me her charge card so I could get some school things. When I told the clerk I'd give her ten dollars, tops, for the forty-five-dollar dress I'd just tried on, she thought I was trying to bribe her into letting me steal it." It hadn't been funny at the time, of course. It hadn't been funny until she was back with Pops and told him the story. Gillie shook her head, smiling. "Pops really hooted over that one."

"Your mother was still alive when you were twelve?"

She looked at him, surprised. "Of course. Why would you think otherwise?"

"You've never mentioned her. I thought she was dead."

Gillie grimaced and picked up her stick again, stirring the dirt with it. "I haven't mentioned broccoli, either, but it's still around."

"You don't like broccoli, I take it."

She shrugged. "Mother and I don't have much in common. She's a very pretty woman, very delicate and feminine. I haven't seen her in—" *five years and two months, plus or minus a week or two* "—in quite a while. We exchange Christmas cards." Her mother always put a check inside. Gillie always tore the check up. "She wrote me once, right after Pops died."

"And what did she say?" he asked softly.

Anger stirred, a small, familiar flame. "That I could come

live with her and Miles and the kids—that's her family now, her husband, Miles, his son and their two daughters—if I wanted to. Good grief, I was twenty-five. I didn't need her to put a roof over my head. Besides, we'd already tried that. It didn't work out.''

"When you were twelve?"

Gillie didn't like the direction the conversation had taken, not at all. "Hey, why are we talking about my mother, anyway?"

"We're talking about why you're still a virgin," he said calmly. "Your mother has something to do with that, I think."

She rolled her eyes. "You trying to play shrink or something?"

"You don't think she does? Then why did you lead the conversation in this direction?"

Had she done that? Gillie shook her head, confused. "I just didn't want to talk about—you know, the other. But there's no deep, dark secret about why I haven't…been with anyone. I'm really not the sort of woman men pursue, so it isn't like I've been tempted that often. And…"

"Yes?"

She shrugged. "Pops and I moved around a lot." Gillie made friends easily and often, but always with the knowledge she'd be moving on, leaving them behind. That sort of life didn't lead to intimacy.

He nodded. "You wanted a relationship, not just a good time. That doesn't surprise me. But is it love you've been waiting for, or promises?"

Suddenly angry, Gillie flung the stick away, off into the darkness. "Why does it have to be one or the other?"

"Am I wrong?" he asked. "Maybe love isn't important to you. Maybe you aren't upset that I want to enjoy you physically without promising you anything. What about it, Gillie? Does it matter whether the first man you have sex with loves you or not?"

She scowled. "You're assuming way too much. And I hate that phrase—'have sex.' You *have* tea. You have a doughnut or an appointment or a flat tire. People aren't snacks. Love isn't—'' She cut herself off.

He looked at her steadily. "I know, Gillie. But people do have sex without the blessing of either love or marriage."

She knew that. She didn't want to hear it, though. Especially not from this man. A puff of wind shook the flames. Gillie shivered. She hugged her arms around herself, and suddenly she knew how to name the fear that clung to her. "Is it so terrible," she whispered, "to want something to last? Someone who will stay?"

He didn't answer. Somewhere far off a coyote sang to the hidden moon. Across the fire Rafe watched her, and she couldn't tell what he was thinking. She had no idea at all. "I don't want you to touch me tonight," she said. "We'll be warm enough with each of us using a blanket. We'll have a fire."

"You have a question coming," he said, speaking without answering. "Do you want to ask it?"

She shook her head. What would she ask? *Are you going to seduce me tonight? Will you put your hands on me? Where?* How could she take the risk of asking anything? Yet she needed to know. She *needed* to. "At least," she said, curling her legs up underneath her, "tell me how you came to be here, on the run from a drug gang."

"Do you believe what I've told you so far, Gillie? Will you believe whatever else I tell you?" He shook his head. "Never mind. I'm here because I was trying to get information about the U.S. end of the gang who's after me. They were using my import business without my knowledge to smuggle their products into the U.S. When I found out, I wanted them stopped. They'd used what belonged to me, you see. I couldn't let them get away with that. They framed me for murder. I escaped."

"Whose death did they frame you for?"

"My foster brother's. He was managing the company for me."

She stared across the open fire at him. His terse answers raised dozens more questions, but she was tired and suddenly chilled, too tired to chase down the truth.

Or to deal with the ache of sympathy his story woke inside her. She stood, dusting her jeans off. "I'm tired. I want to sleep. And I want to sleep by myself, Rafe. Don't press me." She made herself meet his eyes. "Not tonight."

The wind blew harder, tugging loose a strand of his inky black hair, blowing it across his face. He didn't smile or speak. He just looked at her, and her breath caught in her chest. Her heartbeat speeded up, and she ached down low, where he'd put his hand that afternoon.

For a moment she thought he wouldn't have to come to her or even touch her, to persuade her. All he had to do was look at her the way he was looking right now. She nearly went to him, nearly offered him—anything. Everything.

"Good night," she said quickly, and picked up a burning brand from the fire to light her way into the small, dark room they would share.

Gillie lay awake for what seemed like hours. She curled up on the hard ground in her single blanket, facing away from the fire he'd laid earlier and she'd lit with her brand. It *was* warmer inside the little room than their last two campsites had been. With the fire, it was almost warm enough to sleep alone. Almost.

For a very long time she lay there and stared into the darkness of the empty doorway, waiting. But she fell asleep before he came.

Chapter 7

"So are we going or staying?"

"I haven't decided. Finish your breakfast."

Gillie made a face. Smoked rabbit was a pretty uninspiring meal. "I am finished," she said. "I think we should go."

"If it rains, we're better off here." He bit into a strip of meat.

Gillie glanced overhead. The sky was the color of dull steel, as if someone had put a lid over their corner of the earth. She had a pilot's appreciation for the power of weather, yet... "It is the dry season. Even if it does rain, it shouldn't be much of a storm. And the road you spotted is so close." He'd seen it yesterday, but he hadn't told her about it until this morning. She was definitely irritated about that.

"Not that close. One or two days away," he said. "We'll have to cross some pretty rugged country to get there, and we're not likely to find shelter as good as we have here."

Gillie glanced at the sky again. "But won't the chance of rain decrease as we get farther east? We'd be heading into drier country."

"For someone who doesn't care for hiking, you're certainly eager to pick up your pack and go."

"I want to get back to civilization. Is that so strange? I want plumbing and Mamacita's burritos, and I want to see my friends again."

"And you want to get away from me before you do what you're afraid you're going to do."

Blast him. He saw inside her too deeply, too easily, while she could scarcely see past the dark mirrors of his eyes. "You can sit around and stroke your ego if you like," she said, and stood. "I'm going to go to the spring so I can wash up and brush my teeth."

Gillie's toothbrush and toothpaste were in her pack in the little cave room. She took her time getting them. For comfort she let her fingers stroke the familiar carving on her treasure box.

At the moment she couldn't decide which she disliked the most about Rafe—his arrogant assumptions, or the fact that one or two of them were all too accurate.

She did want to be loved. She'd wanted that for a long time now, and couldn't imagine trusting her body to the hands and hungers of a man without it. At least, she'd never been able to imagine it in the past. Lately her mind had begun leaping off in all sorts of bewildering directions.

Of course, there was no way she'd admit her longing to him. She didn't want to look like a fool. Rafe had made it clear that tender feelings played no part in what he wanted from her, and she knew well enough that love was a long shot for a woman like her.

"My little ugly duckling," her mother used to say fondly when Gillie was small, back when they were a family. Gillie had been a skinny kid, all angles and energy, never one for the ribbons and lace her mother had adored...though Linda Appleby had seemed to love her anyway, back then. Before Linda got sick and went to the States to recover, and never came back.

As for his other assumption, that she was afraid of what she might do—oh, yes. He was right there, too, blast him. After waiting so long to be loved, Gillie was very much afraid she might settle for being wanted. Because Rafe wanted her in a way she'd thought no man ever would.

She came out of the dark, cramped room into the relative brightness of the overcast morning. Rafe was shoveling dirt on the fire with the metal box they used for digging. He looked up at her.

Her heart gave a funny hip-hop. "You put the fire out. Does that mean we're leaving?"

"No," he said, and stood. "I'm going to walk over to the spring with you and check my snares. I didn't want to leave the fire unattended."

"I'd rather go by myself."

He didn't bother to discuss it, just gave her one of his looks and reached for the shoulder holster that held his .45. He never stirred far without that gun.

She sighed, knowing there wasn't much point in arguing. "You have to stay out of the grotto, though," she warned him as she started toward the spring. "I intend to wash more than just my face and hands this time."

He shook his head and fell into step beside her. "You have no sense," he told her. "None at all."

"Oh, really? Are you so overwhelmed with lust now that you'll sneak a peek at me?"

"No." He bit the word off. "I won't."

She nodded. "You're an egotistical idiot, but you're not a Peeping Tom."

He didn't answer, so she decided she'd won that argument.

Rafe's snares were set in the underbrush leading to the grotto, not in the grotto itself, so he left her side before she passed under the tall, leaning stone that formed the entrance. The beauty of the place struck her as vividly as ever, but she didn't let herself linger in appreciation.

For a washcloth she had a scrap of cloth from the shirt Rafe had cut into strips to bind his knee. She quickly stripped to the waist. At the edge of the water she hesitated. As much as she wanted to wash all over, being out in the open like this made her feel uncomfortably exposed. Not to mention chilly.

One thing at a time, she decided. She'd wash her top half first, and if she wasn't absolutely frozen after that she'd take her jeans off and at least get her legs and feet clean. She knelt, leaning out over the water in an effort to keep her jeans dry.

She was covered in goose bumps from the waist up and running her scrap of cloth over her stomach when she heard a sound. She turned.

Rafe stood in the stone doorway. Their eyes met for half a second before his gaze dropped to her breasts.

Heat exploded in her belly, a quick burst of fire curling up from her middle and spreading with alarming speed. Instinctively she crossed her arms, covering herself—painfully aware that part of her wanted to drop her arms and let him look. But following fast behind the heat was disappointment, sharp and bitter as the cold air that tightened her nipples into hard peaks.

He had said he wouldn't look.

He pulled his gaze up to her face at the same time she noticed what he held in his hand: the revolver. "I'm not here for the view," he said. "Get dressed. You got your wish. We're leaving."

"Wh-what?"

"One of my snares had a rabbit in it—until a puma found it. The blood's fresh, which means the cat is close."

Gillie shot to her feet, turned her back and grabbed her clothes, yanking her T-shirt over her head. "How close?" She slid her arms into the sleeves of the second shirt, scanning the rocks around them for movement while her fingers stumbled over the buttons.

"I don't know. I'd seen the tracks before—"

She made an angry sound that came out muffled by the sweatshirt she was pulling on.

"But I didn't say anything because they were old tracks. I didn't want to alarm you if the animal was nowhere near."

"But it is near." She turned to face him.

"I think so. The big cats aren't predictable. It might ignore us, but it might not. We're better off risking the rain."

For once, they were in complete agreement. She started for the doorway.

He didn't move. She had to stop or walk right into him. She lifted her chin haughtily. "Do you mind?"

"It won't make any difference," he said.

"What are you talking about?"

"Leaving now won't make any difference as far as what you fear, Gillie. I still intend to have you."

She scowled at him. "I'm not a cup of coffee. You can't *have* me, just like you can't *take* my virginity."

"I could, though. We both know it. But you're right, in a way. Last night I was awake for hours, wanting you, wanting to be inside you. But I stayed away. I realized it's best if you come to me."

She blinked. "I beg your pardon?"

"I'm not going to touch you. You'll give yourself to me freely. Waiting for you to come to me won't be easy, but I can do it. That way the debt I owe you will be less. You don't believe me," he added, "but you do want me. In the end you'll come to me for what you need, Gillie."

No doubt about it. She hated his arrogance most of all, because there was no way, absolutely no way, he could be right with *that* assumption.

Rafe's knee hurt.

They'd been heading steadily downhill for two hours. The going was rough, but he'd found what was probably an old Tarahumara footpath to follow. His mother's people were famous for traveling everywhere on foot, often at a run, and he and Gillie were at the northern edge of their territory.

The country around them now was noticeably drier, but they were lower, so there was more underbrush. As the pine and fir trees thinned, yucca and century plant, live oak and mesquite had begun to appear, giving the land an oddly mixed look.

Rafe rounded a stand of saw-toothed agave and paused. The trail ahead vanished in a treacherously steep slope that looked like the dried remains of a mud slide. He took a moment to study the landscape in front of him, but couldn't see where the trail picked up again.

His knee hurt more when he started down the slope. He was leaning heavily on his staff when Gillie spoke for the first time in two hours.

"You're limping."

Since that was obvious, he didn't respond.

That, of course, didn't discourage her. "Your knee's worse, isn't it?" He could track her progress behind him easily by listening as she slid and stopped, slid and stopped. "Did you wrench it somehow?"

"I don't know."

"You think it's just the stress of walking on it, then? All this hiking can't be good for it." She was silent a moment— at least, her voice was silent. The rest of her made enough noise on the loose dirt of the slope to frighten away small animals for miles around. "Maybe we should have stayed in the meadow."

"Your opinion comes a little late to do much good." He reached the bottom of the slope and stopped. The trail had disappeared. He stood in a wide depression between the steep slope behind and more gently rolling land ahead. From above, he'd seen that the shallow hills ahead rippled down to what was either a small river or a good-size stream. The waterway made a likely goal if he couldn't find the road he'd spotted before descending.

He had hopes for the road, though. There were few trees of any size nearby, and a great many stumps. The area had been logged, and badly overcut, at one time. Not recently, he judged, looking at the height of the new growth. But there should be a logging road somewhere. Even if it was unused and overgrown now, it would lead them to some sort of town.

If they could find it.

He turned to wait for her to catch up, his knee throbbing. Her concern, he reminded himself, was justified. If he couldn't keep going, she'd be stranded along with him. "I may need to rest my knee for a while when we stop for lunch," he told her as she skidded down the slope toward him, "but I'm not incapacitated."

"Maybe we should stop and rest it now."

At the bottom of a former mud slide, with rain threatening? "No."

She slid into place beside him, grimacing either with effort or aggravation. "You're doing that one-word thing again."

"So? You didn't talk all morning." And it had bothered him. Ridiculous as it was to be troubled because she hadn't pestered him with questions, her silence had pulled at something inside him. He didn't like it.

He started walking, leaning on his stick. The scrubby new growth made the going rough.

"I was mad," she pointed out, following. "I still am, actually, but you aren't, so there's no excuse for those one-word answers of yours."

"Why are you talking now if you're still mad?"

"I'm bored. And besides, I wanted to ask you a couple of things."

He smiled before he could stop himself. She was asking questions again.

"Why did the gang try to frame you instead of trying to kill you? Where do you live when you're not on the run? And why did you leave me alone last night?"

Because she'd cried. He felt it again, the same gut punch of emotion that had robbed him of breath yesterday. He'd fully intended to take her, there on the bare ground, when that tear had rolled down her cheek. It had stopped him as effectively as a blow from a two-by-four.

He couldn't touch her now, either. What if she cried again? What if she cried *afterward?*

Last night that image had paralyzed him, kept him by the fire instead of inside, with her. Inside her. He'd been at a loss to understand why it acted on him so powerfully until he realized, with relief, that it was his sense of self-preservation operating. He'd been very close to incurring the sort of debt that couldn't be paid.

Fortunately he'd stopped in time, and had figured out what he needed to do. He had to wait for her to come to him.

Behind him Gillie sighed. "You've gone from one word to no words, Rafe."

He got his breath, and his control, back. "I told you why last night." He paused, and decided to answer one of her questions. The safest one. "I live in Las Cruces, New Mexico, near the Texas border."

"Hey, I've been there!" She sounded delighted by the connection. "I fly into El Paso pretty often, and Las Cruces is only about twenty minutes away. Pretty town. I drove over there once with a friend who wanted me to check out this fancy restaurant. The food was pretty good, but the prices!" She shook her head, obviously appalled. "Is your import business there?"

"No. It's thirty miles away, in a border town called Dolores." Or it used to be. With Steve dead and Rafe on the run, there wouldn't have been anyone to keep the doors open the past two months, no one to fill orders and write paychecks. "It may be bankrupt by now. I have other business interests, of course." And money. He had that. He wouldn't let the import business stay closed for long.

"In Dolores?"

"No."

"Why is your import business there, then?"

Good God, she was nosy. "I grew up there."

"Oh. I guess you wanted to give something back to the town."

The wind was picking up. Rafe looked around, but saw nothing nearby that offered shelter if the weather continued to worsen. He drew on the patience he'd cultivated for so long, and kept to a slow, steady pace up the hill. Pain was a warning, he reminded himself. If he didn't heed it, he could lose mobility completely. "I had debts to pay."

"The people there were good to you, then? They helped you and your mother?"

He made a harsh noise. "Helped? Federal law insisted that kids like me—children of illegal immigrants—be given an education. And I was a citizen. I'd been born in the U.S."

"This may be a dumb question, but if people knew your mother didn't have a green card, why wasn't she picked up?"

"She worked for old man Holbrook, and he owned half the

county. I don't know if he actually bribed officials to look the other way when he hired domestics and agricultural workers, but no one ever checked his people out.''

"Did your mother never apply for citizenship?"

"She died." He swallowed a sudden, surprising swell of emotion. It was so long ago.... "She wanted to be a citizen so she could give something back to the country she'd made her home, but she died before she could."

"What about you?" she asked softly. "How old were you when she died?"

"Seven. I went into foster care. But the government couldn't make the people of Dolores like paying for a 'wetback's brat.' '' Rafe heard the bitterness in his voice and fell silent. Why had he said so much?

"But you thought you had a debt to pay, anyway. You didn't like the townspeople, but you still felt you owed them?"

Some debts were complicated. Rafe's business paid taxes that supported the school system that had educated him, but the name he'd given that business, the name that residents of Dolores saw when they drove past the warehouse on Highway 132 to Las Cruces, paid that debt in another way.

Pia's, he'd named it.

No, he wouldn't let it stay closed for long.

The wren hadn't run out of questions. "Did you go in the service because you thought you owed your country something, too?"

"You're reading too much into a simple comment," he said curtly.

"I don't think so. You're fixated on this idea of debt, and I think you had a rough time growing up. I can understand that. People can be pretty clannish. They don't let outsiders into their groups easily, but it's hard to explain that to a child."

She spoke so matter-of-factly. Was he imagining the wistfulness hiding behind that practical tone? "Do you speak from experience, Gillie? Did you have trouble fitting in as a child?"

"Well, of course. I lived in too many places to really be part of any one spot. Baseball helped me make friends, though.

Did you play any sports? People open up when you're on a team together.''

"Did you play baseball when you lived in the U.S. when you were twelve?'' The wren's habit of asking personal questions must be contagious, Rafe thought. He didn't mind having caught it, though. It was...rather pleasant, actually.

"Darn right I did. I was the pitcher.''

They'd reached the top of one of the low hills. The wind had taken on a bitter edge that cut through his clothes. He glanced at the sky and frowned as he started down. "So how many times did you live in the U.S.?''

"Well, I was born there, and then we moved back when I started school. Pops was trying to please my mother, who hated moving all the time, but he couldn't stay in one place to save himself. I don't know why she married him. Anyway, just before I entered the third grade he got a job offer and talked Mother into going, so we took off for Bolivia. A few months later, Mother got sick.''

The sky worried Rafe. The sullen overcast was breaking up into a dirty, wind-whipped pile of clouds building up in treacherous banks of pending storm. He kept his pace steady as they worked their way downhill. "Was she very ill?''

"She was at first. It was a tropical bug, and she just couldn't seem to kick it. She and Pops told me she had to go back to the States to stay with her folks awhile so she could recuperate properly. I've never been sure if that was the real reason she left, but I guess it doesn't much matter. She never came back.''

"Did you want to go with her?''

"Oh, no. Her parents hated Pops. They didn't mind taking her in, but they didn't want me around. Not that I minded,'' she added hastily. "I didn't want anything to do with people who would treat Pops that way.''

Or with people who hadn't wanted her. She'd been their granddaughter, but they hadn't cared. Rafe stopped partway down the hill, silently studying the land around them, thinking of an eight-year-old girl whose mother didn't come back.

He heard Gillie come to a stop beside him, but didn't look

over at her. The wind whipped his hair in his face and cut through his clothes.

"We're going to have trouble from the weather, Gillie, and I can't find any shelter," he said. Quietly he added, "As far as I know, I've never met my grandparents. My mother's parents died. As for my father's parents—whether they knew about me or not depends on who he was."

Her hand rested on his arm, creating one warm spot in an increasingly bitter wind. "You don't know who your father was?"

"My mother wouldn't tell me." He'd wondered, though. For years he'd wondered. "Most of the townspeople thought it was old man Holbrook." He shook his head and started moving again. "Let's get going. It's going to get bad, I'm afraid." And he couldn't move quickly. He was slowing them down.

She stayed at his side without speaking for a few minutes. "Looks like we're going to get wet."

"Looks like." He wondered if she realized how dangerous it was for them and their belongings to get soaked. Freezing temperatures weren't likely at this elevation, but the weather didn't have to drop below freezing for them to be in danger from hypothermia. Prolonged, damp cold could do it.

A single cold drop fell on his cheek.

Twenty minutes later, rain lashed the air, sky and ground. Lightning burst like hellfire across the sky, and thunder cracked overhead. Gillie and Rafe trudged through storm and mud in the lee of one of the hills, which provided some scant protection. They might have been slightly drier had they huddled beneath one of the short, dripping oaks scattered around, but not safer. Not with the frenzied lightning.

Rafe kept his arm around her as they walked, but there was nothing sexual in the contact. They both needed the warmth.

Gillie's left foot landed in a particularly sucky spot of mud that tried to keep her tennis shoe when she lifted her foot. "Damn," she said tiredly, and stopped. She shivered. "Did I mention that I really hate to be cold?"

Rafe paused with her. "Yes."

She glanced at his stony expression through the curtain of rain as they started moving again, one slow step at a time. He limped badly now. "It's not your fault we got caught by the storm, Rafe."

He said nothing.

"It's not your fault!" she repeated, louder so he couldn't pretend not to hear her over the storm.

"Of course not," he said without looking at her. "I'm not so egocentric I think I could have prevented the storm."

Oh, no, not at all. He wasn't blaming himself for the storm, just for not having found them a place to get out of it. Or maybe it was his knee, and their slow pace, he blamed himself for. Gillie sighed.

There was a great deal she didn't know about the man at her side, but she was beginning to understand a few things. He spoke of debts, but he meant responsibilities. How many people would have felt impelled to take action against a drug gang the way he had? They'd used his business to bring their filthy products into the country. For Rafe, that had made it his fight.

Rafael Stormwalker was a man who took his responsibilities very seriously indeed, and Gillie was pretty sure he numbered her among them. He was no doubt busy blaming himself right now for not finding shelter where none existed. He was probably trying to total up how much of a debt he owed for having allowed her to get wet.

For some reason that thought depressed her as much as the weather did. "Next time build a house," she muttered.

He glanced at her, his eyebrows pulling together. "What?"

"If you'd really tried," she said, pushing some of her wet hair out of her face so that the wind could whip it back again, "you could have thrown together a nice little cottage from sticks and such before it started raining. Yes, this is all your fault, all right."

He smiled. Not the all-out smile she'd seen only once, but the small one that softened his eyes. "What is this, reverse psychology?"

"No, it's sarcasm."

"Being cold doesn't bring out your better nature, does it?" he asked, but the softened look lingered. "I'm hoping to find shelter up ahead," he added. "Where this hill butts into the larger one."

She squinted through the downpour. Was it not quite as heavy as it had been a few minutes ago? "Around those boulders, you mean?" The hill that shielded them so inadequately from the weather was rocky, thin-soiled. It merged with another of the low hills up ahead in a crumble of rock, as if the two had crashed headlong into each other in some distant geologic age and left the debris of their collision behind.

"Yes. There may be a crawl space among the rocks, an overhang, even a small cave. We can't count on it, but—"

"Let's pretend we can," she said. "It will encourage my legs. They aren't feeling real optimistic right now."

"We don't want to discourage your legs," he said. "They're in better shape than mine."

They slogged on in silence. The band across Gillie's back where his arm rested was the only warm place on her body. She shivered and tried to remember what it felt like to be warm all over. She looked ahead, at the tumble of boulders marking the place where two hills met, and decided that the storm *must* be easing off slightly if she could see that far ahead.

Lightning blurred the boundaries of the sky. Somewhere behind them, thunder crashed.

Gillie flinched. "What about my other question?" she said suddenly, wanting to focus on something other than her misery. "I asked you three questions earlier, and you only answered one and a half. Why did this gang go to such trouble to incriminate you instead of trying to kill you? If they knew you were gathering information about them—"

"As far as I can tell, they didn't know."

"Then why frame you?"

"It's complicated."

"So? In case you haven't noticed, I'm not doing anything

important right now. Except taking a bath with my clothes on. C'mon—it'll distract you from the way your knee is hurting.''

He shook his head. ''Knowing too much could get you hurt.''

''Not knowing anything almost got me killed when someone sabotaged my plane.''

''Yes,'' he said, ''it did.''

It may have sounded like he was agreeing, but, since he didn't say anything else, Gillie suspected she hadn't won that argument. She glanced at him.

The closed expression on his face made her sigh. Now he was blaming himself for something else he couldn't have done anything about. ''Or doesn't the crash count?'' she said, hardly aware she was thinking aloud. ''I mean, you hadn't made me your responsibility yet when the marshal brought you aboard the plane.'' Maybe the sums and balances he kept in his head didn't include things that happened when he wasn't free to act.

''What on earth are you talking about?''

Gillie shook her head, irritated. She didn't know why it seemed so important to understand the boundaries of what Rafe considered his debt to her. ''Never mind.''

As they drew near the boulders that were Rafe's goal, the size of some of those jagged rocks became more obvious. It looked as if the earth's bones were showing, broken spurs thrusting through the thin soil where two hills had once collided. If Gillie hadn't been so cold and weary she might have been fascinated by the effect.

As it was, all she really wanted was to sit down someplace warm. If she was very lucky, she might get half that wish granted.

They stopped in front of a shadowed hole as high as Rafe's waist. Gillie couldn't see how far back it went, but it didn't look promising. Rafe knelt, the motion made awkward by his bad knee. ''Stand back in case I stir something up.'' He pulled the revolver from his shoulder holster and brought his stick around with his left hand.

She saw that he intended to probe the opening. She backed

up, looking around. That hole didn't look like a good place to sit out the rain to her. Given the direction of the wind, it should be a bit drier on the other side of the collision of hills.

Gillie started around the rocks.

Rafe's probe met the back of the hole all too quickly. He ran his stick around the interior, confirming that the dimensions were too small for the two of them. He stood and looked around.

Dammit, where was she? Let him turn his back for one second and—

"Rafe?" Her voice was thin, high, all but drowned out by the sounds of the storm. And frightened.

He didn't think. He ran, awkward with haste and injury, around the rocks. And stopped dead.

Gillie stood a few feet in front of him, sodden and motionless, facing a shallow cavity in the hills about ten feet high and deep enough for its sandy bottom to be dry. Deep enough to shelter both of them, given the direction of the wind. It was just the sort of place he'd hoped to find.

Except that it was occupied. By a bear.

The beast stood on its hind legs about ten feet from Gillie— a little over one running stride for a black bear that size. Next to it lay the bloody, half-eaten carcass of some small animal. The bear was big and it was angry, and whether the weather or their presence had put it in a bad mood didn't much matter. Not when half a ton of "bad mood" faced off a hundred pounds or so of woman. Not when a single swipe of one of those paws could gut her.

"Hey!" he called. The big head swung toward him. When the lips pulled back in a snarl, he saw long, yellow teeth.

"Step back," he said softly to Gillie. He dropped his walking stick so he could bring both arms up, military-style, to aim the .45. "Slowly. Move sideways, away from me." And pray that the irritated bear was more interested in staying out of the rain than in coming after them, because Rafe wasn't sure how fast even a slug to the brain would stop a creature that size.

Rafe's heart pounded as Gillie took one step back. "Not toward me," he told her. "Dammit," he muttered as she took another backward step straight for him. He'd planned to keep the bear's attention on him while Gillie got away, but she was rapidly sabotaging that idea.

The bear dropped down on all fours. Rafe's breath stopped in his chest, but the animal didn't charge.

Maybe, just maybe, they were going to get away.

Gillie took another step back, drawing abreast of him. He spared a quick glance for her. Her face was moon pale, and her lips were moving. "Nice bear," she whispered. "Nice bear. *Please* be a nice bear."

"Keep moving just like you are," he said softly. "The nice bear seems to be willing to let us go on our way."

"You coming?" she whispered as she took another step. The bear half reared again, then dropped back to all fours.

Rafe didn't answer. He wanted Gillie to be out of the bear's sight on the other side of the rocks before he moved, so he waited, gun leveled, and tried not to think about bear maulings he'd heard of. Black bears weren't usually aggressive, but they didn't have to be more than irritated to do tremendous damage. And this one was edgy.

"Rafe?" came a slightly louder whisper from behind him.

"Go on."

"Not without you."

Oh, Lord, the woman was going to drive him crazy. "I have the gun. You don't. Get out of here, and I'll follow."

"Not without you."

He wanted to curse. He didn't dare. Slowly he took a step backward. Another. "You'd better be moving," he muttered, "or I'll bump right into you."

But it wasn't Gillie that tripped him. His left foot landed on something that rolled under it, throwing him off balance, wrenching his knee. His leg crumpled beneath him.

He fell, landing badly, his fingers clamped hard on the grip of the .45.

The bear roared its displeasure at the sudden movement.

He pushed himself up with his left arm. Gillie—blast the woman!—appeared at that side and tugged on him as if she thought she could pick him up and carry him off. "Get up, get up," she panted. "Lean on me."

The bear charged.

Rafe aimed. He'd only get one good shot before it was on them.

From overhead came a high, eerie screech—half banshee, half scalded cat. A rock the size of a man's fist sailed down from the sky and hit the bear on the side of the head. The animal stopped, startled, and shook its head.

Another rock, even larger, followed the first. This one hit the bear in the shoulder. It jerked, growled—and, confused by blows that came at it out of nowhere, it turned away. When a third rock hit it in the hindquarters, it broke into a lumbering trot, heading for the stream.

In less than a minute it was gone.

The mud beneath Rafe was cold. The rain pouring down on him was cold, too. His knee, on the other hand, burned like blazes.

But he was alive. The woman beside him, both her hands still wrapped around his arm as if she planned to drag him off all by herself, was alive. She was chattering a mile a minute about something above them.

Slowly Rafe lowered the hand that held the gun, keeping his finger on the trigger just in case. He looked up.

Twenty feet above them, on a rocky shelf at the top of the jumble of boulders, stood a man. No, a boy. A twelve- or thirteen-year-old boy. He was naked except for a triangular waist cloth, and he was grinning broadly.

As Rafe stared up at him, he let out another of those ungodly shrieks. Then he called out something in a language Rafe hadn't spoken in twenty-five years.

Not since his mother died.

Chapter 8

The rain stopped before they reached Canuto's home. Which wasn't too surprising, Rafe thought sourly, considering how slowly he was moving. His knee was not in good shape.

At least the sun was shining now. Their clothes were starting to dry, and Gillie had stopped shivering.

He glanced at her. She didn't seem to have much trouble following Canuto's Spanish, though the dialect he spoke was sprinkled with words from Rarámuri—the speech of the Tarahumara.

Rafe didn't know many of those words himself. It had been too long. He'd made himself respond to Canuto's initial greeting in his mother's native tongue, claiming the rights any Tarahumara could claim to food and shelter. Canuto had accepted his claim readily, offering to take them to his home.

"Did you see that old bear run?" Canuto asked now for the fourth or fifth time, turning to walk backward. His arm swung as he mimed throwing. "Pop! I got him right in the head. I meant to hit his nose," the boy admitted, facing front again and taking a few quick steps, "but his ear was good enough."

"You hit him a good one," she agreed. "You got him three times. He didn't want any part of that, did he?"

"He took off," Canuto said gleefully. "Of course, Tielepa is not such a bad bear. He's just old. He doesn't like the wet weather. Like my grandpa. When it's cold and wet like this, his bones ache and he gets grouchy. But I didn't want your man to shoot Tielepa, even if he did steal my fox."

"Canuto," Gillie said, "Rafe isn't my—"

"Don't bother," Rafe interrupted in English. "He knows we've traveled together. As far as he's concerned, that makes you my woman, whether we've been through a ceremony or not."

She gave him one quick, frowning glance, then went back to talking to Canuto. But she didn't correct the boy's assumption.

Rafe glanced at the woman beside him. She was wet, dirty, cheerful...and evasive. Oh, she'd chattered plenty since the boy clambered down from his perch on the rocks, but her chatter had been directed at Canuto, whose initial shyness had evaporated under the sunshine of Gillie's smile.

She hadn't been smiling at Rafe. No, she'd hardly looked at him. No doubt she was relieved to have found a buffer to protect her from him and the things he made her feel. Gillie didn't trust the wildness inside her any more than she trusted the wilderness they'd been forced to travel together.

She was hiding from him right now, hiding out in plain sight. He didn't like it. He wanted her attention directed at him, and he knew he could have it. All he had to do was touch her. One touch, along the back of her hand or her cheek, and she would turn to him.

And then, of course, he would want to touch her again. Elsewhere. He thought of where he might touch her—along the sensitive skin inside her elbow, and in the fragile place where her pulse pounded in her throat. He could make her want him. He could...

Self-knowledge hit Rafe with all the unwelcome force of a stomach cramp.

He'd told Gillie he would wait for her to come to him freely.

But that was a lie. He had no real intention of leaving her alone. Left to herself, she might decide she wanted her fairy-tale dreams of love more than she wanted him. He had to make sure she chose him.

The realization shook Rafe. He didn't understand. He didn't recognize the need that rose in him, didn't like it, didn't want it.

He glanced at Gillie.

But he wanted *her*.

Her face was bright with mischief as she teased Canuto about his concern for the bear. "I think you were more worried about your old friend than about us."

Canuto grinned at her over his shoulder. "I've known the bear a lot longer than I've known you." That shoulder was covered now in a shirt of faded yellow and green that he'd put back on after the rain stopped.

He'd told them how he happened to come to their rescue—or the bear's.... After a morning spent hunting, he'd been on his way home with his kill, a fox, when he came across Tielepa near the rocks. The bear had wanted the fox, and Canuto hadn't argued. "Even with an old bear, you don't argue." Canuto had climbed up to his niche to avoid trouble and wait out the storm.

He'd been amazed when he'd heard Gillie's voice. He hadn't been able to see the bear from above, not until it came out from its dry niche, but he'd figured out what was happening and had gotten some rocks ready to throw.

"You're funny," he told Gillie now. "I didn't know American women were so funny."

She grinned. "Oh, I think women are a lot the same all over. Or am I wrong? Maybe the women you know don't like jokes?"

"My mama did. She was always smiling. And *Tia* Cuca— she and *Tio* Manuelo came to live with us after Mama died— she loves to laugh very loudly. Crucita and Elena are always giggling, but they're just little. And my sister Maria likes jokes, too, but she plays them on me! Some of her jokes aren't very funny. But she is getting married in the spring, so she will have to play her jokes on her husband after that.''

As the boy talked he hopped from one foot to the other, took a few steps, waited and fidgeted some more. It was obvious he found their slow pace a trial.

He'd told them where he lived. Now that Rafe knew what to look for, he could find Canuto's home easily, so he told the impatient boy to run on ahead and let his family know they were coming.

Canuto grinned and took off running. He sprang from rock to rock, grassy stretch to gravel, heading in the general direction of the stream.

"He sure is fast," Gillie said brightly after a moment.

"The word *Tarahumara* comes from *Rarámuri,* which means *foot runners*. They love to run. In a sport called *rarjiparo,* teams of male runners kick a wooden ball in races that cover anywhere from ten to a hundred miles of mountains."

"You're kidding me, right? No one could *run* for miles through these mountains."

"The Tarahumara carried the mail through the western Sierra Madres before the railroad came. A runner took six days to cover three hundred miles." Rafe remembered his mother telling him these things, telling him where she had come from so he would know where he came from, too. She'd wanted him to be proud of his heritage. Especially after he started school and started getting into fights.

"We can't expect too much," he warned Gillie now. "They are a private people. Most Tarahumara don't consider themselves Mexicans, and resent having outsiders intrude on their affairs. Canuto's family probably has more contact with the outside world than some, since they live on the edge of Tarahumara territory, but they may not be happy to see us."

"Canuto seems friendly," she protested.

"He's only twelve." Twelve and male, and therefore susceptible to the unrestrained warmth of Gillie's smile.

"I see."

Silence fell between them. It wasn't a comfortable silence. Rafe was conscious of everything about her, from the barely heard sound of her breath, to the movement of her body as she walked beside him, to the tension around her eyes and mouth.

That tension, he was sure, came from the fact that she was equally conscious of him.

"You probably should see a doctor for that knee," she said after a few minutes. "I'll bet you need X rays."

"You do realize we aren't going to a town, don't you? Not even a village. Canuto's family lives out here alone. They'll be able to give us directions on how to get to the nearest village, but that's all."

"Still," she said, "we're practically back in civilization now. You'll be able to do…whatever it is you need to do." She gave him one quick, worried look. "What will you do, Rafe?"

Rafe caught himself wondering if her tension might come from worry for him. The thought was as unsettling as it was unrealistic. "I won't make the mistake of turning myself in again, so I suppose I'll need to find a way into the country illegally."

"Again? You mean—they didn't just catch you before? You turned yourself in?"

"I called the American Embassy in Chihuahua to set things up. The Federal Marshal's office agreed to send someone to the place I'd picked out." He frowned, feeling the weight of guilt and debt. "That mistake of mine set a great deal in motion."

"Well—but—you still want to go back, then? You're going to let them put you in jail for something you didn't do?"

She *was* concerned. About him. She believed he was innocent. He felt her concern like a string tugging at a place deep inside him. "I can't live on the run."

"I don't think you'd like living in prison, either."

"No." He glanced at her. She was gnawing on her lip. Worrying. Rafe had to reassure her. "The DEA agent I was working with won't let the situation go that far. I only ran in the first place because I needed evidence and because, once the sheriff got his hands on me, I wouldn't—" He broke off suddenly, appalled by what she'd tricked him into saying—and by what he'd almost said.

"You wouldn't *what?* What is it?"

"How did you do that?" he demanded angrily. "How the hell did you do that?"

"Do what? And why didn't you tell me you were working with the DEA?"

He couldn't believe he'd told her now. "I'm not going to tell you anything more, Gillie. No more questions."

"You're angry," she said wonderingly. "I've never seen you get really mad before, Rafe. You keep everything so close."

Oh, yes, he was angry. He was also in danger of losing patience, losing control, and that made him even more angry.

He couldn't afford it—not the anger, not her blasted concern, none of it. He looked straight ahead and focused on what was real so he wouldn't get tangled up by foolish dreams. Reality was the mud beneath his feet, the pain in his knee, the pure smell of mountain air scrubbed clean by storm…and the ache in his groin that wouldn't go away.

Not until he'd had the woman now walking beside him, at least. Then, he would be the one to go away.

Canuto lived with his father and grandfather, his aunt Cuca and uncle Manuelo, one nephew, three sisters and a brother in a one-room house built of adobe bricks on a stone foundation. The two small windows high on the south side had wooden shutters. It was a sturdy, modest house flanked by two outbuildings—a storage shed and a chicken house—and set in a fantastic landscape of rock, piñon pine and yucca.

Gillie was used to finding common ground with people from other cultures. She liked Canuto's family right away, and they weren't as standoffish as Rafe had warned her to expect.

Maybe he'd really been warning himself. Maybe he'd been worried about how his mother's people would receive him.

When she and Rafe arrived, the family was about to take their noon meal. They insisted that she and Rafe sit and eat. Their "dining room" was a group of rocks set in a rough circle in a sheltered area between the house and a house-size boulder that flanked it.

Gillie sat next to Rafe and tried to tap into the relief she knew she must be feeling. After days of anxiety, days when she was totally out of her element, days and nights spent alone with the man beside her, she was safe. She *must* be feeling tremendous relief.

Yet she seemed to be feeling edgy, instead. Apprehensive. Since she thought she knew why—was very much afraid she knew why—she did her best to ignore the feeling and focus on the conversation. It did take some concentration.

She darted Rafe a look out of the corner of her eyes. He wore his most closed-off expression.

Her lips tightened. She wanted to shake him. He was unfailingly polite when someone spoke to him, and answered with his usual one or two words. When they first got here, those terse answers of his had excited their hosts for some reason, and for a few minutes they'd spoken to each other and to him in their own language. But Rafe had switched to his rather limited border Spanish to thank them for offering shelter.

Apparently they'd established that Rafe and Gillie would be staying the night. Rafe took little part in the conversation after that, so it was no wonder that everyone gradually shifted their attention to Gillie.

Darn him, was this any way for him to get to know his mother's people?

Gillie talked in between bites, and laughed, and asked her own questions. After watching the others, she was able to eat as they did, using a rolled-up corn tortilla to scoop the thick stew of beans, corn, onions and peppers into her mouth, eating her "spoon" along with her stew. It was delicious.

Canuto's aunt, Cuca, had sent one of the little girls into the house to get Gillie a thick shawl to wrap around herself for warmth. Gillie was sure, from the bright, unfaded turquoise of the tightly-woven material, that this was Cuca's best shawl, so she ate very, very carefully. The combination of warmth on the outside and hot food inside did wonders.

During the meal Gillie exchanged questions with people as curious about her as she was about them. They all seemed to think it was a great joke when she said she was a pilot.

After they ate the beans and tortillas, Rafe got out the M&M's and passed them around, which pleased the adults as much as the children. Gillie felt guilty for the small handful she'd had yesterday, and wouldn't eat any.

Then Rafe stood, thanked them for the meal and asked where he might hunt to help fill the pot for supper.

The edginess plaguing her suddenly swelled, sending Gillie to her feet, too. She put her hands on her hips as she faced him. "You've got to be kidding," she said in English.

He looked at her. "People who live on a subsistence level don't joke about food. I'm not taking theirs without trying to contribute something."

"I've got some money—"

"No. That would be an insult. They have given us *korima.*"

The word he used wasn't one she'd heard. "That means hospitality, I guess?"

"Something like that."

"But your knee, Rafe! You need to stay off it. I'm not going to carry you piggyback into town."

One corner of his mouth turned up. "It would be interesting to see you try, but you're right. I'll have to rest my knee before we can walk to the nearest village. But not this afternoon. This afternoon I hunt."

Gillie watched, aggravated, while he spoke to the men about where and what to hunt. Aware that she'd been rude, she turned to Cuca and said in Spanish, "Please excuse me for speaking English, but he has no sense. He makes me so angry!"

Cuca was a short, rounded woman with eyes as merry and mischievous as her nephew's. Like the other females of the household, she wore bright colors in a mixture of prints in her long skirt, long-sleeved blouse, and the cotton kerchief that covered her braided hair. When she laughed, she laughed just like Canuto had said she did—loudly, as if she really liked laughing. "Of course he makes you angry. He is a man, isn't he?"

Gillie had been right about Rafe needing to stay off his knee. By the time he returned from his hunting trip with a wild turkey, he could barely walk. Cuca told him he must rest his knee for at least two days before leaving for Pocodá, the nearest village, and the men of the household accepted her judgment. Rafe looked frustrated, but he didn't argue, not even when Cuca mixed a nasty-smelling poultice to put on it.

Being right didn't please Gillie. Not when it meant taking food from people who had so little to spare.

Not when it meant sleeping with Rafe.

Oh, she was safe, for there was no privacy. That night they lay together in their blankets on the packed-earth floor of the adobe house, surrounded by the others on their sleeping mats. The children, from four-year-old Roberto to fifteen-year-old Maria, slept together in a big sprawl of blankets and bodies. The two widowers, Canuto's father and grandfather, slept near the door, while the boy's aunt and uncle shared a pallet in the far corner.

Not far from the sleeping children, Gillie lay curled into Rafe's big body spoon-fashion and knew herself for a thief and a coward.

Earlier, she'd seen the hunger and the challenge in Rafe's eyes. He'd made it clear he intended to go along with what their hosts expected and sleep with her that night, as they had done on the trail. He had made it difficult for her to insist that she wasn't really his woman.

Difficult, but not impossible.

She hadn't protested. No, she hadn't said a word, because she wanted to lie with him this way. Safely. She wanted him, but she was too much of a coward to give them both what they craved, and so she lay there in the dark and stole his scent and his warmth, drawing both into herself.

Oh, yes, she was safe. And frustrated. And frightened. So very frightened.

Her name was a breath of warmth stirring her hair, a whisper so soft she knew only she heard him. ''Gillie.''

''Mmm,'' she said, trying to sound like she was so near sleep that speech was impossible.

''You're not sleeping,'' he whispered. ''No more than I am. We both ache, don't we, little wren?''

''Rafe,'' she whispered, ''don't do this.''

''I said I wouldn't seduce you, but I want to touch you. It can't go any further than a touch, after all, not here and now. Will you let me touch you, Gillie?''

She didn't answer. She knew that her silence was answer enough.

His hand, which had rested chastely on her stomach, slid up underneath the two shirts, dry now, that she'd left on. His palm was warm and slightly rough against her skin as it slid up to cover her breast. Her breath hitched. For a moment he just held her, cupped in the callused warmth of his hand. Then his palm moved, creating a small, delicious friction against the tip of her breast. She bit her lip.

He took her nipple between his finger and thumb and squeezed. Desire arced, white-hot, between her breast and her groin.

He played with both of her breasts until her chest heaved with the breaths she fought to keep soundless and private, until she felt the sweat on his skin as well as on her own. It was a quiet, delicious agony, a pleasure as cruel as it was sweet. His breath was as tortured as her own when at last she gasped, ''No more, Rafe. No more.''

His hand stilled. He rested his forehead against the back of her head.

For several minutes neither of them moved. Then, slowly, he straightened her clothing and placed his hand, once more, at her waist, on top of her clothing.

Gillie lay awake staring into the darkness for a very long time, aroused and hurting and ashamed. She'd deceived Rafe. Not in words, but in what she'd let him do, what she was letting him think, and her deceit shamed her.

She wasn't going to give him what they both wanted him

to take. She couldn't. He'd already taken something from her—something she had no name for, something she hadn't known was missing until the moment he fell, and the bear charged.

The bear. She could smell it still, the rank, wet odor of the animal mixed with the smell of her own terror. She'd thought she was going to see Rafe killed right there in front of her, killed in a particularly bloody and terrible way. She'd thought she would be killed, too, and she'd been afraid for herself.

But for a second, for that first flash of a second, she'd been more afraid for him.

No, she couldn't give him any more pieces of herself, not when he already held some small, essential portion of her soul. Not when she knew that soon, very soon, he would leave and take that part of her with him…and she, for reasons that eluded and bewildered her, would let him have it.

The next day was sunny and warmer than any Gillie had seen since she landed her plane on top of a mountain. They had eggs for breakfast, courtesy of Cuca's chickens, scrambled with peppers and wrapped up in some of yesterday's tortillas.

Gillie found plenty to keep her busy. She stayed away from the house, because that's where Rafe was. In the morning she went fishing with Canuto. After a lunch of beans and tortillas, she went with Maria to find agave plants. The fifteen-year-old wove beautiful baskets from strips of the long, sharp-edged leaves, and seemed shyly pleased to demonstrate her skill for Gillie.

Of course, Maria had to return home to do her weaving, but she was willing to work on the other side of the house from Rafe.

"Your man makes me nervous," she confided to Gillie after a few minutes.

Her man. Gillie bit her lip. "Rafe isn't really so bad," she said. "He's big, and I guess he can look a little scary, when he gets that look on his face. You know the one I mean—it's the same expression your mountain wears," Gillie said, gesturing at a prominent, rocky peak to the west.

Maria giggled. "Yes, he does look like that sometimes. But I don't think he is bad! It is just that I am so silly, and he is so important."

"Important?" Gillie's brow wrinkled.

"I worry that I'll say something wrong, and then he won't buy my baskets or Grandfather's flutes."

Several questions later, Gillie knew a few things about Rafe he hadn't seen fit to tell her. She excused herself and went to find him.

He wasn't far. He sat with Canuto's grandfather beside a stunted oak that had somehow scrabbled out enough room for its roots between the rocks. The older man was carving something while Rafe patiently sharpened an ax head with a small whetstone.

Gillie stopped when she saw the two men sitting together. She was so used to thinking of Rafe as a loner that it hadn't occurred to her he might not be alone.

He looked up. For once, she could read what was in his eyes. Hunger.

Her traitorous body responded immediately. In spite of that, she walked toward him.

Canuto's grandfather, Julio, was about fifty years old, though he seemed older. He was a foot shorter than Rafe and fifty pounds lighter, as sturdy and wizened as the tree they sat beside. His hair was thick and straight and still mostly dark. Like his son and his two grandsons, he wore his hair in what Gillie thought of as a very short bob.

She wondered what the old man thought of Rafe's long, tied-back hair.

Julio greeted her politely. Rafe said nothing.

"Good afternoon," Gillie said politely. The two men looked so alike, and so very different, sitting next to each other. Rafe was younger, of course, and much bigger. He also looked more European. Oh, the tribal blood he shared with Julio was obvious in their slanted cheekbones and coppery skin, but for the first time she clearly saw his father's heritage, too—in the shape of his mouth, and in something about the way his eyes were set in his face.

Mestizo, he would be called here in Mexico—mixed blood.

She thought of what he'd said. He'd never known who his father was, but the people in Dolores had thought it was "old man Holbrook." The man his mother had worked for. What did it feel like to grow up in the house of a man who might be your father, knowing that even if he were, he would never acknowledge you?

"That is a very handsome flute you are making, *Viejo,*" she said, squatting on her heels near the two men. Several more flutes sat on the ground beside him, spread out on a cloth. "Is it perhaps for sale?"

Rafe gave her a quick, hard glance.

The old man chuckled and agreed that it had been for sale, but no more. Not when her man had just bought all of them. He asked her if, in addition to flying planes, she played the flute, too, and chuckled again.

Gillie grinned to let him know she got the joke—as if a woman would play a man's instrument like a flute!—and asked him casually where he had heard about Rafael's company.

"Oh, everyone knows," he said vaguely. Perhaps it had been at a *tesgüinada* a few seasons ago when he first heard about the man whose company paid good money for Tarahumara crafts. Perhaps it was at the Easter celebration in Pocodá last year.

"So, Rafe," she said in English as she picked up the flutes one at a time, smiling at them in admiration for the benefit of their maker, "why didn't you tell me that your import business imported Tarahumara crafts?"

"Why would I?"

That hurt. She was glad she wasn't looking at him. "You started it because of your mother, didn't you?"

He didn't answer, so she knew she was right. "Whose money were you planning on using to buy the flutes? You don't have any." She wondered if he would be able to bring himself to borrow from her in order to discharge his other debt, the one he felt he owed Canuto's family.

"Actually," he said, "I have quite a lot of money, though

it may take a while for me to get payment to Julio. There is a great deal you don't know about me, Gillie."

And that was how he liked it, wasn't it? She held the flute up to her mouth and blew a few high, clear notes. The old man laughed. "I'll pay Julio for his flutes and you can pay me back."

She could sense his struggle, even if she couldn't see it on his face. "All right," he said after a moment. "It is better for them to have the money right away."

Gillie set the flute down and said a few words to Julio. She told him how good his work was and how fortunate Rafe was to be able to buy such excellent flutes.

Then she stood and turned to Rafe. "I know why you didn't tell me about your business," she said in English, lifting her chin in an effort to keep her courage up. "You don't want me to know you. You want me to let you make love to me without knowing who you really are. You're afraid I might get a piece of you to keep, too."

He met her gaze steadily. "What we will have when you come to me will be very hot and very sweet," he said softly, "but don't call it making love, Gillie. Love won't be part of it."

"I'm not," she said, feeling panic stir. "It isn't—I don't like the cruder words, that's all." Love? No, surely not. Surely she couldn't think she was falling in love with this man. She *couldn't.* "You're wrong," she told him, almost blind now with panic. Quickly, she turned and walked off.

Rafe didn't ask that night.

Gillie lay in his arms in the illusory privacy granted by darkness. Just as she had the night before, she pretended to sleep. When they'd lain there quietly for some time and the sounds the others made in the darkness had all died away, Rafe's hand slid up beneath her shirts.

Her heartbeat went crazy. "Rafe?" she whispered.

He flicked his thumb lightly over her nipple.

She bit back a moan. "This is not a good idea," she whispered.

"Probably not," he whispered back, and took her nipple between his thumb and forefinger. "I'm going to be awake for a long, long time again."

"Rafe…"

He squeezed lightly.

"You hate the very idea of love, don't you?"

His hand froze. After a long moment he answered, his whisper so quiet she felt it against the back of her head as much as she heard it. "*Hate* is too hard a word for it."

"What, then?"

"Love…makes promises."

She swallowed. "I believe in promises, Rafe."

After a moment his hand moved again. Out from under her shirts. He smoothed the cloth he'd disturbed and rested his hand back at her waist. And said nothing.

It was a very long time before she slept.

The swelling was down in Rafe's knee the next day. He would have left that morning, but Cuca made it clear she would be insulted if he did.

He didn't really mind waiting another day. Part of him would have liked to linger there a week or more. The pace and the people fed something in him.

And then there was Gillie.

She avoided him that morning. He wasn't surprised, though he'd hoped—but hopes were no more than a silly variation on dreams, so he paid no attention to his disappointment when she announced that she would go with the younger girls. They were going to gather some goats that had gotten out of one of the enclosed fields.

He spent the morning with old Julio. The two of them pulled and straightened nails from some scrap lumber Julio had found a couple of years ago. The old man gave him advice about women.

Since Julio's advice included such gems as "never tell a woman you do not like her teeth," and "do not whistle when you are inside a woman—it shows a lack of respect," Rafe rather enjoyed listening. At least, he did until Julio's generalized advice got personal.

"You should marry her," the old man said, hooking the nail head with a bit of wire from a clothes hanger.

"What?" Startled, Rafe missed with his hammer and chipped a bit of rock instead of tapping the bent nail.

"You should marry her," Julio repeated. "You think I do not know how things are *outside*—" he used a word that meant, roughly, everywhere-that-isn't-here "—but I do know. Gillie is not your wife, not in the way of the Church, is she?"

Rafe hesitated. "No," he said tersely, and repositioned the nail.

Julio nodded, shifted his grip, and pulled, grunting with effort. The nail came up a fraction of an inch. "She is a good woman. A little odd, perhaps, but a hard worker, with a good heart. Her eyes follow you," he added, tugging and grunting again. "Like water runs downhill, her eyes follow you."

Pain was a snake, a stealthy constrictor waiting to squeeze Rafe unexpectedly—as it did then. As it had last night, when Gillie asked if he hated the idea of love. "I will think about what you have said, *Viejo*," he said with as much courtesy as he could muster.

Julio sighed. "That means you have no intention of being wise and doing as I tell you. Here, hold this board for me so I can get a better grip."

They worked together in silence after that, until Cuca told them to come eat lunch. Gillie wasn't there. She and the two youngest girls had taken food with them.

They returned early in the afternoon. Rafe was whittling a new handle for a metal spade head he'd found in the storage shed. He watched as Gillie stopped to speak to Cuca, then went inside the house. When several minutes passed and she didn't come out, Rafe's curiosity began to bother him. There wasn't much in the little house to hold her interest. The family used it mostly for sleeping and storage.

Gillie wouldn't be sleeping at this time of day—unless she were ill.

Rafe set down the handle, pocketed his knife and limped toward the house.

Chapter 9

Rafe paused in the doorway.

It was like looking into an old, sepia-toned photograph. The house was a study in shades of brown, from the earthen floor to the adobe walls to the woven baskets lining those walls.

So was the woman. Gillie sat in the flat square of sunlight from one of the two windows, looking at the framed picture she held. The hand holding that photo was smooth, tanned, as lovely a combination of form and function as those baskets. Her hair was as cool a brown as the shady parts of the house, and her old yellow sweatshirt draped her body like a patch of faded sunshine.

Several small objects shared the square of light with her: a wooden ball, an embroidered pouch, a hairbrush, a small, ugly doll with lavender hair and a carved wooden box the size of a shoe box.

He remembered her concern about that box. He'd glanced inside it when he was organizing their packs before leaving the crash site. The collection of odds and ends had seemed pretty trivial to him, not worth the space the box would take in her pack, but he'd made room for it anyway, because it had seemed important to her.

Rafe didn't make any sound, nor did his shadow fall inside the house. Yet suddenly she looked up.

There were tears in her blue-sky eyes.

He crossed the space between them quickly. "What's wrong?"

"Oh, you know," she said, setting the photograph face-down beside her and wiping her eyes quickly. "Memories." She sniffed and smiled. "They can make you all happy and sad at the same time. It's hard to know what to give up," she added, picking up the wooden ball and letting it roll from one hand to the other.

He knelt beside her. "You don't have to give any memories up."

"Oh, no." She shook her head vigorously. "No, I don't mean that. I mean that it's hard to know which of my things to give up. Like this," she said, holding out the ball. "I think Cuca's little boy might like it, but I'm having trouble talking myself into parting with it."

He took the ball. It had been carved by hand from some hard, dark wood, perhaps ebony. Age and handling had mellowed the wood, giving it a silky patina. He stroked his thumb over the smooth surface. "Where did you get it?"

"Kenya. We lived there for a while when I was five. Bura and I were best friends, and when I left he gave me his ball. His father and his grandfather had played with it before him, so it's kind of special to me." She smiled. "I've always loved the feel of that ball. Playing with it probably got me started as a pitcher."

The wood was pleasant to touch, but Rafe suspected it was more than tactile pleasure Gillie wanted to hold on to. "Then you should keep it," he said, handing the ball back. "What's that?" he asked, gesturing at the ugly doll with the lavender hair. "It looks mass-produced."

She chuckled. "Mary Jane's big sister used to let us play with her troll dolls. She had quite a collection, and for some reason Mary Jane and I just loved them. When I left, she let me take my favorite…I wonder if she still has hers." She stroked her finger along the troll's cottony hair.

He asked about some of the objects still in the box—a hand-made birthday card, a small shiny stone, a silver pin, a tiny seashell. She had a story about each one. He heard, not about objects, but about people. People she'd cared about. People who had cared about her.

"But much as I love it," she was saying as she tucked the tiny seashell back into its spot in her carved box, "this wouldn't be a very special gift for Cuca."

Looking at the wistful expression on her face, he said, "All of these things mean too much to you to give away."

"But I have to find a present." She brushed a long strand of hair out of her face and picked up another of her objects, the little pouch. She ran her fingertips over the embroidery covering it. "I don't have enough things with me to give each of them a present, but I think they'll understand, don't you?"

"*You* don't understand," he said, upset by her assumptions. "We can't pay Canuto's family for what they've freely given, true, but by buying Julio's flutes I have—*we* have made sure they won't suffer for having given us hospitality."

She glanced up and smiled. "Oh, I know that. It was wonderfully done of you, too. But that isn't the same as a guesting gift." She opened the little pouch, tipped it, and gold spilled into her palm.

It was a chain, he realized, a very delicate gold chain, with a small, pinkish pearl attached. "May I see?"

She held it out.

The chain was lovely, delicate, tiny. It looked too small for a necklace, too large for a bracelet. He glanced at her, puzzled.

"Pops gave it to me when I was three," she said softly. "I outgrew the chain a few years later, but I loved the necklace too much to have the pearl put on another, larger chain. I always thought—" she broke off, embarrassed.

"What did you think, Gillie?"

"Oh," she said, and shrugged. "You know how children are. I had this idea I could give it to my own little girl sometime. Kind of like an heirloom."

Rafe listened to what Gillie said and what she didn't say, and he understood. Gillie wanted children. Most women did plan to have children someday. But he saw the silent hunger in Gillie's eyes and knew this was more than an idle "someday" for her.

She should be surrounded by children, he thought, not objects that, however precious the memories attached, couldn't love her back.

She needed to be loved.

This time the pain was so strong that, for a moment, Rafe had no defenses against it. He could only sit and absorb a blow that came from nowhere, and seemed to have no reason behind it, except...what Gillie needed from a man was something he couldn't give.

Fortunately she wasn't looking at him. After a moment he was able to ask, his voice only slightly husky, "What about the brush? What memory does that come from?"

"Nothing important," she said, and picked the small hairbrush up. The handle was a faded pink plastic, and the soft bristles were an age-yellowed ivory color.

She started to put it away. He reached out and stopped her by gripping her wrist gently. "Everything in that box is important to you. If you don't want to tell me the story behind the hairbrush, say so, but don't say it isn't important."

She shrugged and didn't look at him. "It's no big deal. My mother used to brush my hair with this when I was little, before she left. Every night at bedtime she'd come to tuck me in, and she'd brush and brush my hair...." Her voice trailed off. She ran her fingertips over the bristles.

"You've said you stayed with your mother when you were twelve. Did you not get along?"

"She didn't like me." Gillie shrugged. "That sounds kind of childish, but it's true. I think she *wanted* to like me. She tried, and I tried, but I didn't do or say or even think anything right. One night I heard..."

"What did you hear, Gillie?"

"She was talking to Miles—you know, her husband?"

Rafe nodded. He'd noticed she never referred to the man as her stepfather, but as her mother's husband.

"Well, I knew things weren't going so great with us, but I was really trying...Pops thought I should, you see. He wanted me to be close to her, and he worried about taking me with him as I—well, as I got older. Some of the places we went were a little rough. Anyway, Mother was telling Miles about how sad it made her feel to have me around. How guilty. She thought I'd been ruined—that was the word she used, *ruined*— because she'd let me stay with Pops when they split up. She didn't think there was much hope of civilizing me."

Rafe heard the pain and anger of that younger Gillie. "So what did you do?" he asked, certain that Gillie would have done *something*.

"Why, I left," she said, as if it were obvious.

He raised his eyebrows. "Just like that?"

"Oh, it took a while. First I wrote Pops, but he wanted me to stay put a little longer. See, he was in Panama, and the situation wasn't too stable just then. So I forged a letter from him. I had lots of his letters to look at, so it just took some time and practice. Then I got a friend in Mexico City to mail it to Mother, so it would have the right postmark. It asked her to send me to him. It went on about how he had this real stable job, talked about the school I'd go to, all the stuff she thought was important. A few days later I was on a plane for Mexico City."

Absurdly, panic brushed him, over events that had taken place years ago. "But your father was in Panama! Did he know you were coming?"

She shook her head. "No, I surprised him. It wasn't easy getting from Mexico to Panama, but I had friends in both places, people who knew Pops and helped out. And I had money. Mother had given me some to ease her conscience."

"Good God." He shook his head. "Was your father furious when you showed up?"

Her grin came and went. "For about ten minutes. He really yelled. Then he grabbed me and hugged me and—see, I knew that's how it would be. He loved me, yeah, but he liked me, too. He really liked having me around.''

Rafe was silent. He thought about a twelve-year-old girl who had made her way to Panama alone, during a time when the country was ''unsettled,'' because she'd wanted to be with someone who ''really liked having her around.''

Gillie was silent, too, her fingers absently brushing the bristles of the hairbrush. Finally she said, rather too cheerfully, ''You know, Cuca might like this, now that I think of it.''

''No,'' he said, and took the brush from her hand. ''Find something else.'' He settled the old brush in the box with as much care as he would have had it been truly memories he handled—the memories of a time when she'd felt wholly loved. ''Gillie, you don't have to give up any of your things.''

''Yes, I do. People always give gifts to show appreciation for hospitality. In the U.S. you might bring wine to a meal or send your hostess flowers. Food, jewelry, entertainment— those are common presents. Here—'' she shrugged. ''I don't know just what the custom is here, but I think they'll understand if I don't do it exactly right.''

He shook his head. ''You don't owe Canuto's family anything.''

She reached out, laying her hand on his. ''Rafe,'' she said gently, ''this hasn't got anything to do with debt. Just with giving. I *want* to give them something that matters. It's okay if it hurts a little.''

He was angry. He shook his head, trying to dispel the unreasonable emotion, but it clung to him. He didn't want her giving away things that it hurt her to lose. After a moment he stood and said stiffly, ''You must do what you think is best.''

Rafe went back outside and worked steadily on the handle until Gillie left on some chore with Canuto. Then he went back inside the little house, opened her backpack and took out her box. He pulled out the one object she hadn't told him a story about, the object she'd tried to conceal.

The photograph.

It was a black-and-white picture of a man, a woman and a child. The little girl looked about four. She wore a ruffled dress and sat in the woman's lap, smiling up at the man who stood slightly behind the woman and child, grinning down at them. The grin on the man's face looked just like Gillie's—wide and free.

The woman…ah, the woman who held the child was as lovely as a watercolor princess in a book of fairy tales, delicate, pale, feminine…and fragile. The bones of her shoulders and wrists were tiny. Her eyes were huge in a narrow face framed by hair as long and blond and curly as that of any fairy-tale princess.

She looked about sixteen.

Someone had tried very hard to fix the little girl's hair to match the mother's. Crimped curls straggled over her shoulders, and a big hairbow was perched unsteadily on one side. Even in the stop-motion of the photograph that bow looked about ready to finish its slide to the floor at any second.

Rafe smiled at the little girl who had grown up to be the Gillie he knew, a little girl who hadn't been much suited to ruffles and bows. He looked at the terribly young woman who held the little girl, and thought about a mother who had lovingly brushed her daughter's hair every night when she tucked her in. Until she left, and didn't come back.

His mother had tucked him in at night, too. Until she left, and didn't come back.

She'd had no choice, of course. A drunk driver had taken all Tolopia's choices away from her. Yet death was still abandonment to a seven-year-old boy.

Rafe looked at the woman in the picture and wondered if that weak and fragile lady had been as unwilling to leave her child as his own mother must have been to leave him. Maybe she'd been just as unable to stop it from happening, if for different reasons. He looked at the little girl with her straggly hair and wondered if anyone had told her how nice she looked on that day when she got her picture taken.

It seemed obvious to him that neither of her parents had had the sense to tell her how pretty she was when her hair wasn't curled, when she had dirt smudging her cheek and a baseball cap on.

What Rafe felt as he studied the photo wasn't like the sudden, constricting pain he'd felt earlier. This ache was so familiar he didn't really notice it at all.

Rafe looked at the little-girl Gillie and thought about how his wren seemed to lack all confidence in herself as a woman. He thought about a young girl who hadn't been valued for who she was. Gillie thought that because she wasn't pretty in the way her mother had been, no one would love her.

Understanding came from deep inside, from the place where the ache lived. Gillie didn't think she deserved to be loved.

Maybe, he thought, carefully putting the photo back in Gillie's treasure box, he couldn't give her the love she wanted. He'd found something else to give.

That night when Gillie went to lie down in the blankets she shared with Rafe, she didn't know what to expect. Not from either of them.

She heard the others moving around, finding their places. Rafe was still outside with the other men. Gillie had come in with Cuca and the children to give herself a little time to think.

Not that thinking had helped her so far. Not when all she could think about was last night—last night, when Rafe had pulled back. She'd accused him of hating the idea of love, and he'd stopped touching her.

Gillie felt tense and fragile as she lay down in the darkness and waited for him. She thought she couldn't stand it if he touched her breasts again, as he had the last two nights. Regardless of what he'd said, he was seducing her—oh, yes, he was, and wasn't he good at it, too?

He intended to have her, he'd said. He intended to leave her, too.

How could she want a man like that?

Only…she wasn't sure if she could stand it if he didn't touch her. Because she ached for him. For his touch, yes, but even worse, she ached for Rafe himself. For the smell of him. For his smile and his strength, and even for his stupid, stubborn insistence on seeing everything that mattered in terms of debt and payment. She craved the whole man, God help her, the difficult parts as well as the careful, caring parts he hid behind his stony exterior.

He was a man with secrets he had no intention of sharing, a man who had kissed her as if he needed her...oh, yes, he had, hadn't he? Rafe had kissed her as if she were as necessary to him as air.

How could she not want a man like that?

When the other men came in, Rafe was with them. She heard him softly bid them *buenos noches*. A moment later, she felt him lift the covers, felt the heat of him as he lay down behind her.

His arms came around her and gathered her close. His breath was soft and warm in her ear. "Gillie," he whispered, "we're leaving tomorrow."

"Yes," she managed to whisper after a moment. "I figured we would be."

"The nearest town with any public transport is San Juanito, which has a bus station. Canuto will walk with us into Pocodá and introduce us to a family who owns a truck and can take us to San Juanito. They have relatives they can stay with overnight there. We'll have to pay them for their time and gas, of course."

"Look," she said softly, "if you're worried about money, I've got five hundred dollars American and a few thousand pesos with me. I can cover everything. I know it bothers you to use my money, but you don't have much choice right now. I'll let you pay me back," she assured him.

His arms tightened around her briefly. "I want to take a hotel room when we reach San Juanito."

"Okay," she said, puzzled by his intensity. "It shouldn't cost much in a town that size, though it probably won't be much of a hotel, either." Still, there should be plumbing. Gillie was counting on having plumbing again.

"One room, Gillie."

Her throat closed. "Do you mean—"

"I mean that I want you to come to me tomorrow night. I want to be one of those memories you carry with you, Gillie. I want to be the very sweetest and best of your memories."

She swallowed. His right hand rested at her waist. She put her hand over his. "You're asking for an awful lot, Rafe," she whispered. Did he know what he was asking for? Not just her body. If that were all, it would be only too easy—not simple, but easy—to share it with him.

He was quiet for a long moment. When he answered, his whisper was so soft she barely made out the words. "I need a memory, Gillie. A memory of you I can keep."

Pain squeezed her around the heart. "Rafe—"

"I will pay you back, you know. Whether you say yes or no, I'll pay you back. For everything."

Gillie stared into the darkness, holding her eyes wide so they wouldn't tear up. "Sure," she whispered. "I know you will." She knew he meant what he said. He just didn't understand.

Some things come only as gifts, given freely or not at all. Even when there was a price involved. Even when that price was staggeringly high, the only one who could pay the price was the one who gave the gift.

Things like laughter. And memories. And love.

San Juanito was a lumber town. They passed stacks of timber on their way in, as well as several small stores, a church, two bars, a PEMEX gas station and a handful of *comedores* or tiny diners.

Everything was closed except the bars and diners when the ancient pickup owned by José Rodriguez pulled up in front of the Hotel del Barrancas at a little before nine the next night. The faint scent of wood smoke made Gillie think of other, colder lands as Rafe helped her from the back of the pickup, where the two of them had ridden with the kids.

Not that she needed help. But she liked the feel of his hands at her waist.

José and Maria called out advice as the old pickup crept sluggishly away from the curb, and the children all waved. Gillie held on to her pack with one hand and waved back with the other, postponing the moment when she would have to face Rafe.

"I'll get us checked in," he said.

She turned to look at him. The light was poor, but she didn't need much light to take in the clean, beautiful sculpture of his face and body. Rafe was as dirty as she was, his clothes as poorly matched. It didn't matter. He would turn heads, anyway. Despair was a quiet voice in the back of her mind, whispering doubts and certainties she didn't want to hear.

He was so far out of her league. She remained astonished that there was even a decision to make. Yet he did want her.

Tonight.

It was more than she'd ever expected, but it wasn't enough.

"I have money," she said, "and ID. You don't. As ragged as we look, they're apt to ask for both. It will raise fewer questions if I talk to the clerk."

Gillie expected him to protest, or at least to ask questions— one question in particular, about the number of rooms. But after a pause, Rafe nodded.

She let out the breath she'd been holding. "Why don't you walk over to the *comedore* Maria recommended and order us some supper? I'm starved."

A faint smile flickered over his face. "Why am I not surprised? But forget about walking there on your own. The streetlights don't go that far. I'll wait for you here."

Gillie considered pointing out that she'd been down a lot of dark streets in her life without him in the past, and would be again in the future. "San Juanito is a pretty quiet little town," she said instead. "I'll be back in a few minutes."

A guidebook might have tactfully called the Hotel del Barrancas "rustic." It wasn't bad, really, Gillie thought as she pushed open the screen door and stepped into a tiny lobby that smelled of pine-scented cleaner. The tiles covering the floor were faded green linoleum. There was a small shrine to the Madonna in one wall, adorned with plastic flowers. Everything was a little old, a little shabby, but clean.

No, not bad at all, Gillie concluded as she stepped up to the counter that served as a reception desk. Not much different from any number of places she and Pops had stayed in over the years.

A single, bare bulb glowed a few feet above the bald head of the sleeping desk clerk. He awoke with a jerk when Gillie tapped the bell on the counter. He was a small man with a tidy mustache and a spotlessly white shirt. Gillie approved. The fussier the desk clerks, the cleaner the hotel.

From the look on his face, however, he didn't much approve of her. Gillie knew her appearance fell somewhere between disreputable and ridiculous. She was wearing the same jeans, long-sleeved shirt and sweatshirt she'd worn, waking and sleeping, for days.

She did have Cuca's lovely turquoise shawl for warmth. Cuca had insisted that she keep it. Gillie had been very glad she'd chosen the silver pin as one of her guest gifts, as well as the troll doll she'd settled on for the two younger girls and an inexpensive barrette she'd found at the bottom of her backpack for Maria.

"We do not rent our rooms by the hour," the clerk said shortly, in Spanish.

Gillie almost laughed. If the prostitutes in little San Juanito looked and dressed like her, they must have a hard time earning a living. "I don't know why you would," she agreed in her fluent, badly accented Spanish.

The clerk straightened and lost his sullen expression, just as she'd expected. Mexicans, like people everywhere, expected foreigners to look and act a bit crazy, and so made allowances.

"Pardon me. You are interested in a room, *señora*—ah, *señorita?*" he corrected himself with a glance at her ringless hand.

"Do you have bathrooms?" she asked.

He puffed out his chest, affronted. "Of course. Very clean bathrooms, one on this floor, two on the second floor. Very excellent plumbing. Do you wish a room for yourself or…" He glanced outside. Rafe was leaning against the wall near the door, clearly visible. So were their packs. The clerk looked back at her with a smug, knowing little smile. "Will that be a double, then, *señorita?* For yourself and your, ah, companion?"

Gillie's heart pounded. Her palms were clammy. She

wanted to wipe the man's smirk off his clean and shiny face. "Yes," she said firmly, rubbing her sweaty palms on her jeans. "Yes, I'd like...two rooms, please."

The tiny diner had a single patron when Rafe and Gillie arrived. An old man sat in the corner with his newspaper, a beer and a plate of the spicy tamales that was the *comida corrida,* the meal offered that day.

Rafe watched the woman sitting across the wobbly table from him as she dug in her backpack for her wallet. Either their appearance or local custom had persuaded their waitress to ask politely for payment up front.

Rafe was betting it was their appearance. He looked like a bandit down from the hills himself, and as for Gillie...

Her clothes were none too clean. They covered a body that was slim bordering on skinny, a body that hardly seemed big enough to hold all the strength and passion he knew she was capable of. Her face was pointy at the chin, wide at the cheekbones and tanned all over...and pretty. Not beautiful, not in the usual sense, at least. Pretty, in the way of wildflowers in the spring or the first star on a summer evening.

Until a few days ago, he hadn't known he'd been hungry, starving, for *pretty.*

In the past Rafe had chosen women with more obvious attractions, lush, full-hipped women who knew what to expect from him. Gillie was far too innocent to understand or accept the kind of agreement he'd always had with the women he took to bed. It didn't matter. He wanted her with a burning determination that left most of his conscience in ashes.

Most. Not all. He was drawn tight between the opposing poles of his own, baffling needs and the certainty that Gillie deserved better.

Rafe waited to speak until the motherly waitress, who was also the cook and, probably, the owner, had moved away. "I'd like it if you would loan me some money now, Gillie, so I can pay as I go. That way I can keep track of how much I owe you."

Her eyes met his. "Is that the real reason, Rafe? Once you

have money, it'll be that much easier for you to leave, won't it?''

''I could take the money without asking after you're asleep, if that's why I wanted it.''

''You're assuming we'll be in the same room.''

He hadn't asked. Maybe part of him hoped she'd had the sense to get two rooms—and to lock the door to hers. He wasn't going to ask now. He met her gaze, silenced by his own oppositions.

She looked away. ''All right,'' she said. ''All right, have it your way.'' She opened her wallet and took several bills out. ''I don't imagine it'll make much difference to your plans, whatever they are. Here. That's two thousand pesos you owe me, Rafe.''

He took it. ''I owe you more than that,'' he said, raising up enough to slip the folded bills in his back pocket. Rafe intended to repay her for everything. From the clothes she'd ruined, to the fare José Rodriguez had charged them, to the time that she'd spent unemployed—all because of him. He would see she was paid.

It wouldn't be enough. He knew that. But if money was what he had to give, he could at least be generous with it.

At least, he could, once he had access to his money again. ''It may be a while before I can get the money to you, Gillie.'' Particularly if he were killed. Rafe had a lawyer he trusted as much as he trusted anyone. He would send the man a letter with a handwritten codicil to his will to cover that possibility, but probate took time.

She shook her head. ''It doesn't matter.''

''You do realize you can't go back to your job at Ventura.''

She rolled her eyes. ''Oh, no, really? And here I'd planned to go confront Montaldo in person.''

''Gillie—''

''I'm joking,'' she said. ''Or being sarcastic. Yes, I know I can't stroll in to work when someone there did his best to kill me. I suppose you want me to lie low awhile, give you time to get back to the States before I go to the police about the sabotage.''

She was being reasonable. Calm, unemotional. He frowned.

"I've got plenty of money saved up," she added. "Don't worry about me. I can get more, once we get to Chihuahua and I can use a cash machine."

The waitress came with their drinks and a basket of corn bread. Gillie grabbed one of the golden squares and sliced it open. "I'll admit," she said, spreading the butter lavishly, "a few days ago I would have been upset about having to tap into my savings, but the plane I wanted has probably been sold now."

"You had your eye on a plane?" Rafe's tension eased slightly, buffered by relief. There *was* something material Gillie wanted, something he could get for her. A plane. Of course.

She nodded. "A Piper I'd heard about. It was so cheap I'm sure it'll be long gone by now."

The waitress came back, carrying steaming platters whose scent made Rafe's stomach growl. He thought about getting Gillie a plane. The idea comforted him. "Where should I send the money?" he asked. "Will you stay with friends?"

She set her fork down after a single bite. "It doesn't bother you at all, does it? Talking about saying goodbye. It's just no big deal to you."

"It bothers me," he said quietly. "I would like more time with you. But even if we had that time, I would leave, Gillie. You have to accept that."

Her eyes had a blind, hurt look when she lowered them to her plate. She started eating, but he could see that she ate mechanically.

She was trying to weave fairy tales around him, he realized. A muscle jumped in his cheek as the tension inside him tightened. Suddenly he was glad their time together would be so short. In a single night, she couldn't dream too many hopelessly impossible dreams about him.

"So what are your plans?" she asked, looking at her food, not at him.

"I can't tell you that."

"I suppose you think you're protecting me, or something like that." She stirred her beans around with her fork.

"Something like that." *For God's sake,* he wanted to say, *stop making this so hard on us both.* Except it wasn't her fault that it hurt him to see her hurting. "The first Estrella Blanca bus leaves for Chihuahua at nine-thirty tomorrow morning."

"I guess that means you don't plan on dumping me until tomorrow. Oh, I shouldn't say that you're dumping me, should I? I'm not your girlfriend or anything. Just a woman you want to take to bed."

"Do you want to go into Chihuahua City together, Gillie?"

Her chin tilted up. "Yes."

"All right. I won't leave without you, then." Rafe met her eyes steadily when he gave her the only promise she would ever have from him—and the only lie.

The obnoxious desk clerk had been right. The hotel's plumbing was excellent, the water hot and abundant, and when she sank into the deep, claw-footed tub Gillie felt as close to paradise as she'd felt in days.

Except for the nights when she'd lain in Rafe's arms, balanced between heaven and hell.

She glanced at the neatly folded pile of clothes she'd brought into the bathroom with her. Before coming back to the hotel, she'd asked their waitress where she could buy some things. None of the little stores were open, but Gillie hadn't been surprised to learn that her waitress had a cousin who would be glad to open up his shop so the *norteamericanos* who had been backpacking in the mountains—as Gillie had explained—could buy what they needed.

She'd sent Rafe on to the hotel while she did her shopping, and, surprisingly enough, he'd gone. Now, though she hadn't seen him, she knew he was in his room. He was waiting to see if she would come to him.

Looking at the small pile of clothing sitting on the wooden chair near the door made Gillie's heartbeat accelerate. She took a deep breath and sank beneath the water, then came up, water streaming from her face and hair.

All at once was usually the best way to do things.

The hotel wasn't the sort to furnish amenities like shampoo

and cream rinse, but Gillie had bought a few other things when
she got her new clothes. She lathered and rinsed and was lying
in the tub, eyes closed, humming a snatch of Beethoven's Fifth
and trying not to think, when she heard someone at the door.
"Esta occupado," she called out so the person would know
to use the other bathroom on their floor. She didn't bother to
open her eyes. The door had a decent lock on it.

Then she heard the door open.

She sat up, squeaked, and sank back down—but there
weren't any bubbles, nothing to cover herself with. She
opened her mouth to scream.

And closed it. Just as Rafe closed the door behind him—
and locked it. "Hello, Gillie."

Her heart pounded. Her first impulse was to cover certain
strategic points on her body, but that was such a silly, scared-
virgin thing to do. So she lay there, wide-eyed, her hands
clenched on the sides of the tub. "H-how did you—the door
was locked," she said. "I'm sure it was."

"Blame my misspent youth," he said, leaning against the
locked door. He wore new jeans and a new wine red shirt,
telling her that he, too, had done some shopping. His hair hung
loose, and he didn't look a bit more civilized now than he had
in the mountains. "Before my last foster family managed to
get me straightened out, I learned quite a bit about opening
locks. Were you going to scream?"

She watched him, feeling scared and shivery...and hot and
achy. "Pops always said the first line of defense is a healthy
set of lungs." Her throat was dry. She swallowed. "What are
you doing here?"

He grinned. "Just stopped by to, uh, see you."

The bathroom wasn't very big. In four steps he'd covered
the distance between them. He stopped next to the tub and
looked down. She couldn't help the wave of shyness that
brought her arms up to cross in front of her. She *was* a scared
virgin, after all. "You broke into houses when you were
young?"

"A couple times." He stood there looking down at her
body, not her face. He looked at her belly and her legs...and

other places. She thought she should be embarrassed by his blunt stare, but she wasn't. She was excited.

"I was always trying to prove something in those days," he said, and knelt beside the tub. "You are so pretty," he told her as he took her hands and opened her arms again. "Let me see you, all of you. Don't hide from me."

"Rafe—"

"You have such pretty breasts. Your nipples get hard when I look at them. I like that."

She wondered if he could see the heat that swept through her at his words. "My breasts are too small."

"Kittens are small. And diamonds. And plenty of other perfect things." At last he met her eyes. "I'm sorry I couldn't let you decide," he said softly, and what she saw in those dark eyes shook her. Had she doubted his need?

He held her hands, held them wide apart as he bent and kissed her, sweetly, on the forehead. Her heart turned over. "I meant to let you make the decision," he said, and pressed his hot, dry lips to first one cheek, then the other. "I wanted to leave you free to choose. But I couldn't. You chose two rooms, Gillie," he said reproachfully.

"I didn't want—"

"It doesn't matter," he said, and his breath was warm and sweet on her skin. His tongue came out and traced the outline of her lips. "I was being selfish. It's better if I seduce you. This way the blame is all mine, so you needn't have any regrets, Gillie."

His tongue came into her mouth at the same moment his hands left hers—and closed warmly over her naked breasts. She jolted. He rubbed her breasts and licked the inside of her mouth. "This is what you want, isn't it, sweetheart?" he whispered as he nibbled at her mouth. He pinched her nipples lightly. "You want me to make you feel like this."

Gillie forgot thought, speech, everything except the sweet fire sweeping through her. Hunger expanded into need. She moaned and threw her arms around him.

He drew her wet body up against him, and she moaned again. Or maybe he did. "Rafe—"

"It will be beautiful, Gillie. As beautiful as you are. Let me touch you. Let me show you…" His hand swept down her body, down below the water along her bare hip. She shivered and clenched her fingers into his shoulders. "Please," she said.

"I do intend to please you." His mouth laid a slow trail of kisses along her jaw, down her throat. "Pretty Gillie, there is so much that I intend to do to please you."

"Rafe." Her breath caught in her throat, tangled with the wildfire in her blood. Her heart pounded so hard she thought it was blinding her, then realized her eyes were squeezed shut. She forced them open, forced herself to speak. "Rafe, I have to tell you something."

"I bought protection," he told her, his mouth now skimming deliciously, deliriously over the swell of one breast while his hand slid over her belly, going to the place that ached for him.

"So did I."

His head lifted. He looked at her in astonishment.

She smiled and stroked his cheek. "I bought a nightgown, too. It's there on the chair. I was going to come to you, Rafe."

"But you got two rooms."

Faint heat rose in her cheeks. "I chickened out, that's all. That clerk was smirking at me, and I just couldn't tell him I only wanted one room." She'd felt as if she were being called on to announce the loss of her virginity to the world. "I wanted this to be…private."

"Gillie." When his hands rose to cup her face she was amazed to feel a slight tremor in them. "It will be." He kissed her.

She kissed him back, helpless to do anything else. She stroked his hair, his jaw. She thought of touching him in other places, and shivered.

"Cold?" he asked, his voice husky. He bent to kiss her throat.

She shook her head. "Rafe, I want you to go back to your room. No, listen." She tugged at him to get him to stop nuzzling her neck and look at her. "I want to come to you. I want you to know there's no blame, not for either of us. That this is my choice.''

He looked at her for a long moment. His expression wasn't shuttered now, but she couldn't sort one feeling from another. They swam too swiftly and strongly through his eyes.

Then he nodded. He lifted her right hand and placed a kiss in her palm, and he stood. For a second he hesitated, and she could see how hard it was for him to trust even this much— that she would do as she said, and come to him.

She wanted to promise him she would always come to him when he needed her, but she knew he wouldn't accept it.

He turned and left, locking the door as he went.

Chapter 10

Rafe lay on the double bed and waited. He was nearly naked, and he was nervous.

The flickering dance of candlelight cast confused shadows on the little room's bare walls. Orange candles, white ones, a tall red taper and a squat purple candle that smelled like violets—the little room was full of candles, nearly two dozen of them.

Rafe had lit them before he went to seduce Gillie in her bath. He'd bought them while she was doing her shopping. He'd hoped to buy flowers, too, but hadn't been able to find any, not at this time of night, not in winter, not in little San Juanito.

He hoped the candles would be enough. He had to show her. He had to make her *know* how pretty she was, how sexy and charming and deserving of a great deal more than he could give.

But he could give her this night. He could do everything in his power to make her first experience of herself as a woman so rich and real she would never doubt herself again.

Rafe leaned against the thin pillows and wondered if the

mismatched candles would look tacky to her instead of romantic. What if she misunderstood?

What if she changed her mind?

He muttered a curse, swung his legs off the bed and stood. *This is ridiculous,* he thought as he paced. He hadn't been nervous about sex since he was sixteen and tried to talk Ellen Armstrong into going all the way in the back seat of his old Ford.

He paced past the small mirror above the dresser. The glimpse he caught of himself in his briefs and nothing else stopped him short. What had he been thinking of? She was a virgin. He wasn't supposed to strip before she came to him. He'd scare her to death.

Rafe grabbed his jeans from the floor. He pulled them on one hasty leg at a time, and was reaching for the zipper when the door opened.

She wore white.

She stood silhouetted in the doorway, clutching a small bundle of clothes in one hand. Her nightgown and robe were white, lace-trimmed cotton, plain, and thin enough to be translucent. Her body made a gentle shadow beneath the soft material, her lovely nakedness underneath the gown as obvious as the uncertainty that lay beneath her smile.

Gillie had chosen him.

Lust, relief and something nameless took over Rafe's mind and his being and froze him in place so that he stood, unmoving, staring into her unearthly eyes.

Gillie met Rafe's eyes, equally caught by the cusp she balanced on. Time lost its fluidity. It gripped them both with talons of pure awareness, holding them motionless and desperately still. Neither wanted to step back. Neither, for one long moment, could move forward.

At first all Gillie saw was the man in front of her. He seemed in that moment to be as beautiful as a volcano or a storm, and just as unknowable. Then, as time slipped and skidded into motion along with her heartbeat, as her blood began to pump again and time to flow, she noticed the candles.

White, yellow, purple, red...she looked around the room

and bit her lip so she wouldn't cry at the sheer hugeness of all she felt. "You got me candles," she whispered. "So many candles."

"I couldn't find flowers."

She looked at Rafe. Nothing showed on his face. He didn't move. Yet somehow she saw behind the granite exterior to the man beneath, a man who didn't believe in love or promises. Yet he'd wanted to give her the magic of candlelight.

She smiled. "Candles are better than flowers." Rafe must have given flowers to women any number of times. But she felt soul-deep certain he'd never lit two dozen candles for anyone else.

His expression eased slightly. "You like them?"

"I love them." She loved *him*. She couldn't speak those words, not now. They would surely send him away. But she could hold them to herself, hold them silent and close and dear.

He started toward her.

Gillie watched the man coming to her with the sure, graceful stride of a big cat. Hunger, uncertainty and the high, fragile note of joy her heart sang blended to make her turn nervously. She closed and locked the door and set her bundle of clothing on the dresser.

Rafe's hand cupped her shoulder.

He stroked slowly down her arm to her hand. "Gillie," he said, his voice husky, his fingers closing around hers. "You look so pretty."

She turned and looked helplessly up into his eyes. She'd almost changed her mind in the bathroom about wearing the nightgown. It was so very *bridal*. "There wasn't much to choose from. You don't think this is too—well, you know— too terribly *white?*"

He smiled a slow, wicked smile. "This will be the last time you have one particular reason for wearing white, won't it?" He lifted her hand and kissed her palm, setting flames to dancing inside her as bright and fluttery as the candle flames reflected in his eyes. "Are you nervous?"

"A little." Not as much as she had been, though. Not now that he was close, looking at her. Touching her.

"So am I."

"Oh, sure." Her smile came and went. "You *know* what to do, what to expect."

"No." He shook his head. "Not this time."

He didn't give her any more time to discuss nerves. His head came down and his mouth caught hers in a kiss as rich with promise as any beginning.

Her lips clung to his, cherishing the startling promise of his mouth. Her heartbeat skittered like a stone skipped across the still surface of a lake. Rafe clasped her hand in his and kissed her, just kissed her, not as if he were seducing her—no, he seemed to need her mouth and the reassurance of the kiss as much as she did.

Instinctively she gave what he needed. Her free hand came up to stroke his cheek. He deepened the kiss, widening his stance and bringing his other hand to the small of her back to urge her closer. Gillie forgot candles and nerves, forgot, even, that she loved and he did not. She knew only the scent and feel of the man kissing her and the first sweet, keening notes of her own hunger song. Her free hand went to his shoulder, to the nape of his neck where the skin was rough from sun and weather.

He scooped his hand along her buttocks and pulled her against him. He was hard, big, fully aroused. The feel of him was frightening. Exhilarating.

The faster her heart beat, the more restless she grew until she just had to use both of her hands to learn him. She sent her hands exploring, testing his textures from the cool, coarse fall of his hair to the hard muscles of his shoulders wrapped in the warm, living leather of his skin.

Touching him excited her. It was a new discovery, a new pleasure. Gillie hadn't realized she could be as excited by touching as she was by being touched. "I like the way you feel," she murmured to a private hollow in his neck, and she thought about tasting him right there. "I like the way touching you makes me feel." Her tongue lapped at his skin.

He groaned and stiffened. "Careful," he said. "I'm not…steady right now."

"You don't have to be. It's like flying, isn't it?" She pressed another kiss to his chest before raising her head. Her hands slid over his chest and she grinned at him with the sheer joy of freedom. "I didn't know, Rafe. You didn't tell me how glorious this is. It's like when I'm soaring and there's nothing but sky and wings holding me up."

"Gillie." He reached up and, with one hand, untied the white satin ribbon that held her robe together. As carefully as if he were unwrapping fine china he pushed the robe from her shoulders. Then he stooped, slid an arm behind her knees and one behind her shoulders and lifted. He carried her to the bed.

There, he followed her down, his mouth speaking word-lessly to her of pleasure and need—his need, and that was more seductive than anything else he could have given her.

She could easily have forgotten her own needs in the heady thrill of his, but he wouldn't let her. With his touch, with his mouth—even with words murmured against her skin as he unbuttoned her nightgown and pulled it down, exposing her breasts—he reminded her of how much she needed what he was giving her.

Rafe didn't take Gillie's virginity. She gave it up, surrendered it, one delirious piece at a time. And a little at a time she lost more than her innocence.

He suckled and she cried aloud, her hands trapped in the thick darkness of his hair as she lost her doubts about her body. They rolled, leaving her on top. When his hands raced over her, pausing here and there to savor, she lost the last, lingering fear that she might not be woman enough for him. A moment later tomorrow was lost in the flavors she discovered as she sent her mouth speeding over him. He tasted like salt and smoke, like dreams and darkness, and she couldn't get enough. When she licked one of his small, hard nipples, his muscles jumped and bunched and she almost forgot what she risked.

Almost.

All at once Rafe rolled over with her. Now he was on top,

looking down. His eyes were fierce as his hand sleeked down her side. He grabbed her nightgown and removed it. He threw it on the floor. She lay there naked and astonished by his sudden haste while he yanked his jeans down. The rough denim followed her nightgown to the floor.

Quickly, he kissed her again, and his mouth was hot, avid. His hand went to her thighs. He pushed them apart. When he touched her *there,* where no one had ever touched her, she squeaked—and, a moment later, lifted herself to him eagerly.

His tongue thrust while his fingers teased. He lifted his head. She looked in the burning darkness of his eyes and was suddenly afraid. He was all that was wild, and she was naked with him in the wilderness.

His fingers moved. One slid inside her. She gasped and grabbed his shoulders. "Rafe—it's too much. Kiss me again. I can't—not with you looking—"

"You will," he said, and his fingers drove her higher. "I want to see. I want to see everything happen to you."

Overwhelmed, she pushed against his chest.

He grabbed her two hands in one of his and held them over her head.

Helpless beneath his skilled fingers and the need she saw in his eyes, she knew herself for a fool. He was at home in this storm, but she—she could only give and give. Her body danced to his tune, a high, mad melody. She writhed and whimpered while he pushed her up, up, perilously high and far, rolling ever up on wings of thunder.

Until the lightning hit.

Her body bucked as she exploded. She went blind and deaf with pleasure as she lost everything, spinning out of control. A few seconds and a universe later, she stared up in astonishment. Rafe looked back with storm-racked eyes.

While aftershocks shimmered through her body, he moved between her legs. He'd donned protection while she lay dazed.

He supported himself on one arm. It trembled. He cupped her hips with his other hand and pushed just inside. Gillie's body, slack with the aftermath of pleasure, tightened, sending intriguing little ripples through her. He paused, then thrust once, hard.

It hurt. Tears sprang to her eyes. He bent and kissed her carefully, and he said her name. Just that, her name, but he spoke it in a voice charged with emotion and regret.

It was enough. She relaxed, and the pain subsided. As it did, the other feelings came back—restless, needy feelings. She gave a little wiggle, testing the sensation of having him inside her.

"Rafe," she said, surprised, "this feels *good!*"

He looked down at her...and smiled. A big, all-out, happy smile like she'd seen only once—a smile as clear and honest as summer sunshine. Then he laughed, and started to move.

And she forgot how to talk.

He thrust. She moved, and soon her body taught her all she needed to know about how to ride this storm with him. Earth and sky tumbled and mixed together in a chaos neither rider could control, or endure for long. Gillie climaxed a second time, convulsing and crying aloud. She took him with her, flying flat-out into the sun.

He held her close afterward, and petted her, and told her how lovely she was.

Gillie believed him. How could she not, when his eyes as well as his hands and his words spoke of her soft skin, her perfect breasts, the wonderful, creamy-smooth feel of the place he touched between her thighs? So she told him as much as she could of what she felt—with her eyes, her lips, her hands. But not out loud. Not in words he would reject.

This lovers' conversation led inevitably to a more intense dialogue, one spoken with very few words indeed. Rafe took his time with their second lovemaking, proving the power of patience by taking Gillie up the peak more than once before he allowed himself to be taken in turn.

Three of the candles had burned out and several others were guttering when Gillie lay, awake and exhausted, in the arms of her sleeping lover.

He held her so close, so tenderly. *Surely,* she thought fuzzily as sleep dragged at her, *surely he's changed his mind.* He couldn't leave her now, could he? Not when he wanted her, needed her—oh, yes, she did believe everything he had told her without words that night.

Need wasn't love, but at the moment she could believe she loved enough for both of them. At least for now.

He needs time, she thought, snuggling her head into the crook of his arm and letting her eyes drift closed. She promised herself she could be as patient in teaching him to love as he had been in teaching her to lose herself in the wilderness of passion.

He would see. Sooner or later he would see that love was real, as solid and dependable as any other of nature's laws. He would understand that promises weren't lies, and dreams were as necessary to the soul as food and water were to the body.

All she needed was a little time.

When the knock on the door woke Gillie in the morning, Rafe was gone.

Chapter 11

The bus smelled of people, chickens and tobacco. The chickens belonged to a heavyset man three seats behind Rafe who had a small crate of the noisy birds. The tobacco smoke came from several people who ignored the hand-lettered sign by the driver's seat that read *Por Favor No Fumar.*

Rafe had a seat to himself. The bus wasn't full yet, and the driver was nowhere in sight. They were going to be late pulling away from the wooden platform that served as pick-up point for the small, rural buses known as *polleros.* That nickname came from the way the buses packed their customers in like the crated chickens currently sharing one of the bench seats with their owner.

At least the bus had arrived on time—7:00 a.m., not the 9:30 Rafe had carefully mentioned to Gillie.

He hadn't lied. Not about that, at least. The first bus from one of the regular bus companies did leave San Juanito at 9:30. But the *polleros* ran intermittently all day long, more or less one every two hours—and they didn't stop at the regular bus station. Rafe intended to take this one as far as the next town serviced by one of the regular bus lines, where he would switch to one of the modern buses for the rest of the trip to Chihuahua.

There was no way for Gillie to know where he was, even if she were to wake up. The note he'd propped up on the dresser would tell her he'd gone to get breakfast. She had no reason to doubt him. He'd told her they would go to Chihuahua together.

Rafe thought of her waiting for him to come back. Believing he would come back.

His fists clenched hard on his thighs.

She'd been sleeping soundly when he'd left. He'd paused in the doorway of their room to look back. Even though he'd known looking back was a mistake, he'd had to see her one last time.

Her hair had been spread across the pillow, her face soft with sleep. Strangely enough, in spite of the night they'd just spent, it had been her innocence that had gripped him so fiercely he'd nearly gone back inside.

But he hadn't. He'd walked out and closed that door behind him. He'd done what he had to do, just like he always did. He was going into a situation where the dangers were largely unknown, but very real. He couldn't take Gillie into such a risky future, and, egotistical as it seemed, he'd been afraid she wouldn't let him leave her behind, not without some sort of trickery.

So he'd lied and he'd left. Someday, maybe, he'd be able to take his memories of her out and look at them the way she looked at the treasures in her box. Someday.

Movement at the front of the bus caught Rafe's attention. A man in a uniform shirt and billed cap swung aboard. The driver, at last. They were leaving. Good. That was good.

Oh, God. He hadn't known it would be this bad. He closed his eyes and thought about Gillie's plane, the one he would buy for her. That helped. A little.

He opened his eyes. He saw who was working her way down the aisle to him. "Hell!"

"Not the best way to greet your lover the morning after." Gillie arrived, breathless, beside him. Her backpack was slung over her right shoulder. Her left hand clutched a paper bag. "Are you going to scoot over and let me sit with you? If you don't," she said, widening her legs for stability as the bus started up, "I'll stand here while I have my say, but I won't go away. That's something you may as well know, Rafe. I'm not going away."

Shock held him silent—shock and a terrible inner jolt that felt too much like relief.

Relief? When she'd made everything so much harder on both of them? "For God's sake, woman, don't you have any pride?"

The bus lurched into motion. She wobbled. He automatically reached out to steady her. Closing his hand around her arm was like closing a circuit. Desire arced between them, so vivid he could almost believe it visible.

"Rafe—"

"Sit down," he said, furious. He moved over and half dragged her into the seat beside him.

For long moments, neither of them spoke. The bus heaved itself around a turn while Rafe grappled for control. Patience wasn't possible, but control *had* to be. "How in the hell," he said, "did you find me? Didn't you read my note?"

"That piece of paper on the dresser? I thought that was probably from you, but I haven't had a chance to read it, Rafe. I barely got here in time as it was." Shifting, she jammed one hand in her pocket and pulled out a much-folded paper. She glanced down at it. "Is anything in it true?"

He hesitated. "No."

"Not much point in reading it then." She opened her hand and let the paper fall to the floor.

"How did you find me?"

She shrugged. It occurred to him that she had yet to look directly at him. "Did you think I lived in Mexico all this time without knowing about the *polleros*? Before I went upstairs last night, I bribed the desk clerk to come wake me if he saw you leave the hotel without me."

"You knew—" He stopped, confounded. She'd known,

even when she came to him, that he'd lied? That he planned to leave her? "You knew what I planned to do?"

"No," she said softly. "Not really, not for certain. I hoped...but I wanted to cover my bets."

Why had she done this to herself—to both of them? Now they would have to go through this all over again. Rafe was bitterly certain that leaving Gillie was not going to get easier with practice. "Doesn't it strike you as a little pathetic to chase after a man who lied to you, seduced you, and then walked out on you?"

"Oh, shut up." She sounded more irritated than heartbroken as she dug into the paper sack. "You didn't seduce me, and I can't understand why you're so surprised to see me. You knew very well that once we made love I was going to stick to you like a burr. That's why you tried to pull this disappear-at-dawn bit. Here." She held out a paper-wrapped burrito. "Egg and chorizo with extra peppers."

Automatically he took it. The spicy scent made his stomach growl. He shook his head, confused by her absurd generosity.

She pulled a paper cup out of the sack and handed it to him. "I hope black is okay. You seem like a black coffee kind of guy." She smiled. "I remembered how much you wanted coffee when we were in the wilderness."

"You're getting off at the first stop the bus makes."

"No," she said. "I'm not."

"I won't let you come with me. You'd be in the way at a time when I can't afford distractions. You could get me killed."

"Don't be ridiculous," she said, taking another paper-wrapped burrito out of the bag. "Over the years I've been chased by cocaine farmers, questioned by rebels and stranded in Caracas with an airplane, a dying man and the equivalent of forty bucks. And I've done okay. I stuck with Pops, and I'll stick with you. Besides, I probably know more about the seamy side of life in a Mexican city than you do."

"I'm not your father."

Her glance was quick, oblique, and told him nothing. "No, you're not."

He looked at her, mystified. "Dammit, Gillie, why have you done this?"

In profile, she looked pale and stubborn. "Can't figure that out, huh? We do have a lot to learn about each other," she said, taking out another cup. "For example, I drink my coffee with milk and just a teensy bit of sugar."

"We don't need to learn a damned thing more about each other than we already know."

"Sure we do. We'll get along better if we know a few little things—likes, dislikes, that sort of stuff." He watched as she pried the lid off her cup. Coffee-scented steam rose. "For example, I don't like broccoli or horseradish, and I hate it—I absolutely hate it—when someone walks out on me." She lifted the cup and sipped. "Man, oh man, that tastes good. I've missed having coffee in the mornings."

The tremor in the hand holding the cup was barely visible.

Rafe set his own burrito down, untasted, on his thigh, and tried to accept her pain—but it was harder than dealing with his own. "Gillie," he said. "Please. What are you doing here?"

"Eating breakfast." She lifted the cup again.

He reached out and covered her hand with his, stilling the barely visible trembling. "Don't burn yourself," he said softly.

"*Now* he tells me," she said, and sighed. "You know, I think I'd rather you didn't touch me, Rafe."

He pulled back. "I'm going to keep asking until you answer me, Gillie. What did you hope to accomplish by following me?"

"I don't know." Now, at last, she looked at him. Her eyes were bleak. Her chin was set stubbornly. "That's not the answer you were looking for, is it? You want me to have some nice, logical reason, and I don't. I just knew that if I let you leave without me I'd never see you again."

Baffled, he sat back. "What are you planning to do once we get to Chihuahua? You won't be able to stay with me five minutes longer than I want you to, not in a city that size."

"Oh, that part's easy," she said, folding back the paper on

her burrito. "You won't leave me again—not until we get to the States, at least." She bit into the burrito.

"And why won't I?"

She chewed and swallowed before answering. "You really haven't thought things through. Mexico is too dangerous for me now. Some drug gang has tried to kill me once already—well, you were the one they really wanted dead, but I'm a witness, now, aren't I? We have to assume that makes me a target. I don't know why you thought Chihuahua would be safe for me. Wishful thinking, I guess. Some of the drug cartels have a great deal of power down here, you know. Tentacles everywhere."

"Gillie, we have no reason to believe your testimony is important enough to the gang for them to make the kind of effort that would be needed to track you down. As long as you lie low until—"

She made a scornful noise. "Turn it around the other way. We have no reason to think my testimony *wouldn't* be important enough, either. No, Rafe," she said, taking another sip of her coffee. "I need to get out of the country without attracting any attention. You're planning to do just that, so I'm going with you."

"Going with me is more apt to get you killed than living quietly in Chihuahua for a couple months."

"No, it isn't, because in Chihuahua I wouldn't have you protecting me." She looked straight at him. "Because of you, my life is in danger. You owe me, and I'm collecting. Take me with you."

He felt sick to his stomach. She was right. Damn it all to hell, she was right.

"Eat your breakfast. You'll feel better," she said, taking another bite of hers.

He didn't want any damned breakfast. "Why the hell didn't you say any of this yesterday? Apparently you knew very well what I was planning."

"For one thing, I didn't *know*. I just suspected, mostly because you wouldn't tell me anything. If you'd really expected us to be together in Chihuahua City, you would have said something about your plans. If nothing else, you would have tried to mislead me 'for my own good.' And you do have a ruthless streak. I was pretty sure you were capable of do-ing…what you ended up doing.''

''But why the game playing? Why didn't you bring all this up yesterday?'' Dammit, she'd let him leave her when he didn't have to, and now the leaving was still in front of them.

She shook her head. ''Come on, Rafe, I can't believe you don't know.''

''Know what?'' he demanded.

''I didn't say anything because I wanted to be wrong.'' She bent her head as she folded the paper back again on her bur-rito. Her face was pale, calm, intent. ''You aren't blind. A little stupid, but not blind. You must have noticed that I'm in love with you.''

His heart continued to beat. He could feel it. He felt his chest move as he drew a breath, so everything was really just the same as it had always been. Yet for one bizarre second the center of his chest seemed to turn hollow, as hollow as the bones of birds, open and empty like the sky. Then it tightened again, tightened down hard, as if his heart had made a fist around her words.

He realized he was staring at her with his mouth hanging open. He shut it, because he had nothing to say. Nothing at all.

After they changed to one of the big Estrella Blanca buses, Rafe fell asleep. Not that it made much difference to the con-versation, Gillie thought. He hadn't talked to her, anyway. Not since she told him she loved him.

Lord, but she could be stupid sometimes.

There was little comparison between this bus and the one they'd just been on. These seats were deep and plush, with armrests, headphones and high, individual seat backs that could be reclined like airplane seating. Gillie had the inside seat, Rafe, the aisle. No doubt, she thought, so that he could leap up and protect her if necessary.

Well, she'd told him to do just that, hadn't she? There

wasn't much point in feeling sorry for herself now just because it made her stomach hurt to think of him feeling *obligated* to her that way.

A lot of things made her hurt right now. What was one more?

Gillie had been amazed at how smoothly her scheme had gone, smooth as silk—except for that horrid empty feeling she'd gotten every time Rafe said he didn't want her with him. Aside from that she'd had no trouble. He'd bought that nonsense about her being in danger if she stayed in Mexico with scarcely a blink. As if she'd have any trouble fading from sight for a couple months—or getting herself across the border, if that's what she needed to do.

But she'd planned well, hadn't she? She'd aimed straight for his weakness and his strength. She'd told him she needed his protection and that he owed her. And oh, that had been hard, really hard. Gillie's mother had taught her how it felt to be an obligation to someone she loved. But she couldn't let him just leave. He needed her. She was sure that if she just had time she could make him see it, too, and accept it.

Almost sure.

This time, she told herself, *I'll get promises first.* This time she wouldn't let him take her to any edges, no, not until he promised to stay, at least for a while. A year, maybe. Surely in a year's time she could teach him to trust her.

She looked out the window. Water stolen from a nearby river for irrigation made the desert fertile here, even in winter. Gillie watched as rows of winter wheat slid by. The stalks were tall and greenish-gold, unripe.

She tried to take pleasure in the signs of civilized cultivation and technology as they drew nearer Chihuahua City. But part of her missed the wilderness.

Strange how things could change.

Rafe shifted. She turned to look at him. He was wearing the wine red shirt he'd bought yesterday. He slept with his legs wide and bent, his big hands relaxed on his stomach. Light from the window fell across dull denim and the brighter blue of the seat between his thighs. Gillie wanted to touch that denim, to test with her fingertips how hot the cloth was from its sunbath—and from the warm flesh beneath. She bit her lip.

Even in sleep Rafe didn't look boyish, yet underneath that hard exterior, she thought, there beat the heart of a Boy Scout who would always and forever be helping little old ladies across streets. He really couldn't help himself.

Of course, he was apt to cuss the poor things out while he dragged them across those streets.

He stirred again. This time his eyes opened.

She looked away quickly so he wouldn't know she'd been watching him sleep. She heard the slight noises of him straightening, shifting, adjusting his seat. There was something crushingly intimate about hearing those small, close sounds made by the man who'd been her lover last night.

"How far do we have to go?" he asked.

Quite a ways, still, she thought. "I don't know," she said. "Maybe half an hour. Rafe, we have to talk, to get a couple of things straight."

"I agree."

He sounded more grim than agreeable. "First," she said firmly, staring at the back of the seat in front of her, "you have to understand that what happened between us last night won't be repeated, not unless things change."

"No?"

She shook her head. "That's not part of our deal. I didn't come after you because you—because I—"

"Because you craved my body?"

The thread of humor in his voice made her hands curl into fists. "Strangely enough, I don't find much to be amused about."

He was silent for a handful of heartbeats. "I'm sorry, Gillie."

She swallowed. It was stupid, she assured herself, to get choked up over an apology that meant so little. Rafe didn't believe in regretting necessity, and she knew he considered what he'd done necessary. "Yes, well, I need to know more than I do about the gang and everything. I need some idea of what to expect."

"The more you know—"

She made an angry gesture. "Quit pretending you're protecting me. The bad guys aren't going to give me the benefit of the doubt. They're going to shoot me on the basis of what I *might* know, not what I do know. So I might as well know everything."

He didn't answer. Gillie could only imagine the battle being waged inside him. His instincts would be urging him to say nothing, trust no one, while reason agreed that she would do better if she knew what she was up against.

At least, she hoped his reason would agree with her.

"I can't take the chance," he said at last.

"Rafe, it really isn't your chance to take. I'm an adult. I make my own decisions. You can't just pick me up, toss me out of harm's way and expect me to stay put."

If she hadn't been looking closely, she would have missed the slight flinching around his eyes. "What is it?"

He didn't answer directly. Instead he pressed the button on the end of the armrest and folded the whole thing up between their seats. "Come here," he said, reaching for her.

When he put his arm around her, she stiffened. "What do you think you're doing?"

He bent his head close to hers. "If we're going to talk about things that people are willing to kill to keep secret," he said softly, "we'd better be sure no one else hears, hadn't we? Any of the people around us might understand English, Gillie."

She flushed, embarrassed by her stupidity. The high, cushy seat backs gave the illusion of privacy, but that's all it was, an illusion. "Sorry," she said, and let him gather her up against him.

They probably looked like an affectionate couple, she thought, cuddled up together like this, his arm around her, her hand resting on his chest. She could feel his heartbeat, strong and steady.

Her own heart picked up speed.

"It started," he began softly, his head bent as if he were whispering love words, "when Steve, my foster brother, came to me for a job."

The story Rafe told her over the next half hour had all the elements of a tragedy—greed and betrayal, loyalty and courage. Steve and Rafe had shared a set of foster parents as teens. But Steve hadn't been as successful as Rafe, not in any sense of the word. From what Gillie could tell he'd been weak rather than wholly wicked, a willing dupe who'd given in to the gang's demands as much because of the money as because of their vague threats.

Eventually, either conscience or fear had driven him to tell Rafe what was going on. Rafe had been furious. He and Steve had been in the warehouse office at the time, separated by a wall of glass from the workers filling orders. Several people had seen, but not heard, the bitter argument that resulted.

That semipublic fight had undoubtedly helped the gang frame Rafe for Steve's death.

"So you let your foster brother take over running the company because you were bored, huh?" Gillie said. "Uh-uh. I don't buy it. I think you were doing him a favor."

"I've never stayed long with one thing, Gillie."

No doubt he meant that as a warning. But her head rested on his shoulder. His arm was curled around her, and his hand rested at the curve of her waist. It felt good. Really good. This being in love was so strange. Gillie felt as if her very skin needed him, needed to somehow soak him up like plants soak up the sun. Yet it felt right, not scary. It was hard to remember that the only reason he was cuddling her was to keep their conversation private. "So what did you do after Steve started running your company?" she whispered. "I can't picture you leading a life of leisure."

"I made money," he murmured back, "except for when I lost it. That's what I do, Gillie. I play the markets—stocks, commodities, whatever takes my interest. I discovered a talent for it while I was in the service."

"I didn't think the Special Forces had much to do with the stock market."

"They don't. I discovered my knack on my own, in the barracks. First I learned to enjoy the mixture of logic and luck involved in gambling. Playing the market was just a step or two away from figuring the odds in craps.''

She frowned, trying to understand, It sounded like a pretty big step or two to her. ''That's all you do? Buy and sell stock and stuff?''

''Pretty much,'' he said, amused. ''I manage to stay busy with it. Sometimes, if a particular company takes my interest, I'll invest enough in it to take a hand in its development for a while. Because I've got a short attention span, I usually resell them quickly. Sometimes I make a lot of money in the process. Sometimes I lose a lot. When I get tired of the whole game, I take off into the desert for a week or two.''

''So—are you rich or something?''

''Sometimes.''

As Rafe talked, Gillie got the picture of a man very much alone. He played with money the way other people played Monopoly, using it as a token, a marker, sometimes a tool in a game that had him on one side of the board and the rest of the world on the other.

He told her about getting in touch with a DEA agent he'd known back when they were in the army. Willis had been glad to hear from Rafe.

It seemed that drug traffic in that region had increased substantially in the past year. The DEA had formed a three-county, multiagency task force to investigate. They'd learned that an established Mexican gang and a smaller, purely American criminal group had joined forces with unprecedented effectiveness.

Shortly before Rafe contacted him, Willis had also come to believe that someone on the task force was dirty. He thought he knew who it was, but he had no proof. In exchange for Rafe's and Steve's help in setting up a sting to catch a dirty cop, he offered Steve immunity from prosecution.

Rafe had persuaded Steve to go along with it. He wouldn't give Gillie any details about the sting, but it involved him ''discovering'' Steve's gang connections and pretending he wanted in on the deal, then pressing for a bigger role in the operation.

Gillie protested, of course. No one who knew Rafe would believe he would become involved with smuggling drugs.

He gave her an odd look. "I don't think the rest of the world sees me quite the way you do," he said, and went on with his story.

The sting had never taken place. They'd still been maneuvering when Steve was killed. "Killing both of us would have raised too many questions. This way, they hoped to get rid of both of us with a minimum of investigation. I figured I would meet with some sort of accident in jail if I let myself be taken into custody," he said. "So I ran. I had a chance to get information about Steve's killer. A slim chance, but still, it was there and I had to take it. Steve died because of me. I had to try."

Startled, she sat up straight. "Rafe, you can't blame yourself for the trouble your foster brother got himself into!"

He pulled her back to him. His voice was quiet, almost meditative. "Oh, but I am to blame. Not as much as the man who pulled the trigger, maybe. But Steve wasn't killed because they found out about the sting. He was killed because he was connected to me."

"I don't understand."

"You don't have to."

Gillie was silent. She could feel the emotions stirred by his self-reproach in the hard, quick thud of his heart beneath her cheek. Rafe was hurting, and she had no idea what to do about it. "So you went to Mexico to get, what—information? Did you find what you were after?"

"I got enough. I sent a copy of what I found to Willis just before I turned myself in. I'll call him when we reach Chihuahua. I hope he'll tell me that Steve's killer has been arrested—not for Steve's death, unfortunately. I don't see any way to prove that, but he's guilty of plenty of other things. With luck, I'll learn he's in jail and my own arrest warrant has been revoked…that it's over."

The tension in his muscles told her he didn't believe it would be that simple. "Who was it, Rafe? Who set you up and killed your foster brother?"

He hesitated, then gave in. "You may as well know. Either he's under arrest or he's still loose, and if he's loose he's dangerous. The local sheriff, Fred Daingler. He's definitely part of the gang, probably in charge of the American side of the operation."

"So the information you sent was pretty solid proof, then?"

"Fishing, Gillie?" he asked dryly.

"Well," she said, "you can't blame me for being curious."

"I could, but there's not much point, given the endless quality of your curiosity. What I sent was basically a list of numbers. Call it the electronic equivalent of a paper trail, showing where large sums of money have been moved. It shows that Sheriff Daingler has had his hands on one hell of a lot more money than he can account for. And he hasn't paid taxes on it."

"So the IRS might be the ones in the white hats this time."

"Unpaid taxes sent Al Capone to prison back during the heyday of Prohibition, and this situation has a lot in common with the days of gang warfare in Chicago. When two big, ruthless criminal organizations are jockeying for power, people get hurt."

She pulled back so she could look at his face. "You said you don't think the gang found out about your connection with the DEA, but you won't say why they wanted to get rid of you. Did you and Steve somehow get caught up in a battle between rival gangs?"

He stared at her. "You scare me sometimes."

"That means I'm right." Her mind jumped from fact to fact as quickly as Canuto had leaped from rock to rock. "One gang must have found out you were working for the other one. At least, the other gang thought you were. So they—the second gang—might have thought you were moving in on their territory."

She thought some more and shook her head. "That doesn't explain why they're so eager to kill you now, though. Eager enough that they didn't mind killing me and a federal marshal along with you, which seems odd if they were trying to avoid investigation. And how did they find out you were in Mexico?

Why would they go to so much trouble to get rid of you if you've already sent the list across the border?''

"I've told you everything it might possibly help you to know. This is not a healthy subject for speculation, Gillie.''

"You tell me what really happened and I won't have to speculate.''

"No.'' He shook his head. "No, we're not going to discuss this anymore. Damned if I can figure out how—but never mind. Now we're going to talk about who's in charge once we reach Chihuahua.''

Gillie could just guess which of them he intended to nominate for that role. With a sigh, she straightened so that they weren't touching anymore. "You know, you're not in the army now. There doesn't have to be someone in charge.''

"I want your agreement to do as I say, no questions asked.''

"Now you know I'm not going to do that. Good grief, Rafe, you're a businessman. Haven't you ever heard of the term *partnership?*''

"Partnerships don't work in survival situations. We can't stop to discuss matters and reach a consensus if someone's shooting at us.''

"Give me credit for a little sense, will you? Besides, we're not in the wilderness anymore. The rules are different in cities.''

His jaw tightened. "There's one other subject we need to clear up.''

"What's that?''

He didn't give her any warning this time. He just leaned over and kissed her.

Gillie meant to pull away...she did. After the first startled second, she definitely intended to put a stop to the kiss. Rafe had hurt her too badly for her to let him in again. Not without a promise. She wanted a chance to change his mind about things like promises and dreams. As his lips moved on hers she assured herself she was going to pull back. Only somehow her hand was on his cheek. His skin was warm, smooth-shaven without being smooth-soft the way hers was. Different.

Wonderful.

She just needed to touch him. Just for a moment she needed the feel of him beneath her hand, the intimacy of mingled breaths. Just for a moment.

When hunger leaped in Rafe, Gillie knew it. She felt it in the catch in his breath, the sudden tenseness of his body. When his lips pressed hers open and his tongue probed, she didn't resist. Rafe wanted her. He needed...

No, she told herself, *no, don't believe it. This is a kiss, just a kiss....* But her heartbeat skipped a pace in order to catch up with his heart's rhythm. The taste and scent of him poured through her system. He kissed her as if her mouth and her being were equally open and essential to him, and Gillie lost her grip on her doubts and her reason. Even the memory of pain slid between her fingers like melted wax, stinging as it went, leaving a thin, hard shell of itself behind.

He lifted his head. "For however long you're with me," he said softly, "we *will* be lovers, Gillie." He traced her lower lip with one finger. It quivered.

She turned away without speaking.

Outside, telephone poles whizzed by. They'd left the green of irrigated fields behind while Gillie was snuggled up with Rafe, listening to the reasons that people wanted him dead. Now the highway sliced through a rugged landscape of yucca, dust and mesquite—desert country.

Maybe, she thought, she hadn't left the wilderness behind, after all. Maybe she'd just exchanged one kind of wilderness for another.

Chapter 12

Chihuahua was an industrious city typical of northern Mexico—dry, colorful, cool in the winter. It was full of busy, early-rising people and a rather charming self-consciousness about its own history. Their bus drove down streets with names like Av. Indepencia and Av. Niños Heroes on its way through town to the new bus station. The cavernous Terminal de Autobuses lay on the southeastern edge of the city, not far from the airport. It was a thoroughly modern building that housed all sorts of services, from a pharmacy to a telecommunications center.

The service Gillie had been most interested in when they arrived was a fairly common one, however.

They argued all the way back from the rest rooms. "Two rooms," she said again, her eyebrows drawn in a tight, angry V.

"Your money is limited, and we have no idea how long you'll need to stretch it. One room." He took her elbow in order to steer her around the crowd. The crowd made him nervous. He couldn't watch everyone.

She jerked her elbow away. "Two." The look she shot him

spoke poorly of his ancestors. "I've got the equivalent of several thousand dollars in savings, and all I need to access it is a teller machine. Good grief, we don't need anything fancy. We can each have a room with a bath, and it still shouldn't cost more than forty bucks. Forty dollars is not a problem."

"Gillie," he said, "do you really think getting two rooms will make any difference to what happens between us?" He didn't believe that, not after all she'd told him. Last night her body had explained, in explicit detail, how much she wanted him. Today...

"Yes," she said, and nodded firmly. "Two rooms will work out best, Rafe. You'll see."

Today, he'd left her. Only, Gillie refused to be left. She'd chased him down and told him she loved him.

She believed it, too.

His chest tightened. Her words had lodged there. They were imbedded inside him like a splinter, or a bullet, or the kernel of dust that an oyster builds a pearl around.

He wouldn't forget. He would never forget that Gillie had said she loved him. Never mind what he believed. She thought it was true. And yet she planned to sleep alone that night. She actually thought he might let her do that. He shook his head. "You said you wanted me to protect you. I can't do that if there's a wall between us."

She opened her mouth. Closed it. And slid him a look of such guilty suspicion he had to smile.

Poor wren. She really couldn't lie worth a damn.

"What are you smiling about?" she demanded.

Rafe knew damned well that Gillie thought she'd exaggerated her danger. She'd done it to manipulate him into keeping her with him. But it didn't matter what she thought. Once she'd gotten on that bus with him she'd sealed her fate. He had to keep her within sight now, because she was right—they didn't know how badly the gang wanted to keep her quiet, and no one else was going to take her safety as seriously as Rafe did.

Including her.

His smile faded. As the people around them shifted, he caught a glimpse of someone behind her. He stopped moving.

"Rafe? What is it?"

"There's a man behind you who seems to be following us," he said. "No, don't turn—"

Too late. She'd already turned around. "Where?"

"By the tobacco stand, heading toward the phones. He—no, never mind. He's moved out of sight."

"What did he look like?"

"Late thirties or early forties, short, dark-complected, slightly overweight." Rafe shrugged, frustrated. "That sounds like half of the men here."

She frowned. "Do you think he's one of the bad guys?"

"I don't know." He called up the man's face, trying to place it in some context, but came up blank. "Let's get out of here."

She started moving—in the direction of the tobacco stand. "Come on. Let's get another look at him. It's better than wondering."

That's what Rafe would have done if he were alone. But he wasn't. He caught up with her in two quick steps and grabbed her hand. When he stopped moving, she had to, too. "We're leaving."

"Rafe," she said patiently, "even if the man is a bad guy and not just someone you saw once when you were here on a business trip, he isn't going to shoot us in a public place."

Maybe not. But the man had been headed in the direction of the public phones. It was just conceivable that he was calling reinforcements.

It was also possible that Rafe had watched too many thrillers. But he couldn't take any chances, not when Gillie was with him. "Maybe I'm paranoid. Humor me, okay?" When she still looked stubborn, he added, "We'll find a hotel with room service and get some lunch sent to our room."

She brightened. "Good idea. But we'll get two rooms, Rafe."

They ended up at the Hotel Nuevo, which was, in contrast to its name, an older building. Gillie had stayed there a couple of times when charters she'd flown had left her in Chihuahua City overnight. The Nuevo had private bathrooms, clean linen, cheap rates and a restaurant—everything Gillie wanted in a hotel. All Rafe really wanted was a place with a phone. He got that, though all calls had to be placed through the hotel switchboard.

The one thing it lacked was a pair of vacant, adjoining rooms.

Rafe smiled when the desk clerk told him that. Since there was no way he would let Gillie stay across the courtyard from him, he told the clerk they'd take one of the single rooms. He expected to hear an immediate protest. When he didn't, he looked up, frowning.

Gillie was all the way across the lobby. She stood in front of the big double doors, talking to one of the ragged children who tried to sell tourists everything from gum to cheap souvenirs.

The desk clerk made an irritated sound and started around the counter. "They are not supposed to bother the guests. My apologies, *señor.*"

"No problem," Rafe said. He picked up Gillie's backpack, which she'd left beside him when she wandered off, and waved at the desk clerk to stay. He started across the lobby with her ragged backpack in one hand and his equally scruffy tote in the other.

He wasn't surprised that she'd drifted away, not when a child was involved. Children and Gillie seemed to have a magical connection. Put her anywhere—even in the middle of the wilderness with rain pouring down and an irritated bear nearby—and somehow a child or two would appear.

This particular child was selling newspapers. Rafe watched as she bought one and the boy moved off, grinning. She'd probably overpaid him.

She looked so pretty standing there, with the bright, white light of early afternoon falling squarely on her. Gillie's hair, Rafe thought, didn't turn copper or brassy or any other hard, metallic shade in the glare of the sun. No, it simply grew warmer. Sunlight sank into it as happily as it did into the rich brown of the earth.

"Rafe, did you see this?" she demanded as soon as he reached her.

"I haven't seen any newspapers lately." When she started to hand him the paper he added, "Tell me what it says, will you? My Spanish is limited to the spoken sort."

"Well, it's about two gangs," she said, her eyes skimming along the article at the bottom of the page. "Or at least the authorities think there are only two drug gangs involved. There have been three assassination-style killings in the last three days, Rafe, two in Mexico City and one here, and there was a shoot-out yesterday in Juárez involving several people. The cops here think they're all connected, that two of the gangs are fighting it out."

Fear slithered down his spine with all the chilly shock of an ice cube. "He told me to expect it, but he wasn't expecting it himself, not this quickly."

"Who told you? What are you talking about?"

"Come on." He gave her the backpack and grabbed her hand.

Gillie protested, but she let him drag her across the lobby, across the courtyard. Maybe she could sense his fear. Maybe, in spite of the years he'd spent perfecting the mask he presented to the world, she could even see it.

He should never have let her come with him. Though how he could have stopped her—still, somehow he should have. The acid of guilt ate lines on either side of his mouth as he fitted the key to the door of their room.

Gillie didn't comment on the fact that he'd rented a single room, but she did give the bed a frown as he hustled her inside. "What is it?" she said as soon as he closed the door. "What got you spooked? That business about the two gangs fighting? Do you think they're going to come after you, Rafe?"

"We should have stayed in the mountains." He looked around.

The room was small and square, with the bed smack-dab in

the center, covered by a violently purple spread. A scarred old dresser flanked the bed on one side, topped by a mirror fastened directly to the wall. On the other side, a cast-iron table that looked like it belonged on a patio did duty as a nightstand. The curtains had probably once matched the blue-violet of the spread before the sun faded them to a dusky shade of twilight.

"I guess you're used to staying at nicer places," she said.

"Sometimes." Rafe tossed his tote on the bed and started to pace. When he realized what he was doing, he made himself stop. He'd fought too hard for too long to control the restlessness that used to land him in trouble. He wasn't going to give in to it now.

"The war wasn't supposed to start for several months," he said abruptly. "I thought there was time, or I would never have let you come into the city. Hell, I wouldn't have come here myself."

"Rafe, what are you talking about?"

He looked at her standing near the door, her backpack on the floor next to her. Worry pulled her soft skin tight around those incredible eyes—eyes that were clouded now, upset. In that moment he would have given almost anything to be able to banish that worry.

Instead, he was probably going to scare the hell out of her, either with the truth, or with a very good lie.

It was a shock to realize, once he stopped moving, that he faced a decision. That was odd enough in itself. He could have sworn there was no decision to make, that he would never tell her about Arturo Andalaro. But the situation had changed.

What was even stranger was that part of him wanted her to know the truth. He struggled to sort out his motives, to decide what was best for her.

Gillie didn't help. She crossed the small distance between them, put her arms around his waist and laid her head on his shoulder.

He stiffened. She didn't speak. She didn't let go. The press of her body stirred desire in his, but something else stirred, too, increasing his confusion. Gillie felt small and warm against him, as vulnerable and vivid as life. She was strong and she was tender and she could die—today, tomorrow—because of him, or from a thousand other causes.

She thought she loved him.

All at once Rafe's arms went around her tightly, and he held on. Just for this little while, he would let himself hold on. "I'm talking about my uncle," he said. "He's the reason I came to Mexico. He's the reason Steve was killed."

He took a deep breath, let it out. "He's also the second in command of one of Mexico's largest drug cartels."

Gillie was stunned. Rafe's revelation slid through her like a wound, stiffening her muscles as it went. She lifted her head to search his face. "I didn't know you had any family."

"No one does." He set her from him and started to pace. "No one was supposed to know, at least. Obviously someone does. Someone unearthed the information somehow, since my foster brother was killed because of it."

"I don't understand."

"It's not complicated. My mother had a brother. She became an illegal immigrant in order to survive after their parents died. He became a criminal. He worked hard, sold poison, killed people and rose in the ranks. Eventually he reached the number two spot in his organization. Quite a success story."

She shivered at the violence in his voice. "Which one is his gang? The one the sheriff is connected to? The one that killed Steve and framed you?"

"No," he said. "No, that gang is relatively new. After it teamed up with its U.S. counterpart, it grew fast enough to challenge the power of my uncle's cartel. Now the two gangs are fighting it out. He told me it would come to this, but he thought it wouldn't happen for several months."

Gillie had never seen Rafe like this, unable to be still, words pouring out of him. In the grip of motion and emotion, he was swift, graceful and a little scary. "He's the one who gave you the information you needed, isn't he? Your uncle. He gave you the list you sent your DEA contact."

"Yes. I sure as hell didn't know any of this when I was bumbling around trying to help the good guys catch a dirty cop. I didn't learn anything useful until it was too late for Steve.''

"You didn't know about your uncle's...business?''

"Oh, I knew about him—at least, I knew he was associated with one of the gangs. My mother hated what he did, but she couldn't forget he was her brother. She wrote him. Until she died, she wrote him once or twice a year, and he always answered. I've got the letters.''

He continued to pace, his movement as rapid as his words. "But she wouldn't take money from him, and she didn't tell him about me. She didn't want him to know about me. One of the last things she said to me was that I wasn't to have anything to do with him.''

He stopped suddenly, his back to her. His hands opened and closed, then stayed fisted at his sides. "So I didn't. I almost forgot he existed. Then, about three years ago, he contacted me. A letter, that's all, just a letter—though how he learned of my existence I don't know. He's written every year since then, though I didn't respond. So I knew about him. I just didn't know how *successful* he'd become.''

She went to him. How could she do anything else? She went to him and laid her hand on his back. His muscles flinched at her touch. "Steve's death was not your fault,'' she said softly.

"No? He was killed because Daingler somehow found out who my uncle was.''

"Why didn't they just kill you, then?''

"Two deaths would have been hard to explain. Framing me for Steve's death got rid of both of us. He—the gang—must have assumed I was a plant for my uncle's organization, and that Steve was working for me. I don't know how they found out. I didn't think anyone knew, not until I saw that scrap of cloth by Steve's body. It had the gang's sign on it. Not Daingler's gang. My uncle's. Whoever shot Steve left it there so I would understand. I got the message, all right.'' He scrubbed a hand over his face. "God, I was so sure no one knew.''

She rubbed her hand up his back, longing to comfort him, not knowing how.

He pulled away and resumed his pacing.

Gillie watched, troubled. He'd reminded her of a big cat the first time she saw him, patient and predatory. Now there was no sign of patience, but he still made her think of one of the big cats—a cougar in a zoo, caged and half-crazy with it.

"Rafe, you didn't arrange your birth," she tried. "It wasn't your decision to be the nephew of a drug dealer. None of this was your fault."

"Wasn't it?" He reached the end of the room, turning and pacing back toward her. "The degree of blame I live with doesn't make much difference, though, because the results are the same. Regardless of who is to blame, Steve is still dead, and I—"

He reached her and stopped. The darkness in his eyes seemed to be burning itself up. "It's just as well I didn't believe in promises, anyway, isn't it, little wren?" he said softly, his hands lifting to scoop up her hair, then drift, slowly, down its length. "I'd be royally screwed if I had, since there is no way in heaven or hell I can make any promises now. Not when being close to me is practically a death warrant."

"You can't believe that! Right now, with this gang war going on, you're in a bad position, but once it gets settled—"

"Steve was murdered before the war started."

"It's not the same," she insisted. "He was involved with another gang."

Rafe sifted through her hair. His fingers brushed her neck lightly. Desire stabbed her, breast to belly to groin, a quick electric charge that sent her heart racing.

"As long as my uncle is alive," he said quietly, "anyone close to me is in danger. My uncle may be a killer, but he has family feelings. The bastard cares about me. He told me so." Rafe's mouth twisted bitterly. "That makes me a tool for others to use against him, which he pointed out when he tried to bring me into his organization. It also makes anyone who matters to me a potential tool. You matter," he added simply.

Her breath stopped in her throat.

His hands slipped from her hair to her shoulders...paused and traveled on down to cover her breasts. "That's why I won't stay. Make no mistake. I'm going to take you to bed again.'' His hands were warm and still on her, intimate and unmoving. ''As often as you'll let me. For as long as we're together. But that won't be long, Gillie.''

She needed to push his hands away—quickly, before the heat hazing her body overwhelmed her mind. Hadn't she decided not to do this again without promises? ''Rafe, what we have—''

''What we have, Gillie, is sex.'' He bent and nibbled at her neck with his clever mouth. ''Great sex,'' he said, squeezing her breasts, ''explosive enough to put a man on his knees, but that's all it is. Would you like to see me on my knees in front of you, Gillie? Shall we try that this time?''

She wasn't sure what he meant, exactly, but it sounded wicked and delicious and made those knees he mentioned turn mushy. But there was a problem. Rafe's hands were shaking, ever so slightly. His mouth lingered and licked at her throat as if he were desperate for the taste of her. And she'd seen the monster that hid deep inside him—the monster he feared, and couldn't outrun. She knew that monster because she'd seen its yellow eyes lurking in the shadows of her own mind.

Rafe was alone, quite desperately alone, and convinced he always would be.

He was the one who needed promises. However little he could accept them, he needed them.

She lifted her hands. ''Rafe,'' she said, threading her fingers through his silky black hair. He rubbed his thumbs across her nipples, and she shivered and cupped his face in her two hands. She went up on tiptoe to brush a soft kiss across his hard mouth. ''I'm not going to leave you, Rafe,'' she promised, ''and I'm not going to let you leave me.''

''You won't have any choice.'' His mouth was hot along her jaw, drifting up over her cheeks as he unbuttoned her shirt. ''Don't fool yourself, Gillie.''

Oh, she was probably a fool, all right, but she wasn't fooling herself. She knew Rafe intended to leave her. She also knew the blasted man needed her.

Gillie grabbed handfuls of hair on either side of his face

and directed his mouth to hers so she could kiss him long, slow and deep while he stripped her shirt from her.

When her shirt fell to the floor, he pulled his head back and smiled at what he saw. "You're wearing a bra."

"I do that sometimes." It was white and lacy, the sexiest one she'd been able to find in the waitress's cousin's shop back in San Juanito.

"I like it," he said. "Now...take it off."

Slowly Gillie reached behind her. Her mouth was dry with the taste of risk, and her bones had turned to molten glass, supple and scalding from the inside out. She felt naked already, naked and fragile and hot.

And pretty. He made her feel so pretty.

The bra came loose and fell to the floor.

Rafe reached for her. She went willingly into his arms. The scent of him made her head dizzy and her heart hurt. His mouth was sweetly, thoroughly carnal, and it stayed on hers as he swung her up in his arms and made the world spin. She shuddered and closed her hands in tight fists in his shirt.

The bed was only a few steps behind her. He took those steps and followed her down, and his mouth found other places to kiss. She fumbled with the buttons on his shirt and, in her haste to feel his skin, tore one off.

It went flying. She laughed, flooded with sudden joy. She was soaring while flat on her back, riding the perilous dip and dive of feelings that blew through her like a hot wind when she was with him. Only with him.

His mouth fastened on one of her nipples and she tunneled her fingers through his hair and said his name, so happy with him that every other word slid together in a tangled heap on the floor of her mind. When he switched to her other nipple, she managed to tug his shirt off. He cupped her between her legs as he sucked, and she groaned.

"Gillie," he said, "Gillie, I want you so much. I can't wait." He pressed up, rotating his palm firmly against her, making her body pitch with a sudden swirl of hunger.

She would have answered out loud if she could have sorted any words out of that tangle. Because speech was beyond her, she reached out to cup him the way he was holding her. He felt big, hot even through the denim, and his body bucked at her touch much as hers had done at his. She stroked him and reveled in the sense of shared power—his over her, hers over him—as her fever went into a steep climb.

His breath hissed between his teeth. He unfastened her jeans and dragged them down. She moved to help him, then the two of them got him naked, too.

Gillie wanted to play, then, to tease them both with the power and the giddy feelings, but he was already moving between her legs. His breath came quick and hard. His hands were impatient as he spread her legs wider and slid his hands under her bottom, raising her. Readying her.

She made a small sound of protest at his haste.

He positioned himself, holding her legs firmly apart, looking at her there. She felt terribly vulnerable until he looked up and she met his eyes—wild eyes, frantic eyes, eyes that held all of the need she felt and more, in swirling patterns of desire and despair. "It's only sex," he told her, and she felt him at her entrance, rubbing up and down the moist center of her. "I don't love you, Gillie. You understand, don't you? I can't. I can't love you."

And suddenly some of that tangle of words sorted themselves out. "It's all right," she said, soothing him, reaching for him, wrapping her arms around him and holding on. "It's all right, Rafe. I love you."

He plunged inside.

Once, Gillie had been caught in a thunderstorm in a tiny Piper Cub, at the mercy of all that flash and power and madness. That's what this was like. Rafe's body pounded into hers with all the raw fury of a storm and none of last night's finesse, flinging them both from one thunderclap to the next. Gillie could do nothing but ride the wild winds and hang on to his sweat-slippery back.

Her climax broke over her as a complete surprise, as if it weren't really her body convulsing, but the storm that had taken her. She cried out.

A moment later he cried out, too.

* * *

Rafe lay on his back with Gillie sprawled atop him, face-down. The air around them smelled of sweat and sex. One of her legs lay between his, and his arms were around her.

He had never in his life felt anything as good as losing control with Gillie. It terrified him.

He'd told her. Hadn't he told her why he couldn't stay? He'd even said he didn't love her. She'd given herself to him, anyway. It was her choice, he told himself desperately.

But it hadn't been her choice for him to take her like a rutting boar. She'd been tight, wonderfully, deliriously tight, still practically a virgin, and he'd pounded into her with all the tender technique of a freight train at full throttle. "Gillie," he said, his voice strained. "Gillie, did I hurt you? Are you all right?"

"No," came the muffled response from the region of his chest, where her face was pressed into his skin. "Or do I mean yes? You have demolished me," she added. Her lips tickled him when they moved. "I died happy, mind you, but now my arms and my legs don't work. I'm not sure I am breathing. You will have to move me so we can check."

Relief swamped him. "You sound like you're breathing."

"You're going to make me do this myself, aren't you?" He felt her sigh against his skin, warm and moist. "All right." Slowly, her head turned to the side. "Uh-oh. I think I'm blind."

He smiled. She'd turned her head, but her face was completely hidden by the fall of her hair. Gently he smoothed her hair back, tucking it behind her ear. "How's that?"

Now she tilted her head to grin up at him. "I'm cured. It's a miracle."

Somehow, the sight of her grin shifted his world. It was the tiniest of shifts, a slanting bit of newness that fell inside him like a ray of light hitting places too long dark. Where the light hit, nothing looked the same. He stared at her face and he wanted something, craved it—but he had no idea what it was. He frowned, baffled.

Her stomach growled.

She looked surprised, then she laughed. "I never did get any lunch."

Rafe was relieved by the prosaic need. That, at least, he knew what to do about. He smiled. "Room service," he said, "was created for moments like this."

"I'm not sure they have room service here."

He rolled them both over suddenly so that he was on top, and pressed a kiss on her startled mouth. "They do now."

They ate fried chicken, rolls and mangoes in bed. Gillie wore a sheet wrapped around her, toga-style. Rafe wore his jeans, since he'd had to get dressed to go get their food from the restaurant.

He'd had his shirt on, too, at first, but she'd insisted that was far too formal for the occasion. Not to mention the fact that she liked looking at his chest.

She liked looking at his face, too. Rafe kept smiling—not constantly, but often. He didn't say much, but he touched her a lot, and his eyes were soft when he looked at her. And he kept looking at her.

Gillie was licking mango juice from her fingers when the phone rang. She glanced at Rafe, worried. Who knew where they were?

His face was wiped clean of expression, all the softness hidden behind stone once more. "I stopped by the desk on my way to the restaurant and paid them for an international call," he said, reaching for the receiver. "This should be Willis."

He listened without speaking for a while, then recited a phone number into the receiver and hung up. "I got his machine," Rafe said. "The number I called is a special line, one he checks often. He should call back soon."

She could feel the world and the choices it demanded pushing in at them. "If he says the charges are dropped—"

"Not now," he interrupted. He turned, his hand closing around her arm. "Not now, Gillie. We'll have to deal with everything soon enough. I want a little more time."

She wanted much more than that. But she would give him

what he asked anyway. How could she not, when she wanted it, too, with everything in her? They would claim this little island of time for themselves, a time when they belonged only to each other, holding back the rest of the world by the sheer strength of their need...and her love.

Smiling, she stretched her arms up, linking them around his neck. "Time for what? Perhaps you should explain. In detail," she added, thinking of some of the details she particularly hoped to enjoy again.

Over the next forty minutes, Rafe added greatly to her appreciation for the power of patience and attention to detail.

They dozed off together after making love the second time, and Gillie woke up in Rafe's arms. She opened her eyes and caught him watching her with an odd look on his face, a look as troubled and intent as grief. Then he smiled, and her heart turned over.

They didn't leave their room. They'd eaten so late that neither of them was especially hungry—and anyway, Rafe couldn't leave. He had to wait on the phone call from Willis. And Gillie didn't want to go anywhere. She didn't want to give up one second of this magical time.

They talked. If Gillie did more of that than Rafe did, she didn't mind. He wasn't used to talking about himself. He wasn't used to teasing or playing, either, but he seemed to like both.

As the hours went by, though, and the phone remained silent, it grew harder to keep the world out. At ten minutes before nine, they sat slouched on the bed, leaning on pillows stacked up against the headboard. He wore his jeans. She wore panties and her yellow sweatshirt. They touched along their hips and at the shoulders.

As they talked, Gillie touched him elsewhere, too—his hand, his stomach, his foot—it didn't matter where. What mattered was that he was close enough for her to remind herself all over again, with every touch, of the feel of his arm, his skin, his warmth.

Rafe didn't touch her that way. He probably wasn't used to

touching, she thought, no more than he was used to talking about himself. He watched her, though. Anytime she looked at him he was looking at her, at her face or her breasts or her hands. He seemed to need to rest his eyes on her as much as she needed to rest her hand on him.

Their conversation had drifted, somehow, to the third grade and the possibility that their respective teachers had been twins separated at birth. Or maybe triplets, with the third sister having had a starring role in Hansel and Gretel's story.

"She scared me to death," Rafe said, and chuckled. "That was the only time in my school career I actually wanted to be sent to the office when I got in trouble. I wasn't sure what Miss Higgins would have done to me as punishment, but it was bound to have been worse than a few licks from the principal."

The phone rang.

Rafe froze for a second before pulling away. He swung his legs off the bed, sat up straight and picked up the receiver. After identifying himself he listened for what seemed like a long time. Gillie scooted around on the bed so she could watch his face.

His expression scared her, because with every second he had *less* expression.

Finally he asked, cryptically, "Why do you say that?" After another pause he asked about checking someone's car and apartment, then listened some more and ended by telling the person at the other end he would be in touch.

He hung up, then he just sat there, unmoving, as if he'd been turned to stone.

She scooted over next to him and touched his back. "Rafe? What did Willis say?"

He looked at her. "I need to go out for a while." He stood.

"You what?"

His shirt was tossed across the single wooden chair. When he picked it up and slid his arms in the sleeves without replying, she jumped off the bed and grabbed her jeans.

He paused, his fingers on the bottom button. "What do you think you're doing?"

"Going with you."

"No." He started buttoning.

She had one leg in the jeans and was hopping on that foot while she got her other foot inserted. "You haven't been paying attention the past few days, Rafe. The only time you've won one of our disagreements was when you kept me from leaving you, back when I was trying to escape. You've been really lousy at keeping me from staying with you." She got the jeans pulled up.

He frowned and reached for his socks. "Gillie, I'm not leaving you. I just have some business to take care of. I should have taken care of it this afternoon."

"Okay." She zipped and buttoned. "I'm ready. You can tell me about that phone call while we take care of it."

"I suppose I deserve your doubts, after the way I walked out on you." He reached for his shoulder holster.

"Listen," she said, walking over and grabbing the lapel of his shirt. "We aren't going to talk about what you deserve. We're not going to talk about when and where and whether you're leaving me, either. I'm getting pretty sick of that subject. We're going to discuss that damned phone call, and just what business you suddenly have to take care of."

He stared down at her. "I need to buy bullets for Winston's gun. I only have five rounds."

"Oh." She let go of his shirt. "Well, that's not going to be easy in Chihuahua at this hour. It would be simple enough in Juárez. But we aren't in Juárez."

"Is that all you have to say? Don't you want to know why I want the ammo?"

"Of course I do." She nodded and looked around for her shoes. "And you'll tell me, too." But not if she let him go off on his own. He was trying to put her into some convenient corner, blast him, to set her aside someplace where she didn't trouble him so much. "I'm not good at staying where I'm put, Rafe. So just get used to it. I'm going with you."

Chihuahua was a business-minded city, not a tourist town, and its nightlife was on the skimpy side. What little there was, though, Gillie knew how to find. She'd been right when she'd said she knew more about the seamy side of life in Mexican cities than he did. As soon as they'd climbed into the cab the desk clerk had called, she'd taken over.

Rafe watched now in silence as she leaned forward, discussing various dives with the driver.

Had circumstances been different, he might have been amused to find himself following her lead. But if circumstances had been different, he wouldn't be out looking for bullets for a gun he'd taken from a dead man.

Gillie would probably be more help than hindrance on his search. He admitted that. Her Spanish was better than his, for one thing, and she'd been determined to go with him. Leaving her behind might have required the use of the handcuffs he still had in his tote.

Rafe was keenly aware of how little logic had to do with some of his actions lately.

He looked out the window, trying to shut her out. It was stuffy in the cab, and he was sweating slightly in the cheap canvas jacket he'd bought to hide the shoulder holster. The floral smell of some spray deodorizer mingled unpleasantly with the stale cigarette smell that rose from the seats like dust from an old carpet.

There was plenty of room between Rafe and Gillie on that seat. He'd made sure of that. He had to get his head straight, and he needed distance to do that. He'd left the hotel because he needed more ammunition, yes—but also to get some distance.

So why was she sitting there in the cab with him?

The cabbie assured Gillie that Paulo's was still around and still owned by Paulo himself. "That should do fine, then," she said, and started arguing with him over the fare. Once the two of them agreed on that, the driver pulled away from the curb. Contrary to stereotypes, he drove slowly and cautiously, and didn't talk again while steering them through the light traffic.

Rafe and Gillie didn't talk, either, for the fifteen minutes it took to reach their destination.

He frowned as their cab pulled up near a low, cement building in an area without sidewalks or much in the way of streetlights. The bar had a tin roof and a flickering neon sign that spelled out the name of a popular Mexican beer. The door stood open. Graffiti decorated the side of the building.

While they watched, two men came tumbling through the open door. Another one strolled out after the first two, rolling a cigarette and watching with mild interest while they rolled in the dirt, pummeling each other.

"Ouch," Gillie said, looking out the window. "That looked like it hurt. Shall we give them a minute to finish up before we get out?"

No way was he taking Gillie in there. "No," he said, and leaned forward to tell the driver to try again. "We're going elsewhere."

Gillie opened the door, letting in a wash of music from the bar. "Pay the driver, Rafe."

"Gillie—" But she was already out, holding the door open, her attention divided between him and the two men fighting five feet away.

He cursed, pulled some bills out and gave them to the driver.

The cab pulled away the moment Rafe closed the door behind him. He took Gillie's arm just as the two men finished their fight. One gut-kicked the other, then staggered backward to lean against the building. The second man collapsed onto the ground and curled up in a tight, miserable ball.

Gillie would have stepped forward to help if Rafe hadn't had hold of her arm. He bent to whisper near her ear, "You're crazy, you know that?"

"Don't be such a snob."

Rafe steered Gillie around the man lying on his side, moaning. The third man took a drag on his cigarette, then bent to help his friend up. The one leaning against the building didn't move.

Rafe kept track of all of them. "It's survival, not snobbery, I've got on my mind."

"I told you, Paulo was an old friend of my father's. He'll

help us. His place is a little rough, I'll admit. I haven't come here since Pops died because it really isn't the sort of place a woman should come alone.''

"No kidding." He eyed the doorway they approached. He hadn't been in a dive like this since he was in the service. "Your father took you here?"

"Sure. Paulo and Pops were drinking buddies before Paulo dried out and bought this bar. Shoot, Paulo baby-sat me here sometimes when I was little. Of course, that was in the day-time."

Rafe switched his grip to her hand. They stepped beneath the low doorway and into smoke, dimness and noise.

It wasn't as bad as Rafe had expected…quite. For one thing the room was dim rather than truly dark, which suited him. He preferred being able to see the people around him. The music was loud, but so were the customers, who laughed, talked and argued openly. In Rafe's experience, the really dangerous places were the ones where people were quiet and furtive. There were two pool tables and a long, crowded bar where a man the size of a small mountain was serving beer.

Most of the faces were male, and Gillie had the only set of purely Anglo features in the bar. Not that she seemed to notice. "Come on," she said, tugging at his hand. They'd stopped just inside the door while Rafe surveyed the place. "I see Paulo behind the bar."

Rafe looked at the man-mountain and sighed. He wondered just how good a friend Paulo had been to Gillie's father, and how protective he might feel about the daughter.

Male faces all over the room were beginning to turn their way, checking them out. Many of those glances lit with the quick gleam of lust when they landed on the cheerful woman in a wrinkled yellow sweatshirt and snug jeans who was holding Rafe's hand.

But she noticed none of it. She tugged again, trying to get him moving. Rafe dropped her hand so he could put his arm around her waist. He drew her close to make his claim obvious and moved with her through the scattered tables.

There was one empty spot at the bar. Rafe let Gillie take it.

He rested one hand on her shoulder and stood close behind her. The men on either side of her shifted. One of them glanced at her, glanced at Rafe and quickly looked away.

The other man kept looking. He was young, heavily muscled through the arms and shoulders, almost as tall as Rafe, and his expression wasn't polite.

Rafe's hand tightened on Gillie's shoulder. He fought back the quick, hot bite of anger. It would be better, much better, to avoid a fight.

Rafe's size alone had kept him out of a lot of fights once he'd stopped looking for trouble. But not always. Sometimes, for some men, another big man was a challenge—a challenge that was even sweeter if there was a woman to be fought over. Rafe saw the excitement in the younger man's eyes and knew it wouldn't be easy to stay out of trouble this time.

The younger man turned sideways, smiled at Rafe and reached for Gillie's hand.

A fist the size of a coconut crashed into the side of the man's head, sending him sprawling. Rafe had to sidestep quickly to give him room to fall.

"No touching," rumbled a deep bass in Spanish.

The man on the floor didn't move, but he did groan.

"Paulo!" Gillie cried happily. "It's been a long time."

Rafe looked at the man that fist belonged to. The bartender was about fifty years old and built like a former sumo wrestler, tall and broad with plenty of muscle beneath the fat. He had a long, fleshy face with a scar down the center of his forehead and a thin mustache that drooped in a permanent scowl on either side of his mouth.

The man behind the bar stared back. "Gillian Appleby," he growled in an English that came straight from the Bronx, "what the hell are you doing in this crummy joint of mine, and who the hell is that summabitch with his hands on you?"

Chapter 13

"Paulo has always been a bit gruff," Gillie said apologetically.

That wasn't exactly the word Rafe would have chosen. "It doesn't matter."

They were sitting at a table in the corner near the bar, waiting for the big bartender to join them. A few minutes ago their table had been occupied by a trio who could have given dock workers bad dreams. Paulo had jerked his thumb, telling them to move, and the three had gotten up and left without a protest.

That told Rafe more about the man than his size alone had. "He looks Mexican, but he sounds like he's from the Bronx."

"Oh, definitely. His family still lives there. His grandparents were originally from Puerto Rico, and I gather they've never been real happy with some of his choices. Don't call him a draft dodger, though. He hates that. He says it implies cowardice rather than conscience. See, he was a protester who came to Mexico during the Vietnam War. He liked it here and stayed. While we're waiting for him," Gillie added, "you can tell me about that phone call. I gathered it wasn't good news."

"No, it wasn't." Rafe kept his eyes on the room, not her. It was safer that way.

"So what did Willis say?"

"I didn't talk to Willis. One of his associates told me he's in the hospital in critical condition. He says Willis was shot by Sheriff Daingler—"

"Oh, no!"

"—who is dead."

"Dead?" Gillie sat up straight, her expression stunned. "But how?"

"The police have decided they had a shoot-out. Willis killed Daingler, but was shot in turn."

"Good grief." She shook her head. "Well, that is terrible news about Willis, Rafe, but darned if I can see why it would send you charging out to buy bullets."

Rafe had used the ride over here to try to decide how much he should tell Gillie about his suspicions. He hadn't had a lot of success. Her reactions were hard to predict. Keeping her completely in the dark, though, would only work if he could count on her doing as she was told.

Fat chance. "The shooting didn't go down the way they're claiming."

"Why do you say that?"

He looked directly at her. It was a mistake. When he saw the worried frown between her eyes he wanted to kiss it away. "The shooting happened two nights ago at Willis's office, right after midnight. The man I talked to said Willis caught Daingler searching his files. They both had guns, and they both fired."

"That sounds reasonable," she said. "Though I suppose midnight is an odd time for Willis to be checking out his office."

"The odd thing is that the list I sent Willis is missing. The man I talked to wanted me to send another copy. Willis's copy isn't in his office, his car or his apartment."

"The list—oh!" She leaned forward. "You think a third person was there that night. That this other person took the list."

He nodded grimly. "And I have an idea of who it was—or, rather, who was probably responsible. He wouldn't have been the one who pulled the trigger, of course."

"Who?"

"Who else?" He tasted bile and blame, a renewal of the sick guilt he'd been fighting ever since he got the phone call. "My uncle."

She looked shocked. "But he gave you that list."

"And then I disappeared, presumably killed in a plane crash. It wouldn't be easy, but a patient man with the right training could use that list to access most of Daingler's little retirement fund. I could do it myself in a day or two."

"I don't understand."

"Daingler had the sense to live within his salary while he was sheriff, but he'd been stashing money away for years. It amounts to a pretty good sum. Once my uncle thought I wasn't in the picture anymore, he must have decided he wanted Daingler's stash and sent someone to get the list so no one would get to the money ahead of him. Or..." He paused and took a sip of beer, trying to cool the anger burning inside him.

"Or what?" she demanded.

"Or he may have planned it this way all along. He could have set up that ambush and arranged for the plane to be sabotaged because he'd already gotten what he wanted—my help in disposing of a business rival. After that, I was just in the way."

"But he's your *uncle.*"

"We're talking about a lot of money, Gillie. Four or five million." He could tell by the stubborn look on her face she wasn't convinced. That didn't surprise him. Gillie simply couldn't comprehend someone, even a professional criminal, selling out his family for anything as unimportant as money.

He switched subjects. "We need to leave the country as quickly as possible."

"Because of your suspicions about your uncle? Or because of the gang wars?"

Both. "The longer we're here, the greater the chance that someone will recognize one of us and that word of our survival will reach people who I hope like hell still believe we died in that crash. Whichever gang they're in.''

''It wasn't a crash,'' she said automatically. Gillie chewed on her lip and studied the man sitting across the rickety table from her. Rafe was close enough that she could reach out and touch him. Her palms tingled at the thought.

He was also unreachably distant, as far away as he could go inside his mind. He'd closed all the doors and windows and put up No Trespassing signs.

Her heart lodged itself in a big lump in her throat. Would he have come back if she'd let him leave the hotel room alone, the way he'd wanted? Or would he have headed for the border without her?

If Paulo hadn't picked that moment to slap a couple of napkins on the table in front of them, Gillie would have asked those questions. She was pretty sure she would have...even though she was, for once, fearfully reluctant to ask what needed to be asked. ''Paulo,'' she said, as the big man followed the napkins with two mugs of beer, ''it's awfully good to see you again.''

He pulled out a chair, turned it around and straddled it before reaching out to pat one of her hands briefly—a real emotional outburst, from him. Paulo was not a touchy-feely kind of guy. ''I was sorry when I heard about Ned dying. He was a good man. I know you miss him.''

''Yeah,'' she said, ''I do, but it's not as bad as it was.''

He nodded. ''Time will do that. Now tell me what the hell is going on. You got better sense than to come here unless you're in some kind of trouble.'' He stared at Rafe as if he had no doubt where the trouble came from.

It occurred to Gillie that Paulo was feeling a bit protective. He actually looked as if he might ask Rafe what his intentions were. She thought that was rather sweet. ''I have to admit you're right. Things are a bit hairy right now. The fact is, we need some bullets for—what kind of gun is it, Rafe?''

He was leaning back in his chair. Someone who didn't know him wouldn't realize that the easy look around his eyes meant he was smiling, not when his mouth stayed serious. "A .45."

"Right. Do you know someone we could buy some ammo from, Paulo?"

"You need bullets?" Paulo looked from Rafe to her and back. "That's why you're here? To buy bullets? You got a damned gun on under that damned jacket?" he demanded of Rafe.

"Keep your voice down, okay?" Gillie said. "We may need to get out of the country quickly, too. You know, kind of…unofficially. I can find someone to help with that on my own, but if you've seen anyone around, someone like Little Andy, maybe, or Manuelo Reyes—"

He interrupted with a long, rumbling string of curses in a creative blend of English and Spanish, ending with, "And now will you tell me just what kind of trouble you've gotten yourself into?"

"Well," she said uncertainly, "I'm not sure I should. I think maybe you're better off not having any idea what I'm talking about."

Rafe straightened. He faced the other man, who was a head taller and a hundred pounds heavier. "It's safer for you and Gillie both if you don't ask questions."

Paulo frowned. He had a mean frown, too, one that went well with his build and his scar. It made even Gillie a teeny bit uneasy. "Where do you come into the picture, pretty boy?"

That made her more uneasy. "Paulo, it's not Rafe's fault."

"Shut up, Gillie," Rafe said. "She's in trouble now because of me," he told Paulo, "and because she's almost as big a fool as I am. She has no sense of self-preservation. She doesn't listen to reason."

"So what are you going to do about it?" Paulo growled.

"Whatever I have to. Whatever it takes to keep her safe."

For a long moment the two men looked at each other. Gillie's heart pounded as if there were really something scary happening—though this was Paulo, she told herself. Surely Paulo wouldn't hurt someone she cared about.

At last Paulo grunted. "Benito down the street keeps a .45 under the counter. He'll sell you some shells and rob you blind on the price. I'll send someone to get some." He pushed to his feet and looked down at Gillie. "You sleeping with this pretty boy, Gillian?"

She blinked, shocked. "I—well, really, Paulo!"

"Never mind. Just be sure he uses protection. If he don't treat you right, you come tell me and I'll teach him manners. None of your pop's old buddies are in the city, far as I know, but I know of a pilot, Sanchez, who'll take any job, long as it pays enough. I'll get word to him." He looked at Rafe. "Sanchez is scum. Don't pay him until he does the job, and keep your gun handy."

Rafe nodded.

"It may take a while for Sanchez to show up. You'll wait here." He turned and walked away.

After a long, silent moment, Gillie said, "Do you think he's disappointed in me?"

Rafe's mouth twitched. "I don't think disappointment was uppermost in his mind just now."

She shook her head. His sense of humor baffled her at times. "Rafe…"

Something about her voice must have caught his attention. The muscles in his face tightened. "What is it?"

"What he said about protection. We didn't use any today. Either time."

His eyes went all blank and stunned. He just sat there, silent as stone, for so long she didn't think he was going to respond at all. Gillie made herself breathe in and out really slowly and keep her lips pressed tightly together so she wouldn't say anything she'd regret later.

At last he said, "I didn't think of it."

"Me, neither."

"I won't ask if this is a safe time. There aren't any really safe times. As for diseases—I never go into a woman bare. Never."

But he had, with her. Twice. She picked up one of the napkins Paulo had tossed onto the table—a nicety that she hadn't noticed him wasting on his other customers. Nervously she began pleating it. "Well, you know I don't have anything."

She waited for him to tell her how he felt, what he thought, what he would do if she were pregnant—which she probably wasn't, not from just one time. But he didn't say anything. He didn't even tell her it was all his fault, or assure her that he would pay his debts. Her fingers started shredding the napkin.

Then she realized his gaze had shifted. He was looking over her shoulder. She turned in her seat.

A skinny man with gold-framed glasses and slicked-back hair was headed toward them, with Paulo behind him. The skinny man wore a blue shirt, wrinkled slacks and expensive athletic shoes.

"This is Sanchez," Paulo said when they reached the table. He slapped a small white box on the table. "These are your shells. Pay me before you leave."

The other man smiled. It looked slippery, that smile, as if it could slide right off at any moment, maybe because he didn't have enough chin to hold it in place. "You sell ammo now, Paulo?" he asked. His English was better accented than Gillie's Spanish, if less fluent.

Paulo's frown was a ferocious sight, with the way it made the scar on his forehead pucker. "What I do is none of your business, Sanchez. The girl is the daughter of a friend of mine. You remember that." He looked at them. "I didn't see any reason to mention your names." Then he turned and made his way back to the bar.

Sanchez pulled out a chair without waiting to be asked and sat down. "Always glad to do business with a friend of Paulo's," he said, and smiled that slippery smile.

It didn't take long to settle things. Sanchez had a '92 Piper Cub that he kept at a private airstrip where no one fussed much about flight plans and destinations. He claimed his regular business was crop dusting, that the airstrip belonged to a rancher just outside Chihuahua with some alfalfa fields he dusted in return for hangar space. Gillie didn't argue and neither did Rafe, but she wondered if the man was running drugs.

That didn't make him sound like a very safe bet for them, but Rafe didn't object, so she kept quiet. For now.

Sanchez wanted too much money, of course, but they couldn't bargain effectively when they were in a hurry and he knew it. She had to be satisfied with getting him to drop his price a couple of hundred.

Rafe wanted to leave right away.

"I can have her fueled and ready in forty-five minutes," Sanchez said.

Gillie glanced at Rafe and swallowed, thinking of her treasure box. "We're not going back to the hotel?"

He met her eyes. She got the silent message: delay was dangerous. "It doesn't matter," she said as cheerfully as she could. She reached for the beer she hadn't touched, because she needed something to do instead of thinking about her little pearl necklace, the hairbrush, the wooden ball.... She took a sip and grimaced. She'd never liked beer.

"We'll meet you at the landing strip in an hour and a half," Rafe said abruptly, and stood. "I'm going to ask Paulo to see that you stay here for the next forty minutes—and that you don't make any phone calls."

Sanchez's smile slipped. "I thought you were in a hurry."

"An hour and a half," Rafe repeated, and slid his flat gaze to Gillie. "We need to pick up a couple of things first."

First they had to get some cash. Paying Sanchez would take the rest of Gillie's U.S. money, plus the maximum from two different banks' teller machines. They didn't have a lot of time, so they headed first for the ATM in the bus station and then the one at the public airport. Both places had ATMs in well-lit, public locations and were close enough together to cut down on transit time.

Rafe hardly spoke. He even seemed to avoid looking at her. Gillie told herself to be patient with his need for distance, but she had needs, too. He didn't have to sit on the other side of the cab from her. He could have held her hand or put his arm around her.

He could have given her a promise. Almost any kind of promise.

She swallowed as they pulled up in the passenger loading zone at the airport. She reached for the handle, then paused, looking over her shoulder at him. "You know, if you're planning on dumping me as soon as we get across the border, you can just forget it."

"I told you before," he said. "You aren't going to have any choice."

She was quiet as they passed into the terminal building.

It was nearly eleven. Chihuahua did have a few red-eye flights, but they weren't enough to fill the terminal with the daytime bustle of arrivals and departures. Just left of the entrance, a cleaning crew had set out their buckets and yellow Caution signs that warned of slippery floors. One man pushed a mop around while the two more pushed a cart of cleaning supplies toward the rest rooms. A handful of passengers were hurrying up the ramp, perhaps headed for the gate where, the loudspeaker assured them in two languages, Flight 307 was now boarding.

All in all it felt like home to Gillie. She headed away from the ramp with Rafe beside her. "The teller machines are near the car rental booths."

"We're spending all of your savings," he said. "I'm sorry. I'll—"

"Pay me back. Yeah. I know. Is that how you'll deal with being a father, if I do turn out to be pregnant?" she asked. "You going to pay cash for your baby, or put it on Visa?"

"We don't know that there will be a baby."

"No," she said, "we don't." It wasn't very likely.

"But if there is, I'll take care of everything. The doctor bills, the hospital—I'll take care of all that."

They'd reached the ATM. Gillie dug her card out of her wallet and stuck it in. She didn't answer or look at him.

"I know it's only money," Rafe said, low-voiced. "But money helps. It pays for a lot of things that children need, things like new clothes and bicycles. And sports. School sports are expensive, Gillie, and the schools don't cover everything, not by a long shot."

Gillie followed the instructions on the screen automatically. The foster care system, she reflected, probably didn't have much room in the budget for extras. "Did you want to play football or basketball, Rafe? Or maybe baseball?" Baseball was a very American sport, and she bet a teenage Rafe would have looked mouth-wateringly gorgeous in one of those form-fitting uniforms.

"We're not talking about me."

Oh, weren't they? "A child shouldn't be an obligation." She thought of her mother, who had traded one husband and child in on a second set more to her liking. She'd been trying to give Gillie money ever since.

For the first time in her life, Gillie felt a twinge of pity for the woman. "You're right. Money just doesn't work for some things. It's absolutely lousy at getting rid of guilt, for example."

"Money is what I have," he said. "It's what I can give."

He made her heart hurt. She blinked to clear the dampness from her eyes while the machine hummed and clucked and counted out her cash.

Gillie stuck the bills in her pocket and turned. "You have a lot more to offer than money, Rafe. You—" She saw a familiar pinkish-blond head atop a stocky body that was ambling down the concourse in their direction. "Uh-oh. Kiss me."

He blinked. "What?"

She grabbed his shoulders and tugged, trying to shift him in front of her. "Kiss me," she hissed. "Timothy Lee is headed this way and we can't let him see me."

He put his hand on her face, bent his head and pulled her close. His mouth brushed hers just once, then it turned needy. Demanding. Her heart stumbled, then took off soaring. His fingers spread wide along the side of her face, while his thumb beneath her chin tilted her head up at just the right angle for him to explore her mouth.

She dug her fingers into his shoulders and held on. His other arm molded her close and his big body wrapped itself around her—hiding her, she thought with one last gasp of coherence before she forgot everything except the sweet, hot welcome of his arms and mouth.

Sometime later he lifted his head.

Her eyes were still closed. The world was doing a weird spin, like a lazy hula hoop in an unsteady orbit. Gradually it settled. She opened her eyes. "I'm not sure it's a good idea to mess with gravity that way."

Both corners of his mouth turned up. "Is Timothy Lee gone?"

She peered cautiously around Rafe's broad shoulders. "I don't see him."

"Do you think he saw you?"

"No." She shook her head and was pleased when the world stayed put. "If Timothy Lee had seen me he'd be here now, bubbling over with questions. You think *I* ask a lot of questions—let me tell you, that boy is nosy."

He took her elbow and started steering her toward the exit. She let him get away with that. "It's quite a coincidence," he said, "Timothy Lee being here at this hour."

"A coincidence, maybe, but not all that remarkable. I probably fly in here four or five times a month. Or I did. I guess I'm supposed to be dead now, which means Timothy Lee is taking my flights, so he's here twice as often, if you get what I mean. Anyway, people who pay for charters are often in a hurry, so you wind up flying at all sorts of odd hours."

He frowned. "I hadn't realized you were here that often. There must be quite a few people at the terminal who would recognize you."

"Well, yeah, it's a risk. I thought you understood that."

"I didn't think it through." His voice was tight. "We'll have to hope that—"

The men's room door opened, and Timothy Lee stepped out right in front of them. His mouth dropped open. "Gillie? Gillie, is that you?"

It took them six minutes and several lies to get away from Timothy Lee. Rafe was grim when he slid into their cab.

"He's probably on the phone to Montaldo right now," he said as he closed the door behind him, adding to the cabbie, *"Andale, por favor."*

This driver didn't share the cautious habits of the one they'd had earlier. He took Rafe seriously when Rafe asked him to hurry. They squealed away from the curb so fast it pressed Gillie back against the seat. "Timothy Lee isn't part of this, Rafe. I'm sure he isn't."

"Even if you're right, he's a man who needs to keep his job. Any boss would expect to be told about it, if an employee they'd thought dead was, instead, wandering around Chihuahua City with an escaped felon."

"I don't think he'll say anything to Montaldo. I told him our lives were at stake." Gillie couldn't help noticing that the light up ahead was red. Their driver didn't seem impressed— not enough to slow down, anyway.

"That crazy story you spun him about international spy rings wouldn't fool a sixth-grader."

Actually, Timothy Lee was a good deal more gullible than the average sixth-grader. She figured he'd bought her story. What worried her was that he was just plain rotten at keeping his mouth shut. "With any luck he won't run into anyone he knows for another hour or two. By then we'll be at ten thousand feet and it won't matter."

He turned his head to look at her directly. The reflected lights from the city slid across the darkness of his eyes. "A great many things cease to matter to you once you're at ten thousand feet, don't they?"

She frowned at him. "What are you talking about?"

"Never mind."

She couldn't get him to say more. He held his silence as their cab speeded through the quiet Chihuahua street toward the Hotel Nuevo. Gillie felt heartsick. He kept pulling away, and she didn't know what to do about it.

"The restaurant's still open," she said in surprise when they pulled up in front of the hotel and she saw the lights. "We should order something to take with us. We haven't eaten since—'' She stopped, biting her lip. They'd eaten in bed that afternoon after making love. "Not for hours," she finished lamely.

"This isn't a good time to worry about your stomach," he said as he climbed out of the cab.

She scooted over and followed him. "I don't like throwing up," she said tartly. "Maybe you've never flown a little single-engine Piper on an empty stomach. I don't recommend it."

He hesitated. "All right. Get whatever is quick, and I'll go to our room and get our things."

"Rafe..." She put her hand on his arm. "Thank you for coming back for my treasure box."

"Don't make too much of it," he said flatly.

She wanted, for one childish instant, to stamp her foot and scream. She gritted her teeth and said, "You may as well quit warning me off, Rafe. I told you. I'm already in love with you."

Artificial light coming from inside the hotel mixed with the hard light of the nearby streetlight to steal the shadows and the color from Rafe's face. He looked oddly naked in that light. Only his eyes still held on to their secrets. "Gillie," he said, "the only person you fool when you say you love me is yourself."

She stepped back, her hand falling from his arm. "I thought you didn't want to love," she said, her voice low and unsteady. "I didn't realize you hated the idea of being loved even more."

"How many places have you lived since your father's death?"

"How many?" He was confusing her, and she didn't like it. "Three, I guess. Four if you count Caracas, where we were living when he died."

"Four places in two years." His voice was soft. "Maybe I'm wrong. Maybe you do know what you feel. From what I can see, you're a very loving person. Only you leave, don't you? You've cared about a lot of people in your life, but you always leave."

Her breath caught. She shook her head, rejecting the words and the pain. Then she turned and walked quickly away.

I didn't leave Pops, Gillie thought as she waited near the register for the hamburgers she'd ordered. No, she assured herself, Rafe was wrong. She'd stayed with her father come hell or high water, right to the end. Rafe was one hundred percent off base.

She wasn't like her mother.

The waitress came out of the kitchen just then, carrying two white paper sacks. She was a cheerful young woman with bright lipstick, short hair and a remarkably wide-awake baby on one hip. Normally, she'd told Gillie, the baby stayed with her grandmother during her shift, but the older woman wasn't feeling well that night. "Two hamburgers with everything," she said, lifting the sacks onto the counter next to the register, "and French fries."

Gillie smiled and tried to work up some enthusiasm. She'd been longing for a hamburger for days, and now—*I am not like that,* she told Rafe in her mind. She was dependable. She didn't walk out on her commitments.

Did she ever *make* commitments?

"Thanks," Gillie said, smiling even harder. "Tell the cook I appreciate this. It's awfully late." The restaurant had stayed open because a private party had booked it until midnight. Several of those guests remained at a long table in one corner, laughing and talking.

Gillie's eyes went to the small, happy bundle on the woman's hip. "Would you mind if I held her? I'm not sick or anything."

"Oh, this one never catches anything. She's like her mama, aren't you, *niñita?*" the young woman said, sliding her darling into Gillie's outstretched arms. "You like babies?"

"Oh, yes." Gillie thought about all the babies she'd held over the years as she savored the small, welcome weight in her arms. She thought about holding her own baby. The longing that swept over her, sudden as a tidal wave and just as unstoppable, came as a complete surprise.

Had she never even allowed herself to think about holding her own baby before?

"You have children?" the friendly waitress asked as she rang up Gillie's order.

No, but I might, nine months from now. A tiny hand grabbed at Gillie's bottom lip and pulled. She chuckled and gently detached it. "I'm not married," she said, avoiding a direct answer.

"Neither am I," the woman said wryly.

"This little angel was a surprise, huh?"

"Oh, how did you know? Her name, I mean—Angelita." The waitress chattered happily and Gillie responded, but her mind wasn't on the conversation. She and Rafe had made love twice without protection. What were the odds?

She thought about swelling up like a watermelon, and about labor. Midnight feedings. First smiles and messy diapers. And bicycles. School sports. And a man who wanted desperately to give, but was convinced he didn't know how. Just like he was convinced Gillie would surely leave.

The people in the corner called out a request to the waitress.

"If you like," Gillie said, "I'll hold her while you see what they need."

"Thanks," the young woman said with a quick smile, and hurried over to the big table.

Gillie had changed plenty of diapers. That part wouldn't bother her. Midnight feedings…sleep deprivation probably wasn't fun, but it couldn't be that terrible to get up in the middle of the night and fill her arms with the warm, welcome weight of a baby. Her own baby. As for the first smile…she smiled herself, dreamy and rapt, and wondered if a baby of Rafe's would smile like its father so seldom did—all-out and as bright as the sun.

No, she told herself firmly. *Do not count on this. It's only a slim possibility.* And shouldn't she be worried instead of hopeful? She was currently unemployed, after all, and getting a job as a pregnant pilot wouldn't be easy. And then there was day care, and…

What was she thinking? Gillie stared straight ahead, seeing

nothing of the cheery little restaurant. If she *were* pregnant, would she carry on with her life exactly as she had always done? Jumping from place to place, whichever way the wind blew her, rootless and homeless, as free as…as free as her father had always been. Free, even, of the obligation to make a home for his daughter.

She shook her head in denial. No, Pops hadn't wanted to deprive her of anything. When he realized she was hungering for a home he'd…sent her away. To her mother. To whom she was an obligation and a reminder of failure.

But he let me come back, she argued fiercely, silently. He *had* loved her. He'd been so glad to see her when she made her way back to him after that brief, abortive stay with her mother.

Maybe he just hadn't loved her enough.

Gillie stood motionless, absorbing the truth she'd denied for so long. Pops had loved her, but he'd been selfish in his love in some ways. He hadn't wanted to change his life in order to keep her in it. It had been up to her to find a way to fit.

And she had. There were a lot of things, she realized slowly, that she really liked about herself that came from the way she'd been raised. Yet…

The baby in her arms gurgled and grabbed for Gillie's hair, calling her attention back to the present. She probably wasn't pregnant. But if she were, she wouldn't do what her father had done. She wouldn't put her needs ahead of her child's, expect him or her to either adjust—or be left behind.

The friendly waitress hurried back to reclaim her baby. Gillie handed the little girl back to her mama with suitable compliments, but her mind wasn't on what she said.

She went to the glass door and pushed it open, the two white bags in her left hand. The air outside was cool and smelled like the city—like pavement and people and exhausts. The courtyard was quiet this close to midnight, the paths lit by low floodlights set among the plantings.

Not that Gillie noticed. As her mind and heart wrestled with new truths, her feet carried her automatically.

Neither the wandering nor the occasional danger had really

been bad for her, she decided. What had hurt was always having to prove herself. She'd known that if she couldn't keep up with Pops—couldn't adjust, couldn't take care of herself—he wouldn't keep her with him. For her own good, he would have sent her to her mother.

For her own good.

As she walked past the wrought-iron bench at the center of the courtyard, seeing nothing, she understood what Rafe had meant. She wasn't like her mother, no. She'd always been much more like her father. But not entirely. She had to make him understand that. She wasn't going to leave him.

And as Gillie walked past the Coke machine near her room, she didn't see the big, husky man who stepped out from behind it. She saw the one in front of her, though—a stubby little man with eyebrows that looked like woolly caterpillars. "Jorge!" She stopped and whirled around.

If Jorge had been alone, she might have gotten away. Instead, she spun straight into the waiting arms of the first man. He wrapped one big arm around her, clapped his hand over her mouth and held her still while Montaldo's flunky plunged a hypodermic needle into her arm. And then she truly saw nothing at all.

Chapter 14

Gillie woke to a dry mouth, a pounding head and darkness.

She was lying on her side on some hard surface. The back of her head rested against something rough and warm. She turned her head.

"Gillie," Rafe said, his voice soft and urgent. "Gillie, are you all right?"

"Sure," she croaked. She blinked, trying to focus, but all she saw was blackness. Then she tried to sit up—and discovered that her hands were tied behind her back. The movement sent a sharp stab of pain through her head. "Ouch!"

"Lie still," he said. "I don't know what they gave you, but if it's the same stuff they gave me your head should feel better in a few minutes."

Rafe sat in the darkness waiting for his heartbeat to slow down. He was so damned glad she'd moved at last. Waiting for Gillie to wake up had made for the longest half hour of his life. At least, he thought it had been about half an hour since he'd come to.

He hadn't known for sure that she would wake up.

"I'm tied up," she said, sounding more peevish than frightened.

"So are my legs." Tied with nylon cord that didn't have a bit of give in it. "They used handcuffs on my wrists." The same cuffs he had once used on her.

"Where are we?"

"A small storage room of some sort." He'd tested the boundaries of their tiny prison while waiting for her to wake up. "There are shelves against two of the walls, starting about four feet up." He hadn't been able to investigate the shelves. With his arms and legs both bound, he'd managed sitting, but standing had been beyond him. "We're facing the door."

"Oh." She wiggled around and, from the sound of it, managed to jackknife herself into a sitting position. The movement took her away from him, and he missed the contact. "Oh, I see. That grayish strip that must be the bottom of the door. I guess that means that no one's on the other side of the door right now. Or whoever is there is as much in the dark as we are." Her voice wobbled.

"Gillie." His arms ached with wanting to hold her. He pulled once, futilely, against his restraints. "We're still alive. That means someone needs us for something." He thought he knew why they needed him. The list, the damned, bloody, treacherous list.

"Well," she said, her voice thin but steady, "that means it probably isn't your uncle, right? I mean, he wouldn't need to keep you alive in order to get to the money."

She was quick. "No, he wouldn't." And neither side had anything to gain from keeping Gillie alive—something she'd probably figured out.

"Jorge was one of the two who grabbed me. Montaldo's flunky."

Rafe's memory flashed an image of the man's face in front of him. The recognition came too late. "Damn my eyes. He's the guy I saw at the bus terminal. The one I thought was following us." He fought back the savage anger that welled up.

"Montaldo must have had him watching it for us."

Rafe knew he should have anticipated something like that and stayed away from the major cities. His mouth tasted sour with blame. "Scoot around so our backs are to each other. I'll try to get you untied."

They both shifted awkwardly in the dark, finding each other by feel. His fingers felt thick and clumsy as he found her hands, then her wrists. The nylon cord was tied tightly, and his fingers had trouble getting purchase.

All at once she burst out, "It's my fault, isn't it? I don't know how they got you, but I'll bet you weren't careless like I was."

"Your fault?" he said, incredulous.

They'd come to the door of the hotel room—two men, one large, one short. They'd knocked, damn them, and waited for him to open the door and see Gillie's unconscious body in the big man's arms. Terror hazed Rafe's mind again as he remembered. "He held a knife to your throat." They'd had a gun, too, pointing at him, but it was the knife touching Gillie's throat that haunted him.

"They used me to get you, didn't they? You wouldn't have been caught if not for me. I didn't even see them, not until they grabbed me."

"None of this is your fault," he growled and shifted, trying for a better angle at the knots. "None of it. I let us be separated. I let you—"

"You didn't *let* me do anything. Dammit, Rafe, when are you going to admit that other people are responsible for their own screwups? I'm to blame for this, not you!"

"You're not to blame. My God, Gillie, you wouldn't even be in this mess if not for me. I shouldn't have let you come with me. I should—"

She made an angry noise and twisted.

"I don't want to hear any more about how you're supposed to be omnipotent, Rafe. Not one word. Do you hear me?"

He was silent as he fumbled along her arms to her wrists, finding the cord. The darkness pressed in on him, and with it, the past. "I hear," he said softly. "But I don't know if I can stop thinking that way, Gillie. I'm...used to it."

"Why?" she whispered.

The darkness. The past. Old fears and new ones locked up in this closet with him, breathing his breath, running clammy hands up his back. He closed his eyes, but he couldn't close any of it out. Not when the darkness he needed to shut out was inside him. "Did I tell you how my mother died?"

"No. No, you didn't."

"It was a hit-and-run."

He heard her breath catch, but she said nothing. She didn't ask a single question, which was surely odd.

What was even more odd, though, was that she didn't have to ask. He wanted—needed—to tell her. "We didn't have a car, but we were used to walking," he began. Patiently, his hands continued to work. The knots were so tight he wasn't sure they could be undone without a knife.

"The Holbrook house was on the very edge of town," he continued, "and there was one stretch without any sidewalks where we walked along the side of the road. It was January and it was nearly five o'clock, so the sun was on its way down. The driver claimed that's why he didn't see us, that the glare from the sunset blinded him."

"You saw it happen," she whispered. "Oh, Rafe, you saw it."

"Not exactly. We were walking along the side of the road when a big blue convertible came screeching around the corner, turning so wide it went onto the shoulder. It was headed straight for us. My mother—" He wanted to stop. He wanted to shut down, close it out, but he'd gone too far. He had to finish.

He took a deep breath. His hands kept working. "I couldn't move. There was a ton of metal aimed at us, and all I could do was stand there, as stupidly frozen as any deer staring at death racing toward it behind a pair of shiny headlights. My mother threw me out of the way. She was a small woman, and I weighed nearly seventy pounds, but she picked me up and threw me into that damned ditch like I didn't weigh a thing."

He remembered, oh, God, he remembered. "The car hit her. I didn't see it. I was lying there with the breath knocked out of me, so I didn't see her get hit. But I heard it." Once in a long while, he heard it again, in his nightmares. The too-little, too-late squeal of brakes. The thud.

"You were just a little kid. Rafe, it wasn't your fault. You were seven. Only seven."

She didn't understand. "We were walking home from school. Didn't I mention that? The principal had kept me after school. He'd asked my mother to come in for a conference because I'd gotten into another fight. I got into fights a lot before...that's why we were on that road at that time. Because of me. Because I was in trouble again.''

"Rafe," she repeated, and her voice sounded odd. She sniffed. "Rafe, it wasn't your fault. You were so little."

"You're crying."

"Someone needs to."

He didn't want her to cry. "I don't think it was my fault, exactly. Not anymore." Though he had. Because it was the simple truth that his mother had died for him. Because of him. "She wouldn't have been there if not for me. Just like..." Just like Gillie wouldn't be here now, if not for him.

"Don't do this to yourself!" She sounded angry now. "What if you'd never been born? Maybe she would have gone back to migrant work and died of some awful disease even younger. Or maybe she would have married a man who abused her. Or maybe she would have stepped in front of a truck on the same exact day."

"If you're talking about fate, I don't buy it."

"Call it fate, chance or God's will. Whatever it is that makes one thing happen instead of dozens of others, Rafe, we can't control it. All we can do is just keep on doing the best we know how."

Rafe didn't speak. Something inside him was pushing up, trying to get out—something small and strong and important, but as nameless as any new thing. He held himself silent and still, waiting to see what it was.

Then he felt her hand on his cheek.

He jolted. "Gillie?" He'd continued to work at her bonds, but he truly hadn't noticed when he finally unknotted them. He'd been too caught up in the past.

"You got me free, Rafe. Let's see what I can do for you."

When the light came on in the other room twenty minutes later, Gillie sat down again quickly, her back to Rafe. "Hurry," she breathed.

He worked pretty fast, considering he still had the handcuffs on. They hadn't come up with any way to get those off. He wrapped the nylon cord loosely around her wrists, tucking the end in without knotting it. If no one looked closely, it would seem like she was still tied.

They hoped.

A bright strip of light glowed beneath the door. She heard footsteps, and a voice that she recognized. She stiffened as the door to their tiny prison swung open. The light was blinding after so long in the dark.

But the voice—she recognized that immediately. "You don't look very comfortable, Gillie," Montaldo said.

As her eyes adjusted, she saw that he looked the same as ever. The same neat little mustache and expensive dress shirt. He was smiling pleasantly when he switched to Spanish. "Jorge, why don't you help her out of there?"

When Montaldo moved aside, Jorge stepped forward. His round face was shiny with sweat and his eyes looked funny. Unfocused. He stretched out his hand.

It held a knife.

She pivoted on her bottom, drawing her still-bound feet back, ready to kick. She heard Rafe moving behind her, but didn't take her eyes off the knife. Her heart pounded with fear and adrenaline.

Jorge giggled. It was not a pleasant sound. "It's for the rope on your feet," he said, rubbing his thumb slowly up and down the hilt of the knife. "You can't walk like that."

Behind her she heard Rafe's voice, very low. "He likes knowing you're afraid. Don't give him that pleasure, Gillie. And don't give him a reason to check your hands."

They'd decided, after some discussion, to leave their feet still tied. It was a risk. Rafe thought their captors would be too much on guard when they first opened the door for an attack to succeed, especially since they couldn't get his hands free. With his build and his Special Forces training, he could do a lot more damage than she could—but not with his hands bound.

So she worked at sitting very still and not hyperventilating while Jorge knelt at her feet. He slid his knife between her ankles, but he didn't do anything. He just sat there looking at her face and grinning vacantly.

Jorge was high on something, she realized. The thought

238 *The Virgin and the Outlaw*

didn't reassure her. She tightened her jaw and did her best not to look scared witless.

"You can play later, Jorge," Montaldo said. "I need to settle a few things first."

That didn't reassure her, either.

Jorge pressed the knife to the cord binding her ankles. It was a very sharp knife. The cord parted quickly.

She had to tolerate him putting his hands on her to help her to her feet. He giggled again, rubbed her shoulders, and gave her a little push when Montaldo told him to hurry up and get "the man out here, too."

She managed not to turn her back to him completely, stumbling out sideways. What she saw didn't surprise her, since she'd had a chance to investigate the shelves a bit—and to pocket something from those shelves. The heavy-duty tape measure fit in her pocket, and it had a comforting heft—about the same as Bura's ball.

They were in an empty airplane hangar. She recognized it as one that belonged to another of Montaldo's little airlines. They were near the back wall, which held lockers, a workbench and a long table. One end of the table was set up to be used as a desk, with a computer and printer. The other end held communication equipment. There were two high windows. The black glass in them insisted it was still night, that Gillie hadn't spent more than a few hours locked up.

The hangar also held a third man, an Incredible Hulk of a man with a weight lifter's build. He had a gun. A really big gun. It was pointed at her face.

"Have a seat, Gillie," Montaldo said, pulling a stool out from the workbench. "Stormwalker, do behave yourself when Jorge cuts your feet free. Luis here will have plenty of time to shoot Gillie in the head before he shoots you in the kneecap. I'd hate for him to have to do that, but the silencer will keep everything private."

Gillie sat obediently on the stool, her back to the workbench. They hadn't noticed how loosely the cords hung on her wrists. Hope tingled through her with the pins-and-needles sensation of returning circulation.

Montaldo stayed well back as Rafe came out. "Over there, Stormwalker. Sit at the chair by the computer."

"You have an odd way of doing business," Rafe said. His eyes were as flat and emotionless as his voice. He advanced to the chair Montaldo indicated, about ten feet away from her. As soon as he sat, he sent his gaze skimming over her. She smiled to let him know she was all right.

He looked back at their captor. "I assume you do have a business proposition for me?"

Montaldo chuckled, but his fingers were tapping his thigh nervously. "That's right, Stormwalker. I'm glad you're bright. Stupidity can be annoying." His mouth tightened. "Daingler was stupid."

"Not too stupid," Rafe said, "since he managed to skim money off the top for years and tuck it away where you haven't been able to find it."

"Stupid," Montaldo insisted. "He didn't have a clue I was setting him up when I sent him to get that list. It worked out well. He killed the cop and I killed him. But then, I knew he wasn't bright."

But Willis isn't dead, Gillie thought. Montaldo didn't know everything. She looked around. Montaldo had practically forgotten about her. The hulk still held the gun steady—didn't that thing get heavy after a while, even for him?—but he was watching Rafe and Montaldo. Jorge was looking at his knife and smiling.

She began wiggling her wrists inside the loosely wrapped cord.

"No, not very bright," Montaldo went on. "After all, he started our troubles by killing the wrong man. He should have shot you and framed your foster brother." He shook his head. "I'd had doubts about the way he ran his side of the operation for some time, but my superiors were satisfied, so what could I do?"

"I take it your superiors' opinions are no longer of much interest."

"Not really. Not with most of them dead or otherwise among the missing. Your uncle's organization has taken quite a toll in the past few days, I'm afraid. I've decided to take early retirement and a nice, long trip."

"Retirement is expensive, though, isn't it?"

One loop of the cord slipped off her hands.

"Exactly." Montaldo paced a few restless steps as he talked. He stood in the middle with his two men at either side.

"I wasn't happy when Gillie took that flight," Montaldo said, "instead of that idiot, Timothy Lee. It was just possible she might manage not to crash the plane. As it turned out, I was right to worry, wasn't I? And I was right to have every bus station between here and Juarez watched. By the time my people located what was left of the Cessna a few days ago, though, the situation had changed." He smiled at Gillie. "Everything is working out for the best, after all."

The rest of the cord started to slide off. She grabbed the loops with her fingers and held on frantically, scowling at him.

"Do you have the list, then?" Rafe said, drawing Montaldo's attention back to him.

"Yes." He smiled and patted his pocket. "Though there are one or two things missing from it, aren't there? Pass codes, for example. I'm sure you know those. How long will it take you?" Montaldo took one eager step forward. "Can you use the computer here? It's got a modem."

"Assuming the software is familiar and you've got a place for me to move the money to—yes, I can do it here."

"How long?"

"About three hours."

Either Rafe had lied to her when he said it would take him a day or two, or he was lying to Montaldo now. Gillie didn't even have to ask herself that question. Which meant he was planning something.

She relaxed her fingers and the cord slid to the floor. It made a slithery sound, but no one else seemed to notice. She waited, mouth dry and heart pounding, for a clue about what Rafe planned.

Some of the strain around Montaldo's eyes eased. "Good. I'm a reasonable man. I'll let you walk away from here safe and sound once you're through."

"I'll do it," Rafe said, "for fifty percent."

Montaldo laughed. "Don't be ridiculous. I don't have to give you a penny."

"You don't hold all the high cards. You've got me, but you can't just shoot me. And you're in a hurry, aren't you?" Rafe's smile was downright mean. "I imagine my uncle knows who sabotaged the plane by now. He's got a surprising amount of family feeling, you know."

Montaldo's fingers started their nervous tap dance again. "The official searchers found the Cessna yesterday, so you may be in a hurry to get out of the country yourself. That other U.S. marshal was released from the hospital just in time to go identify the body of his colleague. He was very upset, I heard. By now he's probably gotten the police here to issue a warrant for you, making you a wanted man in two countries." Montaldo smirked. "Need any help getting out of the country, Stormwalker?"

"Don't worry about me," Rafe said. "I've got my own way of getting out." His glance slid to Gillie.

Jorge giggled, drawing her gaze. He was looking at her and rubbing his fingers up and down the blade of his knife.

"Is she your ticket out?" Montaldo sounded pleased. "What about your uncle?"

"He favors having me follow in his footsteps."

"So he doesn't want you to leave. Well." He glanced at Gillie. She sat stiff and still and wondered how he could miss seeing the cord on the floor behind her.

But apparently he did, because he looked back at Rafe. "I did wonder why you were so worried about her. I knew you were sleeping with her, but no piece of tail is worth risking your neck for. Though I admit I was envious. I always meant to get a little—"

"Forty percent," Rafe said, "and a couple of safeguards."

Montaldo shook his head. "I could let you have a hundred thousand or so, just to keep you off the streets. Though you're a rich man, from what I hear."

Rafe shrugged. "I can't get to my money right now. So if I have a chance to get my hands on some of Daingler's stash, I'm going to be a lot more enthusiastic. You're in a hurry, Montaldo. You want me to be enthusiastic."

"Fifteen percent."

"Thirty, and I move my share first. Then Gillie and I walk out of here."

"You understand," Montaldo said, "I really can't just let you walk. I'd have to have Luis or Jorge drive you out into the desert and leave you to make your way back. That would give me a little time to get started on my own vacation."

Gillie frowned. Montaldo sounded entirely too pleased. She stared at Rafe, willing him to look at her.

"Twenty percent," Rafe said, sounding reluctant.

"Tell you what," Montaldo said. "We'll make it a flat fee of a million."

Gillie listened to Rafe bargaining for guarantees that were no guarantee at all, and suddenly she understood. Rafe knew Montaldo had no intention of letting them leave here alive, but he wanted Montaldo to think he'd fooled him.

He was trusting her, counting on her, to figure out what was going on. To act at the right time. She felt sick and frightened and determined not to let him down.

The men came to an agreement. Montaldo was smiling as he told Jorge to keep an eye on her. He had Luis and his gun go stand next to Rafe.

Jorge ambled over to Gillie. He reached out his hand—the one with the knife—and stroked her hair. And giggled.

She shuddered.

"Hey," Rafe said, "get your goon to stay back."

"Territorial, Stormwalker?"

"I don't want her sliced up."

Montaldo shrugged and told Jorge to stand back a bit. Gillie drew a deep, unsteady breath. Whatever Jorge was on, she told herself, it was to her advantage. He was so spaced-out— and so turned on from fondling his knife—he hadn't noticed the cord on the floor, or her unbound hands.

He was bound to notice it, though, when she stood up.

While the hulk held his big gun to Rafe's head, Montaldo fished the keys to the handcuffs out of his pocket. He unfastened Rafe. "Make yourself comfortable, Stormwalker."

"It's a little distracting," Rafe said dryly, "having a gun pressed to the back of my head. You think you could have goon number two step back a bit?"

Montaldo chuckled and passed the instructions on in Spanish.

This is it, she realized. This is what Rafe had been maneuvering for—a time when he had his hands free and the gun wasn't trained on her. She slid her hand into her back pocket.

Rafe switched on the computer. It made a whirring noise, and the screen lit up.

Now, she told herself. *Do it now.* But it was hard to move with a knife-wielding druggie two steps away. It was hard to believe she could save them with a tape measure. Her arms were stiff from being held behind her so long, too. She wouldn't have a chance to warm up, no practice pitches.

The hulk was on the other side of Rafe. *Only twelve feet,* she told herself. Easy. She closed her hand around the metal tape measure.

A message came up on the computer terminal. It was in Spanish.

Rafe couldn't read Spanish. She was out of time.

In one smooth motion Gillie pulled the tape measure from her pocket, surged to her feet, pulled her arm back and threw.

That big gun went off with an incongruously quiet cough. It wasn't pointed at Rafe, though. The hulk had swung around as she'd moved.

The blow she felt was vast, but painless. Like being hit on the side of the head by a baseball bat. She felt the impact a split second before she saw the tape measure strike the hulk dead center in his forehead. She saw the look of utter surprise on his face. He started to fall, but her body was crumpling, too, taking her to the floor in the oddest slow-motion sort of way.

First she fell to one knee. Then she toppled, gradually, onto her bottom. Then her shoulders hit. Then she was lying flat on her back while pain exploded, belatedly, in her head.

It was a huge, unsteady pain, swelling and retreating with her breath. She heard fighting—she thought it was fighting. *Rafe?* She tried to call his name, but didn't hear herself. More noises. Yelling? A gunshot? She blinked, but her eyes got stuck and wouldn't open. All she could do was listen to the way the noises outside blended with the expanding bursts of pain inside her skull.

It was very confusing. Everything seemed to go on for a long time, but she couldn't be sure, because she wasn't completely there.

"Gillie?"

That was Rafe's voice. She smiled. At least she thought she did.

"Gillie, dammit, wake up." His hands were on her, petting her arms, her shoulders. "Don't you dare leave me. You can't. You said you wouldn't leave."

He was hurting. Somehow she got her eyes unstuck.

His face was right over her. There was someone else nearby, too, she realized—no, lots of someones, moving around, calling out instructions in Spanish in official-sounding voices. One of the someones was on her other side, calling out for a doctor. But she didn't pay attention to that.

Rafe's face was twisted with pain. His cheeks were wet. "Gillie," he said. He tried to smile. "You're going to be fine. The ambulance will be here any second."

"Sure," she said, but her voice sounded tiny and frail. She groped for, and found, his hand. That helped. "I won't leave you, Rafe," she said even as a gray fog swirled up around her. "I promise."

The fog darkened into bat wings fluttering at the edges of her vision. Her head hurt fiercely and she knew she was going to pass out, but she held on to Rafe's hand, held on long enough to see him smile. Really smile.

Then she slipped away into the numbing dark.

Emergency rooms in Mexico were much like their counterparts in the United States, Rafe thought. The staff reminded him of a combat unit—quick, efficient, accustomed to working as a team. The room smelled of blood and antiseptic.

Gillie's blood. It soaked the yellow sweatshirt the nurses were busy cutting off her limp body.

Head wounds always bleed a lot, Rafe told himself as he leaned against the wall, dizzy and sick and determined to stay where he was. He wouldn't get in their way, but neither would he leave. He wasn't letting anyone put walls between him and Gillie. She might need him.

A man in scrubs and a white lab coat bustled in. He glanced at Rafe and frowned. "You must wait outside," he said in heavily accented English. "Your police is in the hall. He has questions."

Rafe just shook his head.

One of the nurses looked up. She told the doctor in Spanish that "the big man" was stubborn but quiet, and the only way they would get him out of there would be to shoot him and drag him out, and they were really too busy to deal with another patient just then. The doctor shook his head, then seemed to forget Rafe's existence as the three professionals fell into what was obviously a familiar rhythm.

Rafe watched from his spot against the wall and told himself Gillie was going to be fine. They draped her in a sheet, which must mean they hadn't found any other injuries, and that had to be a good thing. He couldn't understand their technical jargon, but their voices didn't sound urgent. Surely they would be calling for help, moving faster, if anything were very wrong.

But she was so still. So pale. And there was so much blood.

Gillie wasn't going to leave him. She had promised him that. And as pale as she looked now, she'd looked a thousand times worse lying on that cement floor with blood pooling beneath her head.

He hadn't been able to get to her. He'd seen her shot, and he hadn't been able to go to her. Fear numbed his hands and feet as the horror of that moment blurred into the present.

Rafe had finished off the man she'd hit with a kick to the jaw, but Montaldo had grabbed a wrench and Jorge had been coming at him with the knife. They'd kept him busy, unable to reach Gillie's side or grab the gun. Then the door at the other end of the hangar had burst open and two men had run in. The one in the uniform of the Mexican National Police had stopped with his gun extended two-handed and yelled, *"Policia!"*

The fight had gone out of Montaldo right away. Jorge though—it had taken a bullet from the Mexican policeman's gun to discourage him.

Rafe smiled. He hadn't minded the sight of Jorge's blood at all.

"I won't ask what you're thinking," a deep voice said from the doorway. "You might tell me, and if you're planning to kill anyone, I don't want to hear about it."

Rafe looked at the man who entered—Winston's partner,

who had been shot in the ambush outside San Luis del Corba. He had one arm in a sling. "I answered your questions on the way here," Rafe said. "Anything else will have to wait."

"You have some odd ideas about who's in charge," Federal Marshal John Sutton said, "considering you're technically still my prisoner. But right now, I just want to see how she's doing." He nodded at the examining table.

Sutton had a stubborn jaw and a cop's tired eyes. He was also a man who'd recently lost a friend, Rafe thought, and maybe that entitled him to be here, looking for whatever good he could find in the aftermath of his partner's death.

The marshal had discharged himself from the hospital when word came about Winston's plane going down. He'd spoken with everyone at the San Luis airport, urging them to call him if they saw or heard anything, and that was just what Timothy Lee had done after he ran into Gillie and Rafe in Chihuahua. Sutton had flown up to Chihuahua immediately. As it turned out, the federal police had already been suspicious of Montaldo, but lacked both evidence and the manpower to acquire it. They'd been willing to let Sutton and one of their officers go to Montaldo's hangar, however. The two men had arrived in time to see Montaldo going inside. They'd taken up positions outside, waiting to see what happened.

When the fighting started, both men had been more than ready to break in.

The doctor turned from his examination to look at Rafe. One of the nurses left; the other pulled out a tray of shiny, ominous-looking instruments. "The bullet cut her scalp and knocked her out," he said in his heavily-accented English. "I will sew her up now. If she does not wake soon, we will do more tests."

The doctor took his time. Rafe knew Gillie couldn't feel a thing. He'd watched the doctor inject a local anesthetic before he began. But every time the man passed that curved needle through her soft skin, Rafe winced.

The stitching was less than halfway finished when she came around. "Rafe?" She moved fretfully, ignoring the doctor, who tried to calm her.

That was all he needed. Rafe's heart pounded as he made a place for himself beside the IV machine. He closed his hand around hers carefully so he wouldn't disturb the needle taped to the back of her hand.

She quieted immediately and blinked up at him as if she were having trouble focusing. "You look awful."

He had to smile at that. She looked a good deal worse. "I was in a fight."

"Oh, yeah." Her eyes cut to the doctor, who waited, forceps and needle in one gloved hand. She frowned at him. "My head hurts."

The doctor sighed. "You will ask her to be still, please."

"Yes," Rafe said, studying her intently. They'd had to shave off some of her hair to clean and stitch her wound, and the long, ugly furrow in her scalp still oozed blood where the doctor hadn't yet placed his stitches. The flesh around the wound was bright orange from the cleanser they'd used. Where she wasn't orange, she was rust-red from dried and drying blood.

And she was going to be okay. He knew that for certain as he looked down at the expression on her poor, bloody face. Her eyes didn't have the inward look of someone who was badly hurt. No, she mostly looked aggravated, and a bit wary of the doctor and needle. Rafe's knees turned weak with delayed reaction. He had to grab hold of the edge of the examining table to steady himself. "The doctor needs to finish stitching you up," he managed to say. "Can you lie still and let him do that?"

"I hate needles."

"Don't look. He's already given you a local, so you won't feel a thing."

"Okay." Her fingers tightened on his and her eyes locked onto his face as the doctor resumed his work. "I guess I'm in the hospital, huh? How did I get here? Did you beat up the bad guys all by yourself?"

"You don't remember?"

"I remember you holding my hand."

That part of the day's events was pretty jumbled for Rafe, too. He remembered running his hands over Gillie once he reached her. Had he held her hand when he begged her not to leave him? Probably. "You did half the work with that fastball of yours. Marshal Sutton arrived with the cavalry a few minutes later. It seems we owe Timothy Lee a big thanks.''

"Timothy Lee?"

Rafe explained the circumstances leading up to the arrival of Sutton and the Mexican officer, ending about the same time the doctor finished his stitching. The doctor needed Gillie's attention then. He poked her here and there, asking her if it hurt. She sounded more than a little irritated when she told him "no," "no," "yes," and "dammit, quit that."

He smiled, patted her arm and told her she had a wonderfully hard head and they would be keeping her overnight for observation. When he and one of the nurses left, the other one got out a drafty hospital gown exactly like ones inflicted on patients north of the border.

"Just a moment," Sutton said, stepping forward. "Ma'am, I'm sorry to bother you, but I need to ask you a couple of questions."

"For God's sake," Rafe growled, "it can wait until she's admitted."

"The sooner I talk to her," Sutton said, looking at Gillie rather than Rafe, "the sooner you can stop being a prisoner."

"It's okay," Gillie said.

Sutton was as good as his word. He asked four questions, just enough to make sure Gillie's story matched Rafe's in its essentials. "The Mexican police will want to talk to you, too, of course," he finished. "They'll need your testimony to help convict Montaldo." He started to turn away. "Oh," he said, a hint of a smile appearing on his hard mouth, "if you're worried about a wooden box you left back at your hotel, your man here took care of that. He persuaded the police on the scene to, uh, take it into protective custody."

Gillie turned her head slightly to smile at Rafe. That smile, so free and happy, made him feel like a boy who'd just given his girl a handful of flowers, and was working up the courage to ask her out. He didn't like the feeling. It was nerve-racking.

Especially since he intended to ask Gillie for much more than a date.

The nurse, who had been standing by impatiently, broke in to tell the marshal and Rafe in Spanish that they had to leave so she could make her patient comfortable. This time, Rafe let himself be chased out. When he went back in, the nurse and the IV were gone. So was most of the blood. Gillie wore the faded hospital gown and a sad, tired expression.

"What's wrong?" he said, coming up to take her hand again.

"Nothing." She made an obvious effort to look cheerful. "Except for the guy inside my head with a jackhammer, that is. And the fact that I don't have any insurance to pay for all this."

He knew she was hurting. He also knew that the lost look he'd seen in her eyes had little to do with her physical pain. He didn't think it had much to do with money, either, but he knew how to deal with that problem, so he addressed it first. "I've made arrangements about the bill. No, don't argue. I've got plenty of money, and you don't have any choice. It's already done."

"Bossy, aren't you?" Her thumb stroked along the back of his hand in a restless caress. "There's something I need to know." Her throat worked as she swallowed.

"What is it, Gillie?" he asked gently.

Flat on her back and concussed, she still managed to tilt her chin up stubbornly. "The thing is, Rafe, you can't go running off while I'm stuck here. That wouldn't be fair."

"I'm not going to leave you."

Her eyes went wide and vulnerable. "You mean you're not going to leave while I'm hurt?"

The words were hard to find. He felt half-sick with dread, yet he hardly knew what he dreaded most. Her hand was warm and trusting in his, though, and that helped. "You said you wouldn't leave me. I'm not leaving you, either."

She blinked several times, but her eyes took on a damp sheen anyway, and her voice was husky when she spoke. "Careful. That sounded almost like a promise."

"I know how important freedom is to you," he said. "I won't tie you down. My business—well, I can operate almost anywhere. It doesn't matter, does it? Where we live, how often we move, that doesn't matter. But if you meant it—if you really want to stay with me—" His throat closed up. He swallowed.

Her hand clamped around his tightly enough to cut off the

blood supply to his fingers. "Rafe, are you by any chance proposing?"

He nodded. Yes, that's what he was doing. "I'm going to keep you with me, Gillie, and you said you wouldn't leave me. Promising to stay with each other—that's what marriage is, isn't it?"

"Help me up," she said, pushing up with one hand and promptly losing every bit of color in her face.

He grabbed her. "For God's sake, lie down."

"Not when I'm getting the only marriage proposal of my life," she said, still struggling to sit.

Since she wasn't going to be reasonable, he helped her. It made sense to put his arms around her to keep her from falling. So he did that, and it felt good. So good. "We'll get married right away," he told her, needing to have it settled.

"Bossy." She snuggled close, resting the uninjured side of her head on his shoulder. "I haven't said yes."

He went stiff. "Don't play games."

"Rafe," she said gently. "I told you how I feel about you. I need to know what you feel."

What he felt? He felt so many things. What did she want him to say? Should he tell her he wanted her in a way he knew he would never want another woman? Did he say that she terrified him, or that he would rather die than see her hurt again as she had been that day?

He tried. "I feel good when you laugh. I feel alive when I'm with you. It isn't always comfortable." He was getting it all wrong. He could tell by her stillness, her silence. What did she want from him? Not money. Children? She *should* have children, plenty of them, to love her...

"Oh," he said in sudden, belated realization. He knew what she needed to hear. "I love you."

The muffled sound she made might have been laughter. "Rafe," she said, "we do have a ways to go, don't we? But my answer is yes." She turned her face up to him, glowing like a kid at Christmas. "Yes and yes and yes. I'll marry you. Right now, though, I think you had better kiss me."

Carefully, he lowered his lips to hers. She tasted salty, like tears. Like life. She made his head swim. He ended the kiss slowly, and she sighed and laid her head on his chest again.

"I'm not as much of a wanderer as you think," she said. "That's what I was coming back to tell you when those two grabbed me."

"What do you mean?"

"I moved around all the time because Pops did. It got to be a habit, but I don't have his need to pack up and move on. I'll probably always like to take a trip now and then," she said in what he was sure was a major understatement, "but I know where my home is, Rafe. Right here, with you. The rest doesn't matter."

His throat tightened. For the first time since he was a little boy, he wanted to ask for something—something he still wasn't sure was real. "Is that a promise?"

"You bet. I love you, Rafe."

It felt strange to a man who hadn't thought he believed in tomorrows or promises to know he held his future in his arms, and to discover he trusted that future, because Gillie had promised it to him. He tried speaking again what she'd needed him to say before. "I love you, Gillie."

This time, the words made him smile, too.

*   *   *   *   *

*Watch for Eileen Wilks's next sensuous novel coming
in December 1998 from Silhouette Desire.*

The World's Most Eligible Bachelors are about to be named! And Silhouette Books brings them to you in an all-new, original series....

World's Most Eligible Bachelors

Twelve of the sexiest, most sought-after men share every intimate detail of their lives in twelve never-before-published novels by the genre's top authors.

Don't miss these unforgettable stories by:

Dixie Browning

MARIE FERRARELLA

Jackie Merritt

Tracy Sinclair

BJ James

RACHEL LEE

Suzanne Carey

Gina Wilkins

VICTORIA PADE

MAGGIE SHAYNE

Anne McAllister

Susan Mallery

Look for one new book each month in the **World's Most Eligible Bachelors** series beginning September 1998 from Silhouette Books.

Silhouette®

Available at your favorite retail outlet.

Take 4 bestselling love stories FREE

Plus get a FREE surprise gift!

Special Limited-time Offer

Mail to Silhouette Reader Service™

P.O. Box 609
Fort Erie, Ontario
L2A 5X3

YES! Please send me 4 free Silhouette Intimate Moments® novels and my free surprise gift. Then send me 6 brand-new novels every month, which I will receive months before they appear in bookstores. Bill me at the low price of $3.96 each plus 25¢ delivery and GST*. That's the complete price and a savings of over 10% off the cover prices—quite a bargain! I understand that accepting the books and gift places me under no obligation ever to buy any books. I can always return a shipment and cancel at any time. Even if I never buy another book from Silhouette, the 4 free books and the surprise gift are mine to keep forever.

345 SEN CF2W

Name	(PLEASE PRINT)
Address	Apt. No.
City	Province	Postal Code

This offer is limited to one order per household and not valid to present Silhouette Intimate Moments® subscribers. *Terms and prices are subject to change without notice.
Canadian residents will be charged applicable provincial taxes and GST.

CMOM-696   ©1990 Harlequin Enterprises Limited

PAULA DETMER RIGGS

**Continues the
twelve-book series—
36 Hours—in May 1998
with Book Eleven**

THE PARENT PLAN

Cassidy and Karen Sloane's marriage was on the rocks—and had been since their little girl spent one lonely, stormy night trapped in a cave. And it would take their daughter's wisdom and love to convince the stubborn rancher and the proud doctor that they had better things to do than clash over their careers, because their most important job was being Mom and Dad—and husband and wife.

For Cassidy and Karen and *all* the residents of Grand Springs, Colorado, the storm-induced blackout was just the beginning of 36 Hours that changed *everything!* You won't want to miss a single book.

Available at your favorite retail outlet.

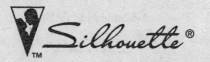

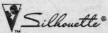